UNDER THE LUPINE MOON

SILVER RAPIDS
BOOK ONE

A. KNIGHTLEY

For those who have an after—keep looking at the moon.

AUTHOR'S NOTE

This book contains descriptions of graphic violence and murder, descriptions of being trapped in a confined space, mentions of past childhood neglect and abuse, mentions of parent death (in the past, during childhood), mentions of past pet loss, mentions of parent alcoholism (in the past, during childhood), and descriptions of struggling with anxiety, depression, and PTSD.

It also contains descriptions of consensual, sexually explicit content that is only appropriate for readers who are 18+ years of age.

If you have any questions regarding the content warnings, or you identify additional content warnings that should be included, please reach out to the author on Instagram (@author.aknightley), or via email (author.aknightley@gmail.com), and I would be happy to discuss.

PART ONE
WANING

CHAPTER 1
JAIME

"Sam. No. You cannot spy on my date by sitting at a different table in the restaurant," Jaime said, shuddering at the thought.

His brother's answer crackled through the phone. "You shouldn't be there alone. You barely know this guy, Jaime. He could be a creep. Who the fuck lives in Silver Rapids, anyway? It's like the nowhere of nowhere. I don't like it."

Jaime rolled his eyes and shut the back hatch of his vehicle, the canvas he'd just loaded carefully covered and padded for the drive into Monroe. "I live outside of Silver Rapids, so if he's a creep just for that reason then so am I. Pick something else to judge him for."

"I would, if you would tell me anything more about him," Sam sniffed.

Jaime sighed. Buckling into the driver's seat, he plugged his phone into the car speakers and waited until he was certain Sam could hear him again. "No. You have his name, the location of our date, and my promise that I will text you when I arrive at the restaurant and when I leave. That's more than enough."

Sam huffed. "Fine. But text me when you are done dropping off the painting, too. Just because they are rich, that doesn't mean they don't have drums of acid filled with people in their basement."

Jaime smirked, tapping in the address of the house he was headed for. "Yes, mother hen."

"Yeah, yeah, call your brother overprotective all you like when you're the one driving all over the state meeting up with strangers," Sam sniped.

Backing out of his driveway, Jaime shook his head and refrained from reminding him that while Sam was older by four years, Jaime was twenty-five and perfectly capable of looking after himself. "I love you, too. Talk soon."

They hung up after Sam told him to be safe one more time, and then begrudgingly wished him a good time on his date.

Truthfully, Jaime was glad for the distraction of his brother's overbearing worry and the task of dropping off one of his commissions in Monroe before he drove back out to Silver Rapids. Otherwise, he might crawl out of his own skin from jittery excitement.

He was going on a date. With Finn. The very attractive and funny *Finn*.

At first, Jaime had wondered how he could be real, with his dating profile looking more like it belonged to an *Eddie Bauer* catalog model than an actual person. Finn had shaggy, sandy blonde hair and rich brown eyes set off by a light golden tan. But Jaime was even more swept away when they'd started chatting, so caught up in his rumbling laugh, thick shoulders, and a smirk that made certain lower parts of him take interest.

What would it feel like to hold on to those shoulders, and kiss that smirk right off his face? Or ride his cock till they were both screaming?

He'd very much like to find out.

But most of all, Jaime couldn't stop thinking about how Finn seemed genuinely interested in him for more than a *"you up?"* kind of night. Not that he was opposed to being intimate with Finn—quite the opposite. He just wanted it to be more than sex. He needed a connection; he needed to know that he was with someone who cared about him and wanted him in more ways than just his dick.

Jaime had dated around a little bit in college, but never found someone he'd really connected with. He'd never found someone who looked at the world the same way he did. Plus, as much as he'd loved Sam's support, he'd been a cockblock.

Who would have thought that having your protective older brother as your college roommate would stop you from getting laid?

So, yeah, Jaime would really like to move this maybe-a-thing with Finn into something deeper. Something real.

And then hopefully have really hot sex.

He blew out a heavy exhale and turned onto the main highway. He needed to focus on the drive, and then on making a good impression on his client before he let himself get distracted all over again by Finn's smile and general broadness, or spiral into worried and anxious thoughts over whether he was actually interested in something real.

The evening light dimmed to a murky blue with dark, overcast skies, and the early spring breeze blew cold off of Loon Lake as he circled around it heading south into town, so he rolled up his window against the chill.

Spring in this part of Alaska was Jaime's favorite time of year, with the purple and blue flowers just pushing through the frost and snow still clinging at higher elevation. Caught between winter's ever-present darkness and the constant, too-bright touch of the midnight sun, Jaime had always found the short, fleeting season precious, and it frequently featured in his paintings.

Most of Jaime's commissions were for his work as a pet memorial artist, where clients shared pictures and stories of their beloved companions for him to paint as keepsakes. People typically found him through his digital art on social media, but he took local watercolor commissions, too.

His ability to support himself fully on his art was entirely due to his brother's help. He'd always had a passion for art, but when Sam's beloved childhood dog, Alfie, passed away last year he'd decided to paint something in his memory for Sam.

It was the first time Jaime had ever seen his brother break. They lost their mom when Jaime was eight, and even though he was only twelve at the time, Sam shored himself up and sealed away all of his cracks to be strong for Jaime throughout the years as they dealt with their absent and drunken father, who'd been unable to handle her loss.

Jaime hadn't been able to bear witnessing his brother's

heartbreak from losing Alfie. He wasn't strong enough to shield Sam from the pain—not in the way that Sam had always been strong enough for him—but he could show him what his love for Alfie looked like.

So, Jaime had painted Alfie in the way he would always remember him, leaping through the field next to their childhood home, chasing all manner of wild creatures until Sam called him inside. He'd painted the joy of knowing that Alfie was forever bounding through that achingly golden field, and he'd painted the deep weight of Sam's grief splashed across the night sky for being without him.

Upon presenting the painting, Sam had pulled Jaime into a crushing hug, before wiping his tears and telling him that he should start posting his art online. Jaime knew that his brother made a substantial amount of money through an online platform he'd started back when he was in college in an effort to financially support them both, but Sam was always opaque about exactly how he did it.

And because Sam only shared what he wanted, when he wanted—despite his near-overbearing protectiveness of Jaime—he'd never pressed him about it. Frankly, Jaime wasn't sure he wanted to know.

Sam shared less of his life with Jaime these days, but his support and love was steadfast. So, Jaime had quit his soul-sucking corporate job and committed to a full-time commission schedule once he'd established himself as a pet memorial artist. He had even bought his own small cabin on Loon Lake, roughly fifteen minutes north of Monroe and just outside the out-of-the-way town of Silver Rapids.

Meeting Finn a few weeks ago had been an unexpected

surprise. He'd signed up for the dating app because he found himself spending most of the time he wasn't at Sam's alone, and he longed for companionship—someone to cherish and make his home warm and cozy with. But he hadn't expected to find someone he clicked with so immediately.

Finn just felt *right*.

They'd shared a surprising amount with each other already, from childhoods with missing and absent parents, to Jaime's close relationship with his brother and his passion for art. Their conversations progressed quickly from the app, to text, and then video chats.

A couple of nights ago, they'd stayed up entirely too late talking about everything and nothing until it was obvious that they should say goodnight, but neither of them did. They'd just laid there, laughing and interjecting conversation into the wee hours of the morning.

Eventually Jaime had started to nod off, and Finn softly wished him goodnight. He had never experienced that kind of ease with anyone before—it was exhilarating and terrifying.

With his heart in his throat, Jaime had texted Finn the next morning.

> Hi. So, last night was fun. :) I enjoyed talking to you. Would you maybe want to go out sometime? With me?

Finn's response was nearly instant.

> Yes!

Maybe tomorrow night? Or the next day?

Or we could wait till this weekend, sorry,
I'm not trying to rush you.

Jaime couldn't wipe the goofy grin from his face for the rest of the day if he tried.

Lost in thought, the drive into town went by quickly. Monroe wasn't big, with only a few thousand people living in the city proper. Most of the town was developed around the local college where Jaime and Sam got their degrees, but it was steadily growing, with a grocery store, a few chain restaurants, and a small hospital.

The town skirted along the base of the nearby mountain range, butting right up against the tree line creating steep, hilly roads. The main town center was home to various local shops that catered to tourists and outdoor enthusiasts passing through on their way into Alaska's interior, but as Jaime drove through the first few stoplights he turned off toward the western edge. New developers had built several communities of large, modern-yet-rugged homes tucked into the mountainside for the influx of affluent people leaving behind Anchorage for their smaller community.

His client, Vera Novikova-Dugan, and her husband Jeffrey Dugan, were one of the wealthier couples to relocate. An heiress to one of the major developers in the Monroe and outer-Anchorage area, Vera was practically Monroe royalty. Jaime was hopeful that a good impression with her commission, a portrait of a golden retriever named Bailey, would lead to more business from her rich friends.

He parked his car along the street outside their house,

one of those colossal McMansion monstrosities with a log-cabin exterior, wrought-iron accents, and giant windows everywhere.

Jaime tried and failed to settle his nerves and excitement for what the rest of the evening would hold, but he couldn't help his broad smile at the thought of finally meeting Finn face-to-face. He'd worn his favorite jeans, the ones that made his ass look fantastic, and he knew the green sweater he had on made his eyes pop, especially on an overcast evening like this.

Commission first, then you can go meet Mr. Swoony Broad Shoulders.

Right. The client.

The air felt still when he stepped out, a hush settling over the neighborhood like a breath waiting to be released. He carefully unloaded the painting and floated up the lit driveway, his thoughts full of warm brown eyes and hope.

A flash of movement caught his eye, and he saw the silhouette of a man shutting an open side window of Vera's house before disappearing further inside—probably her husband closing up against the evening chill.

Sam's warning popped into his head.

Just because they are rich, that doesn't mean they don't have drums of acid filled with people in their basement.

Sam watched too many true crime documentaries. Ready for this quick errand to be over with so he could be on his way to Silver Rapids, on his way to Finn, Jaime straightened his shoulders and rang the doorbell.

CHAPTER 2

FINN

"Do I look ok?"

Finn tried not to fidget with the way his flannel fell over the henley he had on underneath, and checked his phone again to make sure he wasn't going to be late.

Silas looked up from a plate piled high with leftover chicken and broccoli pasta. "You're asking me for fashion advice?"

Finn gave him a look. "I'm asking if I look ok."

Silas shoved a bite of food into his mouth, chewing loudly. "Ok for what? Are you going into town or something?"

Finn huffed. "No, like, for a date. Do I look ok for a date?"

His friend gave an excited whoop and pumped his fist in the air, a stray noodle flying across the kitchen in the process.

"A date! Finny! Tell me everything. Is he hot? Did you meet him on that app you signed up for?"

Finn sighed and dropped down into the chair across from him. "Yes, we met on the app. The one you all but made me sign up for, if I recall correctly."

Silas waved a dismissive hand. "It was time you got out and met someone. You've been moping around for too long."

"I have not been moping."

Yes, you have.

Silas raised an eyebrow, and tucked back into his pasta. "Yes, you have."

Finn huffed again. Fine, so maybe he had been moping. About six months ago, he'd lost his beloved dog Luna, and frankly he was still reeling from the silence and emptiness her absence left in his life.

He'd adopted her after getting out of the service eight years ago. The vet estimated that she was around four years old at the time, and guessed that she was some type of border collie mix. She had been found by the side of the highway. He'd named her Luna because she was a bright spot as he climbed out of a dark place after leaving the military and struggling to find where he fit back into the world, and he was grateful for the laughter, love, and joy she showed him everyday.

But if he were honest with himself, he had been going through the motions for a while even before Luna passed, and one night after dinner a few weeks ago, Silas sat him down and told him enough was enough. He needed to get out and meet people.

"You're a ghost of yourself, Finn. I don't want you to waste your life away like this."

"Oh, and you live your life so fully, do you?" He'd thrown the words back at his friend, and watched Silas close off as they landed.

Fuck, he hated that. He'd immediately apologized, and asked if he had any grand ideas for *"putting himself out there."* Softening, Silas had suggested a dating app, and even helped Finn set up his profile. He'd gone along with it mostly to mend the wound from his barbed words, even if they were true.

It was difficult for them both to meet people. Not only because the small town they lived in, Silver Rapids, had an even smaller dating pool, but because, well, when you could turn into a giant wolf at will, or some jacked-up hybrid version of a wolf and a human, it meant any kind of relationship was short-term and superficial unless you were prepared to share that secret.

In Finn's case, they'd never even got to that point, and usually ended in the same back alley they'd left the bar to go have a quick fuck in.

Sure, there were other shifters and paranormals in Silver Rapids that he could date, but even with them there was always a gentle tug on his heart, the softest pull telling him *not this one, not yet*, whenever he'd chatted up some cute guy.

The mating pull. Or lack thereof.

Some shifters lived their entire lives ignoring it, content to build long-lasting relationships with someone they didn't feel the pull to mate with. But for Finn, it just seemed pointless to be with someone he knew, deep in his bones, wasn't the right person for him.

He wanted the mating bond—needed it. But he was also so terrified of it. What if he felt it, and the other guy didn't? What if he felt the bond with a human, and they laughed in his face, or worse, screamed and ran from him in fright when he told them about what he was? What if they rejected him entirely, not wanting the commitment a mating bond meant?

Or, what if he never felt it with anyone, at all?

Finn's phone chirped, and he hastily pulled up the new message.

> I'm heading into Monroe soon to drop off something for work and then I'll be on my way to Silver Rapids. Does 7pm still work?
>
> I'm excited to see you tonight. :)

Finn replied right away, pride be damned.

> Great! Yes, 7pm at Andi's Restaurant. I'll send you the address. I'm looking forward to it too, Jaime!
>
> See you soon, Finn. ;)

His stomach swooped, and a grin stretched his face so much it hurt. Finn was pulled right out of his anxious worrying at the thought of finally seeing him.

Jaime.

You're all tied up in knots over someone you haven't even met in person yet, you overbearing creep. He'd probably run for the hills if he knew that you woke up this morning hard, wishing it was his warm, sleep-mussed scent and soft, slick ass that you stuffed your cock into instead of your dry hand, in a bed that smelled like your own sweat and cum.

So, maybe Finn thought about Jaime more than was normal for someone he hadn't actually had a first date with, yet. But he just couldn't help it when his wolf went straight for *I bet you smell like mine* the first time he saw the warmth of the man's smile.

Jaime had stood out immediately among the sea of mindless swiping. His cute, knowing smirk and teasing eyes that peeked through cinnamon lashes made something inside Finn sit up, alert, and he needed to know who he was.

He had bright, shiny red hair that Finn wanted to gently rake his claws through; the rich color curled around his ears and set off his mossy green eyes and freckled complexion. He looked lithe and toned, and his movements seemed graceful even through a screen; the muscles of his arms flexing in the picture of him holding a paintbrush, standing over an empty canvas.

The way his fingers gripped the brush with a gentle strength drew Finn's thoughts down all sorts of paths he wasn't prepared to look at too closely right now.

In short, Jaime had enchanted Finn from the start.

He mused that maybe Jaime was some distant descendant of the woodland fae, the ones that had died out long ago but still lived on in cautionary folktales told during bedtime stories and around the hearth fire.

Finn shook off the thought and adjusted himself, already semi-hard as he pictured Jaime wrapping those painter's fingers around his cock instead of a brush, and tried not to think about it too much—even when that pulsing thrum of need shot through him again.

Silas pulled him from his wandering thoughts, voice soft, and Finn looked up to meet his gaze. "Oh Finny, you really like him, don't you?"

He gave a frustrated shake of his head and blew out a breath. "I barely know him, Si. We haven't even met in person yet. Tonight will be our first date."

Silas's look was knowing. "But you've talked, yes?"

Finn nodded. He knew Jaime was an artist, and that he laughed at Finn's jokes and listened when he told him about his toxic mother and how he'd followed his friend into the military to get away from her. He'd told Jaime about Luna, and how sometimes he still expected to hear her padding up to him when he came home.

Would Jaime paint Luna for him, someday?

The hope that came along with that thought frightened him, so fragile and precious, but then Finn remembered the way Jaime looked when he laughed, and the shy way he had suggested that they go on a date, and it bloomed.

Silas smirked. "If you want me to stay out on my run later than usual, leave a sock on the front door."

Finn's face heated. "It's not like that. I really like—" he huffed, "I mean, I want to see where it could go, and don't want to rush things."

The look Silas gave him was so understanding he had to turn away.

I really like him and don't want to ruin it by going too fast.

But of course his brother knew that.

Silas stood, and began clearing up after his dinner. "You're a catch, Finny. You're funny, and smart, and handsome. The parts of you that he doesn't know about yet don't detract from that."

The wolfy parts, he meant.

Finn ignored the nervous twist in his gut, and changed the subject. "So, you're going out for a run this evening?"

Silas regularly ran the perimeter around Silver Rapids in his wolf shift, claiming it eased his mind to know the comings and goings of the paranormal residents in their small town. He wondered if his constant vigilance was because he was a full wolf shifter, where Finn was only half, or from something else. Something that set Silas apart even from the other full-blooded shifters he knew, something that made him *other*.

Sometimes Finn joined him on his patrols, and while he enjoyed the freedom and strength and release of the wild run with his closest friend and brother, the instinct to claim and protect the land surrounding Silver Rapids was muted for him.

Also, the Salt Creek pack, volatile on the best days and violent on the worst, had set up a new outpost twenty or so miles west of Silver Rapids, and Finn thought that their close proximity had Silas on edge. Especially given that it was the same pack that Silas's family had fled when he was just a pup—for reasons Silas had never fully explained—claiming he wasn't sure himself.

"Yeah, I am. That fox shifter came back to town last night, I wonder how long he'll stay," Silas said.

Finn could smell that he was thinking about the last time

that fox shifter was in town. And in Silas's bed. He smirked. "Are you going to try and see him again?"

Silas smiled ruefully and shook his head, but Finn clocked the shift in his eyes. The same look he always had whenever he was distancing himself from something—just a fling that would never last. "That's not happening again, I'm sorry to say."

Finn didn't think he was very sorry about it, but he wouldn't push. Not tonight.

He checked his phone again and saw that it was actually time to leave, so he grabbed his jacket and clapped Silas on the shoulder. "Be safe tonight. Call if you need me."

Silas smiled. "You have fun. I mean it. Be you, Finn. Don't hide yourself away. And hey, it's just a first date. If it doesn't work out, you can let him go and try again with someone else. But if it does, then you'll look back and feel silly for ever doubting it. Either way, you'll never know if you don't try."

Finn nodded, and ducked out the door.

He didn't want to try with someone else, though. He wanted to try with Jaime. Because it wasn't just that he was beautiful, or funny, or kind that had Finn all twisted up inside. Something about him seemed so familiar. He couldn't put his finger on it exactly, only that the sight of him and sound of his voice made Finn's wolf stir and prowl; made the tug around his heart more insistent.

Especially right now, on his way to meet Jaime for the first time—his wolf was practically shouting at him to hurry up.

Go to him. Go.

Find him.

Go, now!

Finn subdued those restless instincts as best he could; he didn't want to come off as overbearing and freak Jaime out. He wanted to give this the best shot that he could.

Because the trouble was, the inner voice that woke up when he thought of Jaime, and howled with the need to find him *right now*, told him that it wouldn't be that easy to let go.

He may not be able to let go at all.

———

SILVER RAPIDS WAS BUSIER than usual tonight.

Andi's restaurant was only a short walk from his house, less if he shifted and ran, but he didn't want to carry his clothes in his mouth and get them all drooly, and he wanted to have his truck nearby in case Jaime wanted to go somewhere after dinner.

He passed groups of intermingled shifters and other paranormals walking toward the town center where a handful of bars held live music nights and various clientele-themed specials. If Finn didn't know any better, he might assume the *Blue Moon's* Vamp Night was a cheeky way to rope in people who really liked overpriced bloody marys and not, well, blood.

Just thirty minutes north of Monroe, Silver Rapids was nestled into the base of the same mountain range, but it was less touristy mountain chic and more grit. The residents mostly kept to themselves, and only ventured out to the larger town when absolutely necessary.

Given that most were magical beings, or some other kind of paranormal creature, they weren't keen on the usual tourist-oriented stores and attractions, but there were a few local shops, including a bookstore that Finn loved to wander through on occasion.

He pulled into a parking spot a little ways off from the restaurant entrance and cut the engine, still fifteen minutes early. Jaime hadn't texted that he was on his way from Monroe yet, but Finn knew he was doing something for work first and probably hadn't had time.

Besides, he wouldn't want him texting and driving on these roads anyway.

Finn shot Jaime a quick message to let him know he had arrived and would grab them a table. Hands shaking, he pocketed his phone and scrubbed at his face.

Holy shit, this is really happening.

Jaime would be here soon, and they would be face-to-face and Finn would scent him and then he would *know*, and oh my God, what if Jaime smelled right? What if he smelled like *mate*?

All of a sudden, Finn couldn't handle the thought of being confronted with his mate, who had no idea what he was or that people like him even existed. His knee-jerk reaction was to turn tail and run. As much as he wanted to know Jaime, as much as his wolf prowled and howled for Finn to find him, the thought of letting him in, letting him see everything, was terrifying.

Wolf shifters weren't something he could casually explain. Most people wouldn't believe him at all, as paranormals had done a good job of hiding the truth of their existence even in the age of modern technology. He couldn't very well expect Jaime to just accept information that would alter his worldview so significantly.

But if he never confided in him...

Finn couldn't be only half of himself. He'd spent his entire childhood living like that for his mother, hiding the true nature of his wolf from her as best he could, and he wouldn't do that again.

Besides, there was something about Jaime that made Finn want to be whole for him—with him. Something that made him long to be seen by him, entirely. And that was a dangerous thing to want, because he couldn't bear the weight of seeing Jaime's disgust or disappointment. Somehow, he'd survived seeing it in his mother's eyes all those years—he wouldn't survive seeing it in Jaime's.

But the thought that Jaime wouldn't be his, that he would smell like every other good-looking man Finn had encountered in a bar hit him, crushing and unbearable, and his inner wolf snarled and recoiled from it.

So, Finn slowed his breathing and grounded himself. Whatever the answer, he wasn't going to find it by working himself into a panic in his truck. Jaime would be here soon, and everything would be better.

Maybe. Hopefully.

With one final deep breath, Finn stepped out and stalked into the restaurant.

The owner and chef, Andi, was behind the counter and waved him back to the booth he usually shared with Silas. They came here at least three times a week for the amazing food, so he figured it would be a nice spot for a first date.

He ordered a couple of waters and chatted with Andi for a bit, but told her to wait a few minutes before bringing any food. She gave him a curious look, so he explained that he was waiting on someone.

She grinned. "A date?"

He shuffled his feet, cheeks hot. Checking his phone, he saw that Jaime was only a few minutes late. He'd probably been caught up with his work thing. He'd text if he wasn't going to make it. "I'm meeting a friend."

She gave him a knowing look. "I'll swing back by when he gets here." He nodded and she sauntered off, back into the kitchen.

Finn checked his phone again, ten minutes late now. Maybe he should ask if Jaime was ok? What if he had a flat tire, or hit a deer on the way here and was stuck on the side of the highway somewhere?

He fired off a quick text.

> Hey, no rush, just want to make sure you're ok.

Nothing.

He waited another fifteen minutes before he stepped out to make sure Jaime wasn't waiting for him in the parking lot.

Forty-five minutes.

Still no word. Finn sent another text, confirming that Jaime had the address. People started to glance over at him with pity. Andi refilled his water once, and then again.

Maybe he wasn't late, maybe he just wasn't coming. Maybe he didn't care enough about meeting Finn, after all.

He carded his fingers through his hair and worried over

every text sent between them in a way he hadn't before. Was it something he'd said? Had he been overbearing? Too much?

Finn scrolled back through their conversations, trying to see where he'd gone wrong. Oh God, what if he hadn't flirted *enough* with Jaime and he thought Finn didn't actually like him?

He sent another message.

> Is everything ok? Have you decided not to come? Are you stuck somewhere?

An hour passed.

Someone leaned over to him, voice filled with pity. "We've all been there, man. Being stood up sucks."

An hour and a half.

Two hours.

He avoided eye contact with Andi as he ducked out of the restaurant. Alone in his truck, Finn stared out through the windshield, fogged over from the heat coming off of him. He heard people laughing together as they walked by, muffled from the distance and closed windows, unaware that he was unraveling a little bit, inside.

Finn closed out of the string of unanswered messages and put a lid on the fragile, hopeful parts of him, his wolf now aching and howling. He stuffed the hurt down, down, down.

Jaime never came, and Finn went home.

PART TWO
NEW

CHAPTER 3
JAIME

3 MONTHS LATER

J aime was trapped in a small, dark room, curled up on a concrete floor. He couldn't see anything through the dark, and he couldn't move his hands or feet, feeling the tight pull of the zip-ties against his skin as he tried to stand.

The room was silent except for the muted sounds of his frantic movements in the enclosed space, his sneakers bumping up against boxes and crates stacked on the dirty floor and his heavy breaths choking behind the gag shoved in his mouth.

But then he was free, scrambling across sticky, wet carpet toward what was left of Vera's body.

She had been standing right next to him just a few seconds ago, telling him how much she loved the painting, *saying that she would be right back, that she wanted to go grab her phone to get a picture of them together with it.*

And now she was torn open and left a bloody heap leaking all over the floor.

Jaime's hands fluttered over her body, helpless, trying to put her back together—failing to scoop her insides back into her ripped torso. The steady beat of his heart was so loud in the narrow hallway.

Thud. Thud. Thud.

There was so much blood. He needed to get up, now, but he felt stuck. He needed to find his phone, needed to call Sam or the police or someone who would come and help him, save him from this.

Step. Step. Step.

Jaime couldn't move anymore, his hands and feet were chained down and dripping blood that wasn't his.

Step. Step. Step.

The steady footfalls grew louder. The man was right behind Jaime, now.

He knew he should turn and look, but he couldn't. He tried, desperately willing his body to move, willing himself to turn his head, to see the person hovering at his shoulder.

A wet, rancid breath exhaled past his turned face. "I'm going to kill you, just like I killed her."

Jaime woke with a sharp inhale, clawing at the sheets that were bunched up around his throat and ripping them off his sweat-drenched body. Panting heavily, he wiped the moisture from his brow and cheeks and stared at his blessedly familiar ceiling.

Home. He was home, and no one was here to hurt him.

He'd gotten out of that house, and was alone in his bedroom. He repeated to himself that he was safe, hoping someday the words would sink in.

He went through several of the exercises from the pamphlet that his therapist gave him on managing his PTSD and anxiety, and slowed his breathing and racing thoughts enough to reach for his phone, dialing the only number he ever felt safe enough to call these past weeks.

"Jaime?" Sam's voice was groggy. Jaime cursed himself when he saw that it was almost three o'clock in the morning.

Voice wet, he croaked, "Sam. I'm, um, sorry for calling so late. I just—I had a bad dream, and needed to talk."

Sam sighed. Jaime cursed himself again for not thinking about the late hour. "Did you do the exercises your therapist gave you?"

Jaime nodded. "Yeah, I did. They helped."

"Good."

Jaime waited for him to say something else, but there was only silence. "Ok. Um, I'll let you go. Sorry for calling you so late. Sorry."

He hung up the phone. It was unfair to expect Sam to be there to help him through every nightmare, every bout of severe anxiety, every bad day. His brother had already done so much for him—hiring a lawyer, and being there for him constantly in those first few days when everything was too much for him to handle alone.

Jaime needed to get a grip. He hadn't been hurt, not really. He hadn't even seen the murder happen. He'd only heard her screams and the sound of her body hitting the floor, just outside of the living room they had stood in together only moments before...

Jaime flipped on the bedside lamp, cutting those thoughts off. He could take care of himself. So, he focused on his breathing, and went through the motions of changing his sheets, tossing the sweat-soaked set into the washer before rinsing off in the shower, swallowing a hydroxyzine tablet, and then he climbed back into bed.

But he couldn't fall asleep, even when he felt the medication soothe his tired mind. Instead he laid there, staring at the moon peeking through the clouds outside of his window. He thought of soft, soil-brown eyes, and that warm fizzy feeling he had when they crinkled in laughter.

Those perfect eyes were lost to him, now. He'd shoved them away in his panic and fear during the first few days after the murder, when Jaime hadn't trusted anyone or anything except for his brother.

But on sleepless nights spent staring at the moon hanging low over the lake, Jaime thought of him, and of all the chances that had slipped through his fingers. Was he staring at the moon right now, too? Did he sometimes wonder about Jaime?

Did he think about Jaime as much as Jaime thought about him?

Longing so fierce pierced his heart—one of the few feelings he allowed himself to sink into anymore. But then the deep, mournful sorrow followed, sounding just like the wolves howling to each other from across the lake and feeling like forever, and Jaime didn't want to think about him anymore.

So he turned away from the moon, and went to sleep.

PART THREE
WAXING

CHAPTER 4
FINN

9 MONTHS LATER

"Hey, did you see the updates that came out this morning on that murder trial down in Monroe?"

Finn grunted, and didn't look up from his computer screen. He needed to finalize the security recommendations for a sporting goods store before it was sent for client approval, and he really didn't want to bullshit about the local news with Silas.

Private Security Solutions, Inc. had been quiet all morning. Their latest hands-on assignment concluded last week—security detail for a politician campaigning for Senator. He'd finally left the Silver Rapids area and another team would be taking over his permanent detail.

Thank God.

The contract paid well, but Finn was happy to see the

end of it. He hated the crowds and non-stop travel that came along with jobs like that, even if they were a distraction from the monotony of his life in Silver Rapids.

He preferred the local contracts. Consulting on home and commercial security risk management plans, mostly, and stepping in as additional body security only when needed or if a high profile client came into the area and their whole team was contracted for the job.

Finn had an eye for assessing security threats; sensing the what, when, and where to build effective risk management scenarios, whereas Silas was the best body security guy in the business. A veritable tank, he stood at least a few inches taller than Finn's 6'1", and while they were both broad-shouldered and solidly built for two thirty-two year olds, Silas's thighs looked more like tree trunks than anything human ever did.

Well, human-ish.

Apparently, Silas took his grunt to mean *go on*, instead of *go away*. "You know what I'm talking about, right? The wife of that Salt Creek wolf who was killed about a year back? And then they arrested one of the low-ranking Salt Creek shifters for it?"

Finn gave up on his ambitions to have the paperwork done by noon, and looked up at where Silas sat in the desk across from him, feet kicked up.

Yes, Finn did remember that murder. He had never met the woman, but he knew of her. She was the sole heiress to her late father's development firm and substantial holdings, and it was widely speculated that Jeffrey Dugan, a high-ranking shifter in the Salt Creek pack, had married her for that connection, to benefit himself and Salt Creek's financial interests.

It was all over the Silver Rapids gossip mill that Jeffrey was good for her murder, not only because *'it's always the husband,'* but because her money and voting power for the development firm would absorb into Salt Creek's assets. But then they had arrested Jackson Bishop, a low-level Salt Creek shifter, and Jeffrey Dugan was still walking around a free man.

Finn knew that Silas kept a close eye on the case because of the Salt Creek connection, but it had also hit the national news cycle and turned into an online sensation overnight.

A beautiful, rich woman married to a slightly less-rich surgeon was killed in her own home under mysterious circumstances, and her husband had a rock-solid alibi.

Toss in how tight-lipped law enforcement was about everything, including the mysterious connection between her and the guy they had finally charged for her murder, and it became the hottest topic in the true crime community for the last year, never-mind that the general public was missing half the paranormally-inclined story.

Finn's chair creaked in protest as he leaned back, racking his brain for the details he could remember. "There was a witness to the murder, right? But that's not who's on trial?"

Silas's brow creased. "Yeah, that's the thing. They've kept everything so close to the vest with this case, even our contacts in Monroe PD have been tight-lipped about it. They didn't even release the identity of the witness when they arrested and charged Bishop."

Finn didn't have a ton of knowledge on criminal law or

the way the trial system worked, but he had been adjacent to a few cases where a client of the security firm was involved. "They didn't make the witness testify during the preliminary hearing? How?"

Silas shook his head. "There was no preliminary hearing. They indicted Bishop with a grand jury and sealed the proceedings. The witness didn't even have to testify, they had a law enforcement officer read the witness statement."

Finn raised his eyebrows. "There must be more that the witness saw, then. More than just identifying Bishop as the murderer. Why else would the police protect their identity like that? Do they suspect the husband was involved at all?"

Silas shrugged a shoulder. "No one will tell me for sure, but reading between the lines, they must. There are enough shifters in Monroe PD for them to know of the Salt Creek connection between Bishop and Dugan, even if they have to go about proving it in some other paranormal-free way. But I'm sure the bastards from Salt Creek that are on the force are doing everything they can to bury the connection. My bet is that the witness is the key."

He leaned forward, dropping his feet from the desk and flipping his phone around, and indicated to an article he had pulled up. "Which brings me back to what just happened this morning."

Finn raised his eyebrows at Silas again, and glanced down. His breath caught, heart stopping. He snatched the phone out of Silas's hand, everything else falling away at the name he saw in the article byline—the face that was staring back at him from just underneath.

Eye witness in gripping Monroe murder trial uncovered: Jaime Lamont saw everything!

Finn tried to read the rest of the article, but his eyes kept circling back to the name. The picture. Jaime's goddamn picture—beautiful freckled cheeks and pink smile and mossy green eyes on full display.

It had been his profile picture before the account went dark.

One year ago, Jaime stood Finn up in his favorite restaurant, stomping all over the fragile hope that had bloomed in his chest at the possibility of something real between them. One year ago, Finn had sent several embarrassingly frantic messages asking Jaime if he was ok, if he was hurt, or stuck on the side of the road somewhere.

It turned out that Jaime just hadn't been interested in him.

Finn had received confirmation of that the next day, when Jaime sent him a single short, pointed text replying to the several from the night before.

Don't contact me again.

It had hit him like a punch to the gut, making it difficult to take a full breath. No explanations or apologies, no hint as to how they could go from late night video calls and flirty texts and plans to... nothing.

One fucking year ago. Right around the time of the murder.

Oh God.

Finn tried to focus on the article, and not the yawning pit of guilt that threatened to swallow him. He leaned onto his elbows, head in his hands, and read:

Sources say Lamont, known in public filings only as 'JL', is the prosecution's key witness set to testify in the upcoming trial of Jackson Bishop, who has been charged for the murder of Vera Novikova-Dugan, heiress of the Novikov Corporation and wife of Jeffrey Dugan. Until now, the prosecution has kept Lamont's identity secret, our sources say, "...to protect his safety and the integrity of the case." Novikova-Dugan was found murdered in her home on April 9th of last year, after a previously-unidentified witness (Lamont) called emergency services...

All thought of risk management plans forgotten, he sat in stunned silence for a few minutes, passing back Silas's phone without really hearing what he was saying.

April 9th. The day they were meant to have their first date. Jaime had texted that he was running into Monroe to drop something off for work before heading out to Silver Rapids, and then he went silent.

While Finn had sat in that booth, hot with embarrassment and anger and so hurt, his wolf whining and pacing in his mind, restless like it had never been before, Jaime had witnessed a brutal murder.

Jaime had been in danger.

What if he didn't just see it? What if he was also hurt?

Fuck. Fuck. Growling, he pulled the article back up on his own phone and scanned every word, but they only ever referred to him as a "witness." He wasn't identified as a victim.

Still... Jaime had, at minimum, witnessed and would testify to the brutal murder of a woman allegedly committed by a Salt Creek shifter, landing him right in the crosshairs of one of the most violent packs in the state. In the country, even.

Certainly *that* was why his identity had been kept a secret for so long. The other paranormals in Monroe PD would know the track record of who Jaime was about to testify against and tried their best to protect him, maybe hoping the Salt Creek shifters on the force wouldn't be able to make a move without outing their involvement when only a select number of people knew who Jaime was.

But now, the world knew his name. He had no protection at all.

Fuck.

He wasn't safe. Not from the general public, and not from the bigger players in all of this. Ones he probably knew nothing about.

Finn needed to find him. To tell him—something. Somehow, he needed to help Jaime without revealing too much about himself. He just needed to find him first, and then—

"Finn. Finn!" Silas was waving his hand in front of

Finn's face, trying to catch his attention. "Are you alright? You zoned out there for a bit."

He cleared his throat. "Yeah, sorry. I'm fine, just tired." He gave a half smile, one he knew Silas saw right through, but thankfully he didn't push.

Resting his elbows on his desk, Finn leaned his head back into his hands and sighed. He couldn't just track the man down and barge into his life, uninvited. In fact, Jaime had specifically told him to leave him alone. And yes, even if Finn assumed the circumstances around witnessing a horrific murder were the instigating factors of Jaime dropping all contact with him, it had still been his choice to do so, and he hadn't reached out since. He didn't want Finn back in his life.

He's not safe. Find him.

Go.

Go.

His wolf clearly wasn't on the same page. And the truth was, Jaime wasn't safe, with his name and face splashed all over the internet as every national news outlet covered the newest breaking story in Vera Novikova-Dugan's murder trial. Especially if Finn and Silas's suspicions regarding Monroe PD's reasons for hiding his identity were correct, and Jaime would be able to testify to more than just Bishop's identity, possibly having information on a connection between Bishop and Salt Creek.

The Salt Creek bastards in the police department were probably the ones responsible for the leak to begin with. What better way to cover up their interest in a key witness linking

Bishop with Jeffrey Dugan, than to splash his face all over the news for the world to see?

Finn shook his head. He was making some dangerous assumptions. He couldn't go publicly accusing the Salt Creek pack of anything without strong, non-paranormal friendly evidence to support the connection between Bishop and Dugan.

What the hell am I thinking?

A year of silence from Jaime, a year of hurt feelings and anger at himself for daring to hope, followed by resignation and the slow settle back into moving through the motions of his life, and not even ten minutes after hearing Jaime's name again, Finn was already planning how he could protect him from the wolves at his door.

Literally.

Fuck, that was another thing to consider. Had Jaime actually seen Bishop shifted? Did he know that he was neck deep in shit with one of the most violent and dangerous wolf shifter packs in the country? Did he know about wolf shifters at all?

Finn needed to slow down, and take a deep breath. He didn't know what Jaime knew. He didn't know who leaked Jaime's identity to the media, and he didn't know why.

All he knew was that Jaime was vulnerable. Media trucks would be swarming his home within hours, if they weren't already there, like vultures flocking to a fresh kill until something newer and juicier came along.

The thought of Jaime unprotected, at the whim of the media and every other intrusive weirdo out there had another involuntary growl rumbling from his chest.

If I sought him out, just to make sure he had even the most basic security protocols in place, would that make me one of those intrusive weirdos, too?

He could do it. It would be easy.

With just a few clicks of his mouse, he would know everything there was to know about Jaime Lamont. He had chosen not to do that a year ago—chosen to respect Jaime's boundaries. He didn't want to invade Jaime's privacy; he wanted Jaime to invite him into his world with open arms, not to burst through the door uninvited.

That's what the weirdos will be doing in a few hours, you fool. Go!

He'd been in this job long enough to know how people behaved when they thought they had access to a person's private life. Half of his job was to make sure those people weren't successful in invading the personal space of their clients. Could he really sit back and do nothing, knowing how much danger Jaime was in?

No, he fucking couldn't.

Jaime might hate him for it, might call him a creep and want nothing to do with him, but he couldn't let him fend for himself. Not now that Finn knew he needed help. He'd look Jaime up, take the day off of work claiming he didn't feel well, and go find him. After that, well.

He'd figure that out in the truck on the way there.

His inner wolf was less agitated now that Finn had made a decision—*the right one*—his wolf growled, but just as he was about to pull Jaime's name up in their database, Sheppard's voice hollered out from his office. He'd been on the phone all morning, and Finn prayed they didn't have a new client to go deal with. It would make lying about being sick more difficult.

Cameron Sheppard, the owner of Private Security Solutions and Silas and Finn's boss, started their team eight years ago after they were all discharged from the service together. When Finn and Silas graduated high school, they were contacted by a shifter representative from the military and recruited into an experimental, covert unit that specialized in '*elimination of threats to national security using shifter assets.*'

Whatever vague bullshit that meant.

They were assigned to Sheppard's unit and joined by only one other shifter on the team—Joe Renner. Sheppard and Renner were three or four years older than Finn and Silas, but after training as a pack, they were soon thick as thieves.

Their shared history and friendship wouldn't stop him from lying about needing to leave to find Jaime, but he would feel guilty about it.

"Winters! Granger! Come in here."

Finn and Silas glanced at each other, eyebrows raised, before they stood and made their way over to Sheppard's door. Finn leaned against the frame while Silas stood just inside, arms crossed and feet planted wide, always ready for assignment.

Finn just hoped this would be quick.

"Sir?" Silas asked.

Sheppard motioned them inside and told them to sit. "We've got a referral from Monroe PD. It's a unique situation, and I want to discuss it with you both before you commit to the contract."

Finn's ears perked up at that. Monroe was not that big, surely there couldn't be more than one *unique situation* happening today? Shooting each other wary glances, Finn and Silas sat in the chairs across from Sheppard.

"When was the last time you 'consulted' us before taking a case?" Silas asked, using his fingers to make air quotes around the word.

Sheppard shot him a flat look. "I assume that you're aware of the murder trial down in Monroe? The one the Salt Creek pack is so wrapped up in?"

Finn and Silas both tensed and nodded, predatory focus honed on Sheppard's next words.

"One of the detectives on the case, Logan Sutton, gave me a call this morning." At Silas and Finn's raised eyebrows, Sheppard shrugged. "She's an old friend."

Right. Cameron Sheppard was a tomb when it came to his personal life.

"She's not in-the-know about our world, but she does suspect a connection between their guy Bishop and Jeffrey Dugan. She thinks he is somehow involved in his wife's murder, but she's run up against some roadblocks in the investigation."

"What kind of roadblocks—"

"What does this have to do with the referral?" Silas and Finn asked at the same time.

Finn's head was spinning. Were they being brought in on the case somehow? Would that mean he would have a chance to see Jaime without having to track him down on his own like a stalker?

Sheppard answered Silas's question first, tipping his chin in his direction. "The kind of roadblocks that would put us on Salt Creek's radar if we take this case."

Silas tensed, and Sheppard gave him an understanding look. "I can't share any more details unless I know that you both are officially on board. It's a tense situation, and Sutton wasn't going to tell me shit unless I took the contract and signed an NDA. You'll have to sign them too, before we can move forward. But I wanted you to know what you were getting into, before you made that decision."

So that's why he'd wanted to consult them first; he didn't want to force Silas's involvement with the case in respect of the tension between him and the Salt Creek pack. Really, tension was putting it mildly—they were going to butcher him as a kid before his parents snuck him away in the dead of night.

Finn knew this would be a tough call for his friend. Silas's parents had sacrificed everything to get him as far off Salt Creek's radar as they could, and as far as Finn knew, Silas never knew why they wanted him dead to begin with. Finn didn't want his brother to be put in danger—didn't want him anywhere near those Salt Creek bastards.

But there was absolutely no way he would pass up the opportunity to be involved in this case. Not if there was a chance to see Jaime. A chance to get him some kind of message to stay safe, even if he couldn't tell him everything.

"I'm in," he said to Sheppard, and turned to Silas. "You should stay out of it, though. Sheppard and I can handle this."

Silas considered for a beat longer. "No, I'm in too. I'll

stay on the periphery as much as possible, but I'm not leaving you two to go into this on your own. If Salt Creek is as far up Monroe PD's ass as we think they are, you'll need someone watching your back."

Finn knew better than to ask if he was sure. Silas would never put his family in danger on a whim, and he was right. They'd need each other. They always had.

He clapped Silas on the shoulder, and turned to Sheppard, who nodded. "Good. Right. Well, sign these NDAs and get ready to head out while I brief you on our new client, Jaime Lamont."

CHAPTER 5
JAIME

Jaime wasn't sure how long he'd been laying in bed. It had been a while, though, because it was dark when his nightmares drove him from sleep, and now the morning sun had risen enough to no longer be streaming in directly through his bedroom window.

He turned to look out toward the lake, the meadow that swept around his backyard separating his lawn from the narrow, rocky beach filled with green lupine stalks, gently swaying in the breeze.

He'd seen fields of them up and down the highway surrounding his home when he moved out here, and fell in love with the blueish-purple blooms. He'd immediately wanted his own lupine meadow, so he ordered packs and packs of seeds and planted them all around his backyard last spring, before...

Before.

They hadn't bloomed. Which was normal in the first

year, sure, but even when fall came and the stalks were still bare, and then crispy and brown, buried under snow drifts in the punishing winter winds, it felt like a cosmic sign.

Beautiful things aren't for you, anymore.

You can't even take care of yourself, let alone something else.

The lupine were doing well this year, though. Jaime thought it wouldn't be too long before they bloomed and saturated his meadow with deep blues and purples. It was a different kind of blue than the one he would use to paint grief; the rich hues of lupine more akin to a peaceful night sky, one that rested and breathed over chilly spring evenings...

Stop.

He turned his head away from the window and the life blooming outside and stared up at his ceiling, thoughts and plans of lupines and emotions and time moving forward drifting away from him.

He didn't want to think about it—not right now.

Not ever, really.

Jaime's therapist said thinking like that wouldn't help him get better. He attended one session a week, to process the trauma and grief of what had happened last year and his resulting isolation.

They helped, really. He'd been a complete disaster in the weeks following Vera's murder and the attack, and now the nightmares weren't nearly as frequent. Still, he would often stay up late into the night, tense and anxious, reciting the facts from that evening over and over.

He would repeat them the same way the police had

made him do in that tiny, cold room filled with stale air and metal furniture. They'd barely finished patching up the cut on his temple when they sat him down and began peppering him with questions before Sam swooped in like an avenging angel, armed with a lawyer and a scowl that cowed even the most hardened detective, and ushered him out.

Yes, she knew I was coming to drop off the commission myself.

No, I don't do that very often, but I did this time because I wanted to make a good impression so that she'd recommend me to all of her wealthy friends.

No, I didn't follow her out of the room when she went to find her phone.

No, I didn't see who murdered her, just the shadow of a man in the window before I went into the house. I thought it was her husband.

No, I didn't see what weapon they used.

Yes, it really did only last a few seconds.

No, I didn't see the murderer before they knocked me out.

No, I don't know how much time passed before I came to, tied up in that closet.

No, they never said who they were talking to on the phone.

Yes, they called her by name.

No, I didn't see their face.

I don't know why they left me alive.

I don't know how I got out of there.

No, I didn't fucking kill her!

Reciting it over and over wasn't about trying to remember details he might have forgotten in the initial panic.

Jaime knew he never saw the murderer, and that no matter how often he thought back on the moment he'd been hovering over Vera's torn and ravaged body, searching for a pulse, helplessly trying to put her insides back inside of her, trying to do *something*, he hadn't seen or heard anyone come up behind him. There'd only been the barest hint of a shadow in his periphery, the most subtle draft along his cheek before he was knocked out cold, only to wake and find himself tied up and gagged in a closet.

He never saw the face of the man who'd murdered Vera, but he had heard his voice, and Jaime was haunted by both.

His therapist said that reciting the facts over and over was a coping mechanism. By doing so, his mind was reminding him that he got out. He survived.

Jaime told her he wished his brain would find a better way of doing that.

And that's when she would suggest he try painting his feelings like he used to.

But he couldn't.

There was no emotion in rote facts. He could repeat them without confronting the deep fear and anxiety lurking beneath the surface, but if he were to try to paint how that night felt... no. Not yet.

It would remind him of why his brother had finally decided he'd had enough of taking care of Jaime, of always having to be there when he couldn't take care of himself. Like he was pathetic and helpless and in need of being managed.

The short, rhythmic buzz of his phone on the nightstand cut through the silence. Jaime reached over and fumbled with the charger before seeing a text from his attorney, Dana Chase. She was one of the few people who had his new number, and one of the fewer who actually used it.

After the case hit national news, Dana had told him that it was in his best interest to change his phone number and stay off of social media for a while. "Just in case," she'd said.

> Jaime, please give me a call when you are available, ASAP.

He rolled his eyes. Dana Chase was a damn good attorney, but she was not a socially adept texter.

Still, Jaime knew how much she had done to keep him from the police's intrusive scrutiny. Not that he had anything to hide, he wasn't the one who fucking gutted Vera right there in the hallway, but when weeks went by and they had no one else to point fingers at, they had become restless.

Then, six months into the investigation, a neighbor came forward with doorbell camera footage from that day showing a grainy man, later identified as Jackson Bishop, entering a first story window in the Monroe-Dugan house a few minutes before Jaime had arrived, corroborating his description of events.

And now he was on the hook to testify in Bishop's murder trial. Assuming that was what Dana wanted to talk about, he called her.

She picked up on the second ring. "Jaime? Are you at home?"

Her voice held a note of alarm that made him sit up in bed, but he breathed through the spike in his heart rate. He'd come a long way in therapy—he could make it through one phone call without panicking. "Yes, I'm home. Why are you calling?"

There was a pause that lasted just long enough to tangle and snarl in his chest. "Jaime, someone leaked your identity to the press. It was all over the morning news cycle. They know you are the prosecution's witness to the murder."

What?

Jaime swung his legs off the bed and padded over to the window, pulling back the curtain. "Holy shit."

A sea of media vans flanked his gravel drive and the road on either side of his house, and people were milling around everywhere. How in the world had he not heard all of those vehicles pull up?

Hastily, he dropped the curtain and put his back to the wall next to the window, like he'd been caught invading their privacy and not the other way around. "What the hell do I do?"

Satisfied that Jaime was alive and safe, Dana's calm and unflappable tone returned. "I've got the District Attorney on the line, he's going to explain the situation. Hold on."

Jaime stood there in stunned silence, turning to peek outside when he heard a car door shut. Impossibly, it seemed like even more news reporters had appeared in the minute or so he'd been on the phone, and he watched as they all talked to a camera, holding giant microphones and gesturing to his house behind them as they spoke.

A low beep came through the phone, and a vaguely familiar voice joined Dana's. "Jaime? It's DA Rivera, and here with me on speakerphone is Detective Sutton, the lead investigator on this case. Are you well? Are you safe inside somewhere?"

He huffed out a breath. "Yes, I'm home. How could this happen? I thought everyone agreed that keeping my name out of the media until the trial was for the best."

He tried not to sound accusatory, knowing the DA wouldn't have done anything to jeopardize the case, but the list of people outside the police department who knew of Jaime's involvement that night was very short. Two others, to be exact—his lawyer, and his brother. Even though his relationship with Sam wasn't what it used to be, he knew Sam would never risk his safety by running his mouth, and Dana wouldn't risk her job or bar status.

DA Rivera gave a heavy sigh, like he'd been asking himself that same question all morning. "That was the plan, yes. I'm sorry, Jaime. I don't know who the leak is, but we've narrowed it down to one unit in Monroe PD. We're running an internal investigation to see if we can root out who talked to the media, but right now our focus needs to be on keeping you safe."

"The media is already swarming his house, Gabriel, it's a little late for mitigation," Dana said in that no-nonsense tone that she always used when speaking to law enforcement on his behalf. It was belied by the use of the prosecutor's first name, though, so they must be on decent terms with each other.

"The media is an annoyance, yes. And will be an even larger headache once we start jury selection, given that this brings the case right back into the public eye just a few weeks out from trial, but we'll cross that bridge when we get to it. They aren't my main concern right now."

Jaime's stomach flipped, and he started to pace around his room, keeping away from the window even with the curtains drawn.

"You know something about that phone call, don't you?" Dana accused. She was referencing the call Jaime had overheard the murderer make after he came to, tied up in Vera's closet.

They had called to report to someone that Vera was dead, but that Jaime was an unexpected visitor, and asked whoever was on the line what to do with him. Apparently, they'd been instructed to leave him alive, because they didn't come back to check on Jaime—they'd just left.

"You know I can't tell you that, Dana." DA Rivera sounded genuinely sorry. "What I can say is we received a tip regarding the murder of Vera Novikova-Dugan that Detective Sutton and her colleague Detective Jones are investigating. We are still confident in prosecuting Jackson Bishop for first-degree murder, but there are open lines of investigation in regards to this crime. We aren't ruling anything or anyone out."

Detective Jones was the asshole detective who had started interrogating Jaime the minute the medics had finished stitching up the wound on his temple. He sat down on his bed with a heavy sigh, and ran his fingers through his unwashed hair.

When was the last time I showered?

Out loud, Jaime asked, "And you think whoever this is will come after me now that they know who I am?" Another pregnant pause, and he couldn't stop his breathing from accelerating this time.

"Yes." That voice belonged to Detective Sutton. She had been more reserved at first, but she'd spoken to Jaime like he was someone who'd just survived something horrific, whereas Detective Jones had been belligerent. At first, Jaime had thought they were doing their own good-cop-bad-cop bit, but after a few weeks, he thought Detective Sutton's quiet observation and subtle kindness were genuine.

"If you know who this is then put a tail on them. Make sure they don't come near my client before you get enough for an arrest warrant," Dana snapped.

"We've hit some roadblocks with the arrest warrant, but we are working around them. It may take some time, though, and we don't want to take any chances with Jaime's safety in the meantime."

"Well what do you suggest, then? He's already essentially housebound, never mind the media circus currently camped in his yard. What else do you expect him to do?"

Jaime winced at his attorney's words. Sure they were true, but he hated the blunt reminder of how isolated he'd become in the last year.

Detective Sutton gentled her tone. "I've called an acquaintance of mine who owns a private security firm up in Silver Rapids. They take both body security and household security contracts, so they'll be able to set up Jaime's home with an alarm system and escort him when he needs to leave the house. Cameron Sheppard is a good guy, and his team is highly competent. They'll be able to handle this."

Jaime tensed at the mention of this private security firm.

How much would that cost? Probably an astronomical amount to outfit his home and pay someone to be with him until the trial in a few weeks. "Why can't you just have an officer come out and keep watch? Surely a police car parked in my driveway would be enough of a deterrent."

He didn't actually believe that. Whoever it was that might want to silence him had enough resources to hire someone to murder one of Monroe's elite socialites. They would be able to find someone who, with the right incentive, wouldn't blink at a police car in the driveway while they snuck in and did the same to Jaime.

But he didn't have the money for private security. Sam was already covering Jaime's bills on top of paying for his attorney, and his brother had clearly had enough of helping Jaime when he was too young, weak, or pathetic to do it himself—he wasn't going to become even more of a burden.

Maybe if he handled something like this himself for once, Sam would see that he could do it. He didn't have to step in all the time and save him, and they could be brothers again.

Friends, again.

"I spoke with the state Attorney General about hiring private security for you Jaime, but the budget's just not there to do it. And given the leak was internal, I think it best we outsource security until the trial. Sutton, are you sure about Cameron Sheppard's firm?"

"Yes, they do excellent work and are very professional. They were on the Senator's detail when he was campaigning in the area last week," she confirmed.

Then Jaime definitely couldn't afford them. "I appreciate your efforts here, but that's not something I can afford to pay out of pocket. I'll take the police cruiser and have a doorbell camera installed. I'll be fine."

Hopefully.

There was an awkward pause, and Detective Sutton cleared her throat. "Did your brother not tell you? The contract is already set, paid for in full. He called this morning immediately after the news broke and we arranged everything. The security team is probably already on their way to you."

Jaime's face flushed hot with anger.

Sam called Detective fucking Sutton before talking to me first?

They'd *managed* him before consulting him, before asking what he wanted. Sam hadn't even called—he just threw money at a babysitter so he didn't feel obligated to come and scrape Jaime off the floor. Again.

He wasn't sure how much of their deteriorating relationship the detectives and his lawyer had picked up on over the past year, but right now he didn't really care about letting on how hurt he was about this.

"Jaime —" Dana began, but he hung up before any of them could say anything else.

Jaime strode over to his closet and yanked on the nearest t-shirt and sweats without really seeing them. Fuming, he stomped down the stairs and pulled out his phone to call Sam while he hunted for his jacket and car keys.

When was the last time I drove myself somewhere?

The call went to voicemail.

Jaime knew things had become distant between them.

Sam had pulled away because Jaime was a twenty-six year old adult who needed to learn how to take care of himself when shit hit the fan. And he was trying.

He was *trying*.

Jaime was going to therapy, and listening to the advice of his attorney, and he would get up on that stand and tell the world how fucking useless he'd been when a woman had been brutalized in her own home. And then he would sell his house, get a job somewhere they didn't know his name so he could pay his own rent, and then maybe Sam would want to talk to him again because he wouldn't feel like Jaime needed him anymore.

Jaime could do that. He could make it so he didn't need anyone.

But Sam didn't even give him the chance. He'd solved the problem and payed the bill before Jaime knew there was a problem, and that made Jaime so irrationally angry that he had his keys in hand and was stepping out the front door to go tell his brother that he didn't need him anymore, before he remembered what was waiting for him on the other side.

The noise roared up around him, sudden and deafening, and the crowd pushed forward all at once.

Hands grabbed for him and people shouted and shoved microphones in his face. Jaime was backed up against the side of his house, the throng shifting him away from his front door, surging closer and closer.

His ears began to ring, and he couldn't get enough air into his lungs. Taking great heaving breaths, Jaime frantically searched for someone, anyone to see that he needed space. He needed them to back up. If they gave him a minute he'd be able to breathe again, and then he could ask them to please let him go find his brother so that he could tell him he didn't want his money—he just wanted Sam.

Jaime's vision grew spotty. Bright flashes in his periphery made it difficult to focus on anyone's face as they all blurred together into one angry, loud mob.

He saw the closet walls closing around him, bodies crowding him and grabbing for him and trapping him. He needed to turn around, needed to look and see the man striding toward him out of the dark so that he could dodge the inevitable blow—

Someone began shouting loud enough to be heard over the mob standing above him.

At some point, Jaime must have slid down the side of his home, and his hands covered his head as he sat hunched over his knees, taking great heaving breaths.

Two massive figures pushed through the crowd. The larger, darker-haired one began shoving people back and away from Jaime, like a guard dog defending his flock. He looked giant from Jaime's viewpoint, curled up on the ground.

The other came toward him, hands extended in the universal language that said, *"I'm not going to hurt you."*

Maybe Jaime was just hoping he wouldn't.

He crouched down, and gently pulled Jaime's hands away from their protective cage and pressed soothing, sure sweeps of his thumbs across his knuckles.

"Hi Jaime. I'm Finn, and that's Silas. We're here with Private Security Solutions, and we're going to help keep you safe. Can you take a deep breath for me?"

His voice rumbled through Jaime; a quiet, familiar blue-purple note of calm that blanketed over him and hushed the bright haze of his panic. Jaime focused on that, followed the sweeping eddy of his voice back out into the gentle calm where he could take several slow, measured breaths.

The man striding out of the dark behind him was gone. Only this beautiful voice in front of him remained.

"Good. That's very good, Jaime. Alright, how about you tell me five things you can see."

Oh, yes, the pamphlet.

For some reason, that nearly made Jaime giggle. "Your voice is blue."

Does that make sense? Probably not.

"Thank you, I love the color blue. Now how about you open your eyes and tell me four other things you can see."

Jaime blinked, not realizing he had closed them. "The sky, it's starting to get cloudy. Your sweater is soft and green. My pants are gray."

He looked up then, and wondered if he had passed out and was dreaming after all, because he knew those brown eyes. He hadn't been able to tell just how deep they were through a phone screen, but now he could see—like sun-drenched soil, offering warmth and life and hope.

"It's you. I see you."

CHAPTER 6
FINN

It's you, I see you.

Jaime's words bounced around in Finn's head as he helped him to his feet and guided him through the front door while Silas pushed back the crowd. The wolf in his head was prowling in circles, a low rumble coming from his chest.

It's him.

Scent him. It's him.

Protect.

Protect.

The tug on his heart went hot and taut, finally tethered. Finn followed Jaime inside, beholden to that tug as it pulled him toward someone instead of away for the first time—for the only time.

Silas locked the door behind them and threw closed the curtains covering the bottom half of the floor to ceiling windows in the living room. Finn took a steadying breath, bracing himself for the full effect of being in the same room as Jaime Lamont.

Hopefully he wouldn't make a fool of himself.

Jaime mirrored his deep, slow breaths, and looked up. A jolt of awareness shot through him when their eyes met.

It's you, I see you.

He opened his mouth to say something, anything, to the beautiful man standing before him, but Jaime spoke first. "You can let go of me now, I'm not going to pass out."

Right. He was still clinging to the younger man like his life depended on it. Finn quickly dropped Jaime's arm, and cleared his throat. "Sorry. Right. Yes."

The whole ride over Finn had been pinching himself, feeling like this was all some surreal dream. This morning, Jaime had been a what-if; a deep regret that he'd messed up somehow and lost his chance.

And now, just a few hours later, Finn was standing in his foyer.

But Jaime hadn't chosen the circumstances that led to him needing a security detail, and he hadn't chosen to reconnect with Finn. This was all a result of the unfortunate events Jaime had survived last year.

Sheppard had filled them in on everything the detective could share before the case went to trial—Jaime had delivered a commissioned painting to Vera Novikova-Dugan's house on that early spring evening roughly a year ago, and wound up shoved in a closet, tied up, and left to suffocate. Somehow, he'd escaped and called for help. As far as the police could tell, he'd been in the wrong place, at the wrong time.

Oh, and he was the only witness to a brutal murder and had overheard key evidence that it had more than likely been orchestrated by someone other than the guy they'd already arrested.

Someone who had a very good reason to want Jaime dead.

Protect!

Finn realized he'd been staring for too long, so he cleared his throat again and fumbled for something to say, but again, Jaime beat him to it.

"Thank you, for... that. Out there. I'm sorry. I just found out that my name was leaked to the media, and I wasn't thinking straight. I'm not... helpless, like that. All the time. I mean, I wouldn't have gone out there at all if I hadn't been distracted. I'm not an idiot." His tone grew increasingly indignant even as he stumbled over his words and fidgeted with the hem of his t-shirt, as if Finn had been the one who accused him of acting recklessly.

Finn couldn't help but think how adorable Jaime's nervous rambling was.

The sight of him being swallowed up by that pack of scavengers currently squatting outside would haunt him for a while, and his hackles rose with the instinct to protect.

He'd been half out of his mind when they pulled up to the house only to realize they hadn't arrived in time to keep Jaime away from the media fishing for an angle on the breaking news. Throwing open his door before Silas had even fully stopped the vehicle, all he knew was the steady pulse inside him.

Protect, protect, protect.

Go! He's there!

Protect!

Finn tore down the lawn, yelling as loud as he could at the group to step away from Jaime. Silas caught up quickly, his giant strides eating up the short distance, and together they parted the crowd like sharks. Seeing Jaime crouched there, with his head tucked in, honed all of Finn's predatory awareness.

He's vulnerable.

Protect, protect, protect!

Luckily, his training in basic mental health triage kicked in, and Finn talked Jaime through slowing his breathing and grounding his senses. It was a pity that all of his training and common sense seemed to have left him now, though, standing in Jaime's foyer while he stared like he was looking at the last golden unicorn.

Which was silly, considering those went extinct hundreds of years ago. Probably. Fuck if he knows.

God, you're an idiot. Say something, you fool!

"I believe you," he ground out, tone gentle. Jaime seemed to like that, before. "This situation must be quite a lot to process, never mind the frenzy outside. I promise you, we won't let them hurt you like that again."

Silas shot him a look.

Right, Finn wasn't usually one to promise clients much of anything, except his professionalism. Or one to be very talkative.

Chatty had never been a word used to describe him.

Jaime nodded, but still had that reserved look. Could there be more to what had happened? What had made him so worked up that he'd walked right out into that feeding frenzy without realizing he'd be mobbed?

Silas cleared his throat. "How about we all have a seat, and Mr. Winters and I will talk you through some next steps. Does that sound alright with you?"

Jaime looked toward Silas as he spoke, taking stock of him for the first time, noting how giant he was. Finn bristled at the once-over, and Silas shot him another confused look.

Calm down, you creep, he's not checking out your friend. And even if he was, he's not yours to be jealous of.

Jaime ran his fingers through his messy hair and motioned for Finn and Silas to follow him, and Finn reminded himself that he was here in a professional capacity, and absolutely should not lean forward to scent him better.

Sweet, like lemon bars. He still smells like warm bed sheets.

What would the bed sheets smell like after I woke him up with his cock in my mouth?

He was so, so fucked.

Finn took stock of the home. For security purposes, of course. An A-frame made up the main structure, with a two-story section built into the side that added a couple of additional rooms upstairs and a kitchen area downstairs. Floor to ceiling windows covered the A-frame section of the house, overlooking the backyard and encroaching wilderness.

They entered a living area off the foyer which connected to the kitchen, an archway dividing both rooms. He circled around the oversized, plush couch, noting the gas fireplace and large built-in bookshelves. Peering into the kitchen, there was a dining nook at the very back, framed by a large bay window, and french doors led outside toward an over-grown garden.

A small shed sat at the back of the lawn, and a green meadow separated the property from the rocky lake shore.

Circling back toward the living room, he noticed the smaller details of the home. Jaime clearly had an eye for making a space cozy and lived-in, with throws and pillows on the furniture and the shelves were full of books and trinkets. There were paintings of all different sizes; some hung alone and some clustered together in an unexpected but artistic way. Most were landscapes, but some were portraits of animals and people.

There were a few pictures of Jaime with another man, shorter than him, but with similar features. His brother, maybe?

Despite the layer of dust and the unruly landscaping outside, the house and property were gorgeous.

And so was the man living there.

Pictures really had not done him justice. Even as he nervously paced the room, fingers tangled in the hem of his shirt, he was graceful. Finn again thought that he could be some far-removed descendent of the fae. Jaime certainly looked the part, all lithe muscle and long legs that went up, up, up...

Finn had gathered the basics of him through their video chats; red hair, pale freckled skin, and green eyes. But standing before him, Jaime was truly stunning. His hair wasn't just red, it was more like cinnamon with highlights that shone copper when he passed by the vaulted windows that flanked the living area. His eyes were a muted, mossy green, accentuated by the red flush of his cheeks. And his freckles were far more pronounced and numerous than Finn had seen before, all nutmeg and spice dusted along his cheekbones, down his neck and arms.

How far did they trail down his shoulders and torso?

The poor man is probably having one of the worst days of his life, and you're wondering if he has freckles on his ass? Focus.

His wolf rumbled.

It is a fantastically perky ass.

He shook his head to clear it, and sat next to Silas on the giant couch. Which was a mistake, because their combined weight tipped them inward toward each other, sucking them so far back into the comfortable monstrosity that there would be no way to stand up.

At least not with their dignity intact.

Jaime sat across from them in an armchair, and the corner of his full mouth tipped up at the sight of the two giant men struggling to look professional while being swallowed by the furniture. So, maybe it wasn't such a disaster.

Silas assessed Finn's tongue-tied state and took the lead on the conversation. "Your brother asked us to do a full security analysis and technology setup of your home, which will be completed by Mr. Winters," he gestured toward Finn.

"Finn. Please call me Finn." He couldn't stand the thought of Jaime calling him *Mr. Winters*.

Silas gave him yet another sidelong glance. "Right, yes. And you can call me Silas." He smiled at Jaime in that way that had twinks throwing themselves at him during their youth, and Finn barely suppressed the growl that rumbled up his throat.

Silas looked exasperated.

Jaime glanced between the two. "Nice to meet you, Silas and, uh, Finn. Please call me Jaime."

There hadn't been a moment for them to address that they clearly knew each other, which Silas seemed to be quickly picking up on, and Finn wasn't keen on having that conversation in front of his best friend. Up until this point he hadn't let on that he had previous contact with Jaime, and he wanted to see how things went before disclosing that to Silas and Sheppard.

Finn cleared his throat. "With your permission, I'll conduct a full security sweep of the home. That includes noting entry and exit points, areas to set up cameras and motion detection technology, and developing a security plan based on the most likely scenarios in case of an intruder. Once you've approved that plan we'll forward it to our technology partners who will install everything."

"You don't set that up yourself?" Jaime asked.

"No, we're a small team and don't have an in-house technology expert right now. But I promise the people we work with can be trusted. All monitoring is done by the bodyguard assigned to you."

There he went, making more promises.

"Bodyguard?" Jaime's eyes darted between Silas and Finn. "Like, someone will be staying here with me? All the time?"

Silas nodded. "Yes. One of our team members will be with you around the clock for now while we assess the potential threats. We'll have to switch out who stays with you on occasion, but one of us will be assigned as your main detail."

"Me. It's me. I'll be staying with you." Finn nearly cut his friend off in his rush to clarify.

He knew Silas and Sheppard had been surprised by his offer to act as main security detail, but he'd played it off, citing his concern for Silas brushing up against the Salt Creek pack. Which was true, but he felt like an asshole for using his concern as a distraction. He just wasn't ready to explain his other reasons.

Mainly, that he would go crazy if he passed up an opportunity to be close to Jaime, even in a professional context.

Jaime wasn't keen on that idea, though. "Is that really necessary?" His fingers tangled in his lap. "I mean, does one of you really have to stay here all the time? If you set up the security cameras and everything, I'm sure I'll be fine. I don't need that part of the contract, you can give my brother his money back for that part."

Finn and Silas looked at each other, then turned back to Jaime. Gently, Silas explained, "Everything is paid in full through the end of the trial, your brother Sam was adamant about that. We will do our best to keep a low profile and not impose. If you're not comfortable with someone sleeping in a guest room, we can station the night shift detail in a van in your driveway—that's no problem at all."

Yes, it sure as fuck would be a problem.

"But even when the media frenzy dies down—and we are making calls about that right now—it's not safe for you to be alone out here until the police know more about whoever was on the other end of that phone call," Silas finished.

"No, no, it's not about someone being in here. I won't make you sleep in the driveway. It's just—" Jaime's phone started buzzing in his pocket, and he scrambled to answer it. "Sam."

His tone completely changed with the greeting, face shuttered. He seemed angry, and... hurt. It was similar to the way he'd assured Finn and Silas that he wasn't an idiot, earlier. Jaime held the phone out as he spoke, like it was a video call.

"We'll excuse ourselves," Finn said, as he and Silas shifted and listed into each other, struggling against the plush cushions for enough leverage to heave themselves up.

"Is that them? Let me see them."

Silas froze at the sound of Sam's demand, and Finn knew his ears would have been perked if he were shifted.

Interesting.

Jaime sighed, irritated, and moved to perch on the coffee table in front of them, angling the phone so that they were all visible. Finn told himself that he leaned in to make it easier for them all to fit in the frame, not to feel the warmth coming off of Jaime.

Liar.

"Yes, it's the security people you sent over. *Without asking me first,*" Jaime snarked.

"I'm sorry, Jaime. I got busy this morning and didn't get the chance to call. I'm glad they are there with you. What are their names? Are you safe? Are you ok?"

"I'm fine. I was fine before. If you had called me first so

we could talk about this, you would know that." Jaime's cheeks were flushed in anger. He turned the camera toward the couch, inadvertently leaning closer to Finn in the process.

His inner wolf preened.

Down, boy.

Get closer!

"This is Finn Winters, and Silas... I'm sorry, what was your last name?"

"Silas Granger. Nice to meet you, Mr. Lamont. Please call me Silas. If you prefer. We were just sitting down with your brother to go over the terms of the contract so we can begin the security sweep. We should have our technology expert out here by tomorrow to install everything."

Well, now who's Mr. Chatty?

At Finn's raised eyebrow, Silas narrowed his eyes.

Finn turned back to the camera. "I'll be leading the security detail. We were just discussing with Jaime whether he would prefer us to set up a van to conduct nighttime surveillance or whether he'd prefer we use the guest room."

"The guest room is fine," Jaime mumbled, ears turning pink.

Is he blushing? Oh God, that's fucking adorable.

Remembering his hesitancy over the security detail, Finn gentled his tone and leaned in. "Are you sure? It's really not a problem to set up nighttime surveillance from a van in the driveway."

It was a problem. Not the van part, they often used surveillance vans based on the needs of the client and they usually had a kitchenette and cot to keep comfortable during the overnight hours. But Finn would be an anxious mess, sitting outside in a van every night thinking about Jaime being *inside*.

Warm, in bed. All soft, sleepy, and alone.

Closer!

Get it together.

"I'm sure. If you're going to be here, I'd rather you not be left outside. The evenings are still chilly," Jaime sniffed, turning his nose up.

Finn chose not to look too hard at why that tone made him shift where he sat, adjusting the crotch of his pants before he embarrassed himself. "Alright. Thank you."

Sensing, *probably smelling*, Finn's predicament, Silas interjected. "Now that we've been introduced to Sam, and with your permission Jaime, Finn and I will begin our security sweep of the main and upper levels. I asked our supervisor to put in a call with Monroe PD to send some cruisers out to block off the road shoulders and driveway, they will be here soon. In the meantime, it's best we all sit tight. It was nice to meet you, Sam."

"Likewise. Thank you for looking after my brother."

Jaime moved back over to the armchair, and with him distracted, Finn gave one last heave and escaped the clutches of the too-soft couch. He offered an arm to Silas, and they were both free and moving toward the stairs.

"You're starting up there?" Jaime asked, voice pitched high in question.

Finn turned back toward him. "Would you prefer we start elsewhere?"

"No, just. Um. Let me clean up my bedroom and bathroom a bit before you go in there. Give me a minute to talk to Sam and then I'll be up. I haven't had company in a while. Not that I usually bring company into my bedroom when I do. Or that I have that kind of company at all!" His ears were tipped pink again. "You can start on the two guest rooms to the left of the stairs."

A chuckle came through the phone speaker, and Jaime glared at the screen and reached for the earbuds sitting on the nearby side table.

Finn chose not to dwell on most of what Jaime had just said, lest he start peppering him with intense and intrusive follow up questions regarding the specifics of who had been in his bedroom and *why*.

"Of course. Let us know if you have any questions."

He followed Silas up the stairs, and they entered the first door on the left. A slightly more toned-down version of the curated chaos of the living room, the guest room was still cozy, with pictures and a mirror hung above a chest of drawers and a queen sized bed covered in a soft quilt, flanked by two windows overlooking the front yard and driveway. It was a far more comfortable sleeping arrangement than he had on many of their past contracts.

Silas shut the door behind them, and Finn closed the curtains before he turned back toward his brother.

Silas gave him a look. "Alright, when were you going to tell me that not only do you know our client, but you are also clearly panting after him like a lovesick puppy?"

"I am not panting after him like a lovesick puppy."

Yes, you are.

"Yes, you are."

Of course Finn wouldn't be able to hide that from him. While Silas wasn't his actual brother by birth, they knew each other better than anyone else in the world, and he couldn't keep a secret from him for long.

Finn sighed and tipped his head back. "Ugh. Fine. Yes, I know him. Sort of. Not really. I don't know him well. We've never actually met before."

Silas looked confused, so Finn waved his hands around and tried to elaborate. "I know him from the internet. That dating app I was on."

"The dating app you were on... over a year ago?"

"Yes."

Silas raised his eyebrows and shot a considering look toward the closed door. "When did you meet up with him?"

Finn shuffled his feet. Right, well, there was no way around this. "We never actually did meet up."

Silas cocked his head. "You're telling me that the tension between you two downstairs was because you both remember each other from meeting on a dating app, but you never actually met in person? That can't be it."

"There wasn't tension."

Yes, there was.

"Yes, there was. He gets flustered with just a look from you, Finn. One word in that low, soft voice—which I've literally never heard you use on anyone else before, by the way—and he turns into a tomato and starts word-vomiting his life story. What, did you two exchange dick pics or something? Is that what's going on here?"

Jesus Christ.

Pinching the bridge of his nose, Finn grumbled, "No, we

did not exchange *dick pics*, you ass. And he does not turn into a tomato, it's just his fair complexion. And I do not speak to him differently than any other client!"

Liar.

"Liar. So, what? You chatted through an app? That's it?" Silas still looked like he had missed something, before the realization dawned. "Oh, that's *him*, isn't it? The one who stood you up?"

Finn looked away, but nodded.

"Oh, Finny, why didn't you say something?"

Finn sighed heavily. "Our date was meant to be just over a year ago. He was going to drop something off for work in Monroe and then head up to Silver Rapids, but he never showed up. When I saw his face in the article you showed me this morning, and the date of the murder..."

"Jesus, Finn. You think that's why he didn't show up? It was the same night as Vera's murder? You think he was there, instead?"

Finn nodded. "I checked the date in my calendar. He was tied up in a closet, fearing for his life, while I sat in a restaurant being angry at him."

Silas's face fell. "Damn, Finny. I'm so sorry."

"I didn't tell you this morning because I was so shocked that it was him, and that the reason he disappeared was because he had seen... and then I just..." Finn trailed off.

Silas didn't need him to elaborate, though. "You needed to be here, to see him for yourself."

Finn looked at his dearest friend, and nodded. "I was planning on finding him on my own before the contract came in."

Silas raised his eyebrows at that, but his tone remained neutral. "Why, Finn?"

"Because he's a client who needs our protection." Truth, but not the whole of it.

"Why were you going to find him before you knew he would be our client? Why did you volunteer to be his full time security detail?"

Finn's gut twisted with guilt. "I'm sorry, Si. It's not a lie that I'm worried about you and your involvement with the Salt Creek pack. I don't want you within a hundred miles of them."

"I know that. But there's more, yes?"

Finn rolled that question around in his head. "Yes, there's more. What that is, I don't know. Or I'm not ready to know. This is the first time I've ever met him in person, it's crazy to say there's more there for me, isn't it? Am I crazy?"

That steady, thrumming beat pulsed inside of him, and tugged him back downstairs to where Jaime sat.

Go to him.

Go. Go. Go.

He looked at his friend, silently asking why he felt like this after just one meeting. Silas always had the answers Finn needed, even when they were boys.

"Only you can say what it is you feel, and when you feel it. But I do know that you're not crazy, and this kind of reaction is not... out of the ordinary for our kind, Finn. Not when we meet someone... special. Not by a long shot."

The weight of that statement hung in the air. Finn and Silas stared at each other, an understanding passing between them as deep as the bond they shared as friends and brothers. As pack.

He smells right.

Finn wasn't ready to say it out loud yet, and Silas sensed that. He moved forward and pulled Finn into a bear hug, tree-trunk arms clapping him on the back. "You've been distant lately, even more than before. I've been worried about you. In there..." Silas pulled away, and looked toward the closed door, his face peaceful. "In there, you were present. You were Finn."

He yanked Finn back to him, harder this time. "Please be careful. For everyone involved. I don't want either of you getting hurt."

Finn didn't know if Silas meant that Jaime might not be interested in him, or that he would tell Jaime about what they were and then he would reject him, or that something bad would happen to Jaime. There were a lot of ways they could be hurt. "I will be."

Silas released him, a knowing look in his eye. "Love you, Finny."

Finn clapped him on the shoulder, and smiled before turning toward the door to start the security sweep. "Yeah, yeah, love you too, Si."

CHAPTER 7
JAIME

Jaime's life was a complete disaster.

The entire world knew his name, and was currently speculating that he could be an accomplice to Vera Novikova-Dugan's murder. Or maybe her heartbroken ex-lover, or her long-lost son, or whatever other wild theory that had spun out of hand since his identity was leaked to the media four hours ago.

His brother no longer wanted to be in the same room with him, and didn't trust him to make his own decisions about his personal safety and well-being. To make matters worse, he'd hired a security agency that seemed to only employ Greek gods, one of which was, hands down, the most attractive man Jaime had ever met.

Who also happened to be *Finn*, the man he'd asked out and then stood up over a year ago because he'd been knocked out and shoved in a closet the night of their date.

Now, Finn was standing in Jaime's bedroom, pointedly *not* looking at the pair of boxer briefs hanging from the hamper that Jaime had frantically chucked all of his dirty laundry into right before they'd entered the room.

Oh, and Jaime had just overheard him exchange *I love you*'s with the other giant, hunky bodyguard standing in his room.

A complete, and total disaster.

Did I really say that his voice was blue? Out loud? God, who says shit like that?

Jaime had made it embarrassingly clear that he remembered Finn, but he hadn't really acknowledged him back. What if he'd spent the last year full of guilt and shame over the way he'd left things with Finn, longing to see him again, only for the man to not even remember him?

Sedate me, please.

The two men made a quick sweep of the room, briefly peering into his closet and bathroom before going back downstairs. He quickly flicked the boxer briefs fully into the hamper, but blushed when he turned to see Finn standing in the doorway, staring at him.

Again.

The man stared quite a bit, and Jaime couldn't decide if it was because he didn't want to say anything, or that he just wasn't very loquacious. Probably the former. Jaime hadn't made a very good first impression, or second, if you counted the time he no-showed on their date and then ghosted him.

First, Finn had to rescue him from panicking at the swarm of foam microphones shoved in his face, and then he had to coax Jaime into seemingly caring whether he lived or died at the hands of a hypothetical hitman.

It wasn't that he didn't care—he very much did not want to die, and he especially didn't want to be murdered. But so much of his life had been out of his control this past year. So many of his joys and passions had been taken from him, he just wanted the option of whether or not to let the two hot bodyguards—*who are in love with each other*—invade his privacy for the next two weeks.

He really shouldn't be so hung up on that last bit, but Finn was still staring and it was starting to give him a complex.

"Um, sorry about the mess. I really have been mostly alone in this house for...a while, now. I'll make sure the sheets in your room are clean before you sleep there tonight."

Finn nodded. "It's ok, really. I understand. Or, well, I don't. I honestly can't imagine what things have been like for you. But I want to. Understand, that is."

Jaime wanted to reach up and smooth out the little crease that had formed between Finn's eyebrows.

Yikes.

Finn went on, "I didn't get the chance to say, before. That I haven't forgotten about you. I wondered where you'd gone, when you... disappeared. I hoped you were ok. And now that I know a little of what's happened in your life since then, I wish that it hadn't. And, if my timing is right, and the night of our—of when we planned to meet was the same night as the murder..." he huffed.

"I'm sorry. I wish I could have done more, then. But Silas and I will do everything we can to make sure no one hurts you, now," Finn finished with a rush, his brown eyes warm and bright.

Damn him, but Jaime believed his earnestness. Clearly, he'd missed the chance for anything to happen between them—Finn was with Silas now. And why wouldn't he choose a strong, capable man who could look after himself instead of someone weak and pathetic like Jaime?

His job is to protect people, of course he's like this with all of his clients.

Jaime didn't want to be anyone's job, anyway. He could look after himself, and he'd show Finn and his brother that. "Thank you, Finn. I appreciate you and Silas for helping. I'll do my best to not be more work for you both." He tried to smile. "And, there was nothing you could have done, then. It didn't feel like it at the time, but, all things considered, everything happened fairly quickly. I wasn't stuck in there for long. You have nothing to be sorry for."

He was the one who should apologize for the way he'd left things, but that line between Finn's eyebrows was back, and before he could say anymore, Silas was hollering up the stairs. "Monroe PD is here to break up the crowd, want me to go out and talk to them?"

Finn shot a concerned look outside, and turned away. "No, I'll do it and bring the truck around when they're gone."

He tromped downstairs, Jaime following behind. Just before opening the front door, he turned around to face them, voice stern. "Hopefully this won't take long. You two hang tight, and stay inside."

Silas's grin was cheeky. "Yes, sir."

Awkward silence descended as Finn left, and the large man turned around to face Jaime, giving him another of those easy smiles that belied his height and stature. Silas seemed more like a gentle giant, than a real monster. Although, given his profession, that ferociousness was probably there, well-hidden under his smiling eyes and the gentle way he moved.

Silas's complexion was darker than Finn's, more of a warm bronze that was emphasized by his near-black hair pulled away from his face and dark eyes, and he was even taller than Finn.

Suddenly, the thought of seeing Silas and Sam next to each other popped into his head. With Sam being a few inches shorter than Jaime's 5'10", their height difference would be quite something.

However, Sam had never been one to be cowed by someone based on size. Jaime had seen him tear apart larger men with one look and a few well placed words, and had loved every second of it. Hopefully the two wouldn't clash too much if they ever met. He might be jealous, but he didn't think Silas was a bad guy and wouldn't wish Sam's quick wit turned sour upon the man.

Maybe just one good verbal jab would be ok...

He wished things between him and his brother were still that simple. "Can I get you anything to drink? Water, maybe?"

"Water would be nice, thank you."

He got the sense that Silas accepted more for Jaime's comfort, as it gave him something to do. They moved into the kitchen, and Jaime poured him a glass of water as they listened to the sounds of the crowd dissipating outside. Finn shouted something over the din of doors slamming shut and gravel crunching under tires.

If only to break the silence, Jaime said, "I'll need to go to the grocery store."

Silas nodded. "No problem, Finn can go with you. He'll probably need to get a few things of his own while he's staying here."

"Is that what you all usually do when you're guarding someone? Get your own groceries and just use their kitchen?"

Silas eased back against the small island, relaxing into their conversation rather than looming. It put Jaime more at ease. "Not often. Most of the time we either camp out in the van and eat fast food, or we are working with clients in shifts and don't eat very much until we are relieved. This is a bit of a unique situation."

Jaime cocked his head. "Why?"

Silas paused, head tilting like he was still trying to listen to what was happening outside. Jaime couldn't hear anything anymore, and assumed most of the crowd had cleared off by now.

Instead of answering his question, Silas asked one of his own. "So, you and Finn knew each other before, yes?"

Jaime went still. Had he really been that obvious?

"It's ok, I'm not trying to catch you out. It's just good for us to know, to get ahead of anything should people go digging into your past. Finn told me that you were talking on a dating app before all of this happened."

"It's all been deleted, so if anyone goes digging around

they won't find much. But yes, we knew each other before. We were talking, but..." he took a slow, deep breath. "It never went anywhere."

"Because of that night? Or some other reason?"

Is Silas jealous?

He shouldn't be. Clearly, he was a better match for Finn. Stronger, more capable. But Jaime was saved from explaining to Finn's current boyfriend that he still carried a torch—or maybe a forest fire—for him, and would have jumped at the chance to date him if not for the whole 'being hit upside the head and shoved into a closet on the night of their first date' thing, because the front door opened and Finn came tromping back inside.

Does he clomp around like a Clydesdale everywhere he goes?

Silas walked out of the kitchen ahead of him, and Jaime rounded the corner just in time to catch Finn shoot Silas a dirty look.

Turning toward Jaime, he schooled his features. "The crowd is gone, and barricades have been set up along the road shoulder fifty yards on either side of the driveway. There will still be increased traffic coming by, and we'll need to be cautious leaving the house, but it's better than it was this morning."

Finn tossed a set of keys to Silas. "The truck is out front. Do you need anything before you leave?"

Silas raised his eyebrows at the dismissal. "I should be asking you that. Need me to bring you anything from the house?"

Do they live together?

Jaime wanted to sink into the floor.

"I've got my go bag from the truck. Thanks, though." Finn lifted the duffle bag he was holding, seeming to deflate from whatever had riled him up outside.

"Call me if you need anything. I mean it. Anything," Silas said, pointing at Finn in emphasis.

"I will, Si. Talk to you soon."

Silas hummed, and then left. Jaime noted the empty driveway as Finn once again shut the door and threw the locks into place.

Feeling awkward at having witnessed their goodbye, Jaime made his way back toward the kitchen. "I'll need to go to the grocery store later today. I usually put in an order ahead of time for pickup; if there's anything you'd like to get, let me know and I can add it to the list."

Finn's heavy steps followed him into the kitchen. "Thank you, yes. I'll write some things down for you. Do you mind if I use your kitchen while I stay here? I'll stay out of your way and do my own dishes."

He leaned back against the island the same way Silas had, and even cocked his head in the same way, as if listening to the truck start up outside and drive off.

They are so similar, even down to their mannerisms.

Well, similar in the sense that they behaved the same and spoke the same, but they didn't look very much alike. Finn's skin also had warm undertones, but it was several shades lighter and his sandy blonde hair shone golden in the light, curling around his ears in a short, shaggy cut.

Sure, they were both on the taller side compared to most, but where Silas was a true giant of a man, Finn was a brick wall. He looked like a linebacker with a dark green henley pulled tight across his broad shoulders, and his rolled up sleeves revealed heavily muscled and corded forearms.

Jaime didn't realize how much of a thing he had for forearms until right now. And hands. What would it feel like for those arms to crowd him up against the kitchen counter? For those hands to bracket his hips, while Finn leaned over and brushed his lips against his neck, grinding into Jaime where they were both hard...

Ok, so maybe he just had a thing for Finn.

"Of course, please use whatever you like. Do you cook very often?" If his voice cracked a bit he blamed it on the rough morning.

Finn's mouth turned up in a half smile. "I do. I'm actually pretty good at it, if I can say that. What about you? What are your go-to meals?"

Jaime tried not to picture Finn moving about his kitchen in socked feet while he chopped and stirred things in relaxed, sure movements. Would he hum to himself while he cooked? Would his biceps flex as he reached up into the cabinets? Would he cook shirtless? Maybe with just an apron on...

Jesus, pull yourself together.

"What?" he asked, blinking at Finn.

His half smile turned into a smirk, eyes twinkling. "I asked what your favorite things to cook are. If you have standard go-to's, I'll work my list around that."

Jaime's face flushed all the way to his ears.

You cannot get caught daydreaming about your body-guard—who's very much involved with your other bodyguard—cooking in your kitchen, only wearing an apron!

The apron would say, 'Kiss the Cook.'

Jaime choked on a cough. "Oh. Right. Um, well, I'm not much of a cook to be honest." He rubbed the back of his neck. "Sam used to bring around take-out quite a lot. Since he's stopped coming over I mostly eat frozen meals. A lot of frozen pizza and chicken pot pies," he chuckled sheepishly.

A muscle flexed in Finn's jaw. "Your brother doesn't come visit you anymore? Why? Do you go and see him?"

The abrupt shift in conversation caught Jaime off guard, even though he was the one that mentioned Sam in the first place. "Um, he just doesn't. He was around for me a lot at the start, right after all this happened. Probably too much. Even before then, too. I think I told you about how our mom died young and our dad checked out, so Sam basically raised me. I imagine it was quite a burden to be a young college student stuck worrying about your teenage little brother."

Deeply uncomfortable, Jaime shifted on his feet, fingers tangling in the hem of his shirt. "I don't blame him for needing space from it all. From me. Always having to take care of someone else is a lot. And I can manage on my own, I'm really not as much of an idiot as I made myself look when you got here this morning. I'd just gotten off the phone with the detective, and everything built up and I needed to go talk to Sam, and I forgot about everyone outside. It won't happen again."

Fuck, he'd worked himself up again. He could feel his cheeks go red with anger and embarrassment.

That crease was back between Finn's eyebrows, and he pushed off the counter and stepped toward Jaime. "He told you that you are too much of a burden to be around anymore?"

Jaime could barely make out the words through the rumble in Finn's voice. "Well, no. Not in so many words. But it was hard at first. I had to stop working, because..." He shook his head. "I wasn't painting anymore, and with bills and groceries and everything, my savings went quickly. I bought the house outright before, so no mortgage, but Sam helped me out so much with the lawyer and everything else, I know supporting me like that takes a toll. Things should be better after the trial."

I hope.

Finn's features softened. "I'm sorry, I shouldn't have brought it up like that."

He took another step toward Jaime, standing just an arms length away now, hands at his side. Jaime had to look up to meet his eyes, noticing little flecks of gold in the chocolate brown color. "I did not think you were an idiot this morning, nor have I ever thought that. And I do not think you are weak. I think you witnessed and experienced something horrible, and have been forced to put your life on hold for an entire year because of the threat it poses to you. There is no weakness in enduring that, Jaime."

His breath caught, and he had to look away or else Finn would see him blinking back tears. "Thank you."

Clearing his throat, Jaime stepped back. "So, unless you want me to up my usual order of frozen pot pies, write down your grocery list and I'll make an order for pickup this afternoon."

Finn stepped back too, seeming to realize how close they'd drifted, but his voice was still gravelly. "How about I cook enough for the both of us while I'm here, yeah? You can't live off of frozen meals indefinitely."

Jaime laughed. It was brief, but real, and made him feel lighter than he had in a very long time. "You certainly can, big boy. But I won't turn down your offer."

Their eyes connected, and electricity zipped between them as he realized what he'd said.

Oh God, big boy? Really?

Before Jaime could stop himself, his gaze skated downward at the implication, eyes widening at the prominent swell in Finn's pants. He shifted so the counter would cover his own lower half, because the blood that had previously flushed his face had descended elsewhere at his choice of words and the visual evidence of just how true they were.

Jaime coughed through the croak in his voice. "Cooking. I won't turn down your cooking. Just tell me to do whatever you want, and I'll do it. Order! Tell me what groceries to order, and I will."

Wishing a sinkhole would open up and swallow him whole, Jaime looked anywhere else but at Finn, waiting for him to scoff and make fun of his rambling or tell him this wasn't going to work, and to look for the sexual harassment complaint in the mail.

Instead, Finn rumbled, "Alright Jaime, I'll tell you what I want."

It sounded like he had a bit in his mouth, his voice low

and choked. When Jaime focused back on his face he sucked in a sharp breath at how dark Finn's eyes were—pupils so dilated they nearly eclipsed his irises.

So, relationship with Silas or no, Finn looked like he was aware of, and maybe shared, the attraction that charged the air around them.

A complete, and total disaster, indeed.

CHAPTER 8

FINN

Finn was so fucked.

It had been years since he'd struggled to keep a lid on his shift, and it had never been the scent of someone's arousal that caused him difficulty. Usually, Finn's wolf only wanted to come out when he was angry, or when it was time to fight.

But the scent of Jaime's desire had been strong since they'd walked into the kitchen, and at his suggestion of *doing whatever Finn told him to*, his fangs descended from his gums and dark talons now tipped his fingers, his wolf ready to *take*.

Ours.

He's ours.

Finn chose not to look too hard at that right now.

Fighting back his shift, and the urge to bend Jaime over the counter and show him exactly how skilled he was in the kitchen, he grasped for a thread of self control. "Where would you like me to set up my laptop? I'll write the grocery list, and then work on the tech report before we go pick them up."

His question sounded choked through his fangs, and Jaime was still looking at him like a rabbit caught in a trap—but he didn't scent fear. No, the only thing he detected was overwhelming want. When Jaime turned, Finn caught a glimpse of the bulge in his pants as he walked to a small table and found a notepad and pen.

Professional. You are a professional, and this is your client. He didn't ask you back into his life. You're a goddamn wolf and instead of finding a way to gently tell him that, he's going to figure it out in a few seconds when he sees the fangs you're sporting, you animal.

That thought slammed into him. Not the fangs, but that he'd skipped right over *if* and went straight to *when* in reference to telling Jaime about his shift.

He was so, so fucked.

He accepted the pad of paper and pen from Jaime, who said he was going upstairs to shower and clean up. Finn nodded, now completely unable to speak without revealing his fangs thanks to thoughts of Jaime in the shower, wet and slick with soap, and only a few flimsy wooden doors between them.

After several deep, calming breaths, he scrawled out enough food to feed them both for a week or so, and left the list on the counter. And if he picked the recipes he was best at to impress Jaime—the ones Andi had taught him himself— well, that was his business.

His phone rang with a call from Sheppard. He could still

hear Jaime padding around his bedroom upstairs and hadn't heard the shower start yet, so he took the phone call outside to the back of the property. He needed to look around anyway before submitting the security report.

Gently closing the glass french door behind him so he didn't startle Jaime upstairs, he answered. "Hey Sheppard, what's up?"

The cool spring air lifted Jaime's scent and cooled his arousal enough that he could think clearly again.

"Did the media clear off alright?"

Finn's mouth tipped up in a half smile—Sheppard had never believed in smalltalk. "Yeah, Monroe PD came out and set up the barricades and shooed them away. A few of the deputies were Salt Creek; they gave me some funny looks, but nothing overly threatening. Silas was inside with the client, not sure if they were able to scent him to report back to the alpha."

Sheppard grunted in acknowledgement. "And the client, how is he? Have you met the brother yet?"

Finn's chest tightened. What Jaime had said about his brother thinking of him as a burden just didn't track with the way Sam Lamont had spoken on the phone this morning, or with the way Jaime had talked about their relationship last year. To Finn, he'd sounded like a devoted brother willing to do anything and pay any amount of money to keep Jaime safe. But it was odd that he hadn't come out to see how Jaime was after the media storm this morning, or to meet any of the security team.

"Jaime seems tense and exhausted, but he's agreed to the tech install and is fine with one of us staying here full time.

I'll let you know if that changes. We met Sam Lamont over the phone—he seems to keep to himself for the most part." He wasn't keen on airing Jaime's messy relationship with his brother, but he had to say something.

"Hmm, well. He sure keeps himself informed over the phone. He told me he expects daily update calls every morning until the trial is over. Maybe he just doesn't leave his house. Some people are like that."

Finn gave a non-committal hum. That's not what Jaime made it sound like, but he wasn't privy to those details and it wasn't his place to speculate. "Yeah, I'm not sure what's going on there."

"Alright, well, keep me informed and keep your head on a swivel. We can't underestimate Salt Creek if their claws are as deep in this as it seems."

"Will do, boss."

Hanging up, he saw that he had a couple of new texts from Silas.

> Dropping off the truck in a bit, Sheppard will follow me there to give me a ride home.

> I haven't told him that you know the client, but you should. You know he'll figure it out anyway.

After their whirlwind of a day, Finn would cross that bridge if they came to it. He was also allowing himself to accept that the reason he wasn't telling Sheppard was because he was afraid he'd try and take him off the assignment—which Finn wouldn't abide.

With a sigh, he pocketed his phone and went to walk the small property and adjacent shoreline. The wooden fence flanking the house offered privacy from the road, but the back was open to the lake.

Not wanting to stray out of hearing range from the house, he only spent a few minutes scanning the surrounding tree line and thick brush that went right up to the rocky shore on either side of the property, almost cradling the private beach. Judging that approaching from either direction would be slow and potentially noisy, he headed back inside.

On the way, he noticed the small shed at the edge of the yard, but when he tried the handle he found it locked. Peering through the glass, he recognized the setup immediately.

This was Jaime's painting studio.

Through the dusty window, the space looked hastily packed up, with canvases stacked haphazardly against the back wall and paint brushes sitting stiff and crusty in dried out jars.

"Don't go in there." Finn whipped his head up to see Jaime striding toward him, the back door flung open.

He quickly stepped away from the window, dropping his hands. "I'm sorry. I was just scouting out the property for the tech report and wondered if this was a space you'd want to put cameras in."

Jaime's face remained tight. "No, cameras won't be necessary there. I don't go in there anymore."

Silence stretched, with only the sound of small waves lapping at the rocky beach and calling shorebirds between them. Finn nodded. "I'll leave it out for now. If you change your mind and would like it to be outfitted, just let me know."

Jaime gave a terse nod, and went back inside.

———

THE AFTERNOON FLEW BY. Finn worked quietly in the kitchen dining nook to submit the security report, and scheduled the tech installation for tomorrow. They usually had the necessary equipment on hand for an install of this size.

After he finished up, he took his overnight bag filled with a few changes of clothes and toiletries upstairs and settled into the guest room, noting the sheets were freshly changed and the layer of dust that had previously coated everything was gone.

He had the sense that Jaime was avoiding him after their tense exchange about the painting studio, which was made even more obvious during their trip into Monroe to pick up groceries. They only exchanged a few words on the drive there and back, and Jaime spent most of the time staring out the window, fingers twisted in the hem of his shirt.

It had been a long day, with even more of Jaime's privacy and sense of normalcy stripped from him. It was no wonder that he was reserved and quiet. So, Finn didn't push him to speak, and they quietly worked around each other while they brought their groceries inside and Finn began preparing dinner.

"I hope you like Shepherd's Pie," he said, as Jaime came into the kitchen after Finn hollered that the food was ready.

"I don't think I've ever had it. Not real Shepherd's Pie, anyway. The frozen dinner version probably doesn't count."

Finn chuckled. "No, I don't think it does. Where are your plates?"

As they fumbled around each other plating their meals and settling into the dining nook, the silence between them settled, more intimate than it was this afternoon.

"Are you ok?" Finn asked. Jaime was pushing his dinner around his plate more than he was really eating it.

Green eyes looked up. "It's really good, I promise. I'm just tired. Sorry. I'm... not myself. Or I am, and this is just what I'm like now."

Jaime said the last part with some bite, but Finn sensed it was directed inward. "This will pass, I promise. There's always some other, newer, more tragic story for the media to move on to. It's sad, but we've seen it enough in our line of work. Just get through these next few days, and things will quiet down."

Finn knew he wasn't addressing the larger threat of the still unidentified phone call and the Salt Creek pack's potential involvement, but he didn't want to burden Jaime more than he already was.

"It's not that." Jaime shook his head. "I can barely even talk about what I saw that night to the cops and to my therapist. How am I going to keep it together during the trial? Up on the witness stand, with a microphone in my face where every word I say will be thrown back at me, and everyone will be judging me and whether I am lying, or hiding something, or—" he took a great, heaving breath.

Finn reached across the table and grabbed Jaime's hand,

causing him to drop his fork. "Hey, it's ok. Let's take a couple slow, deep breaths, ok? There you go."

Jaime's anxiety attack hadn't progressed as far as it had this morning with the reporters, but he could tell the boy was still shaken by it, a slight tremble in the hand cradled in Finn's.

"I'm such a fucking *mess*." Jaime's voice broke on the last word, and Finn's heart broke a little along with it.

"You're not a mess, Jaime."

"Yeah? I can't even talk about talking about it without falling apart! How pathetic is that? I'm not the one who fucking died. I'm not the one who had to suffer while some monster ripped me open and sprawled my insides all over the floor!"

Finn winced and inwardly recoiled at the word *monster*, withdrawing his hand at the harsh way Jaime spat it.

Not because he didn't want to touch him, but because he knew Jaime wouldn't want to be touched by him, if he knew what he was. Of course, Jackson Bishop was a monster for what he had done. For killing Vera, and for doing it in such a horrible, frightening, and painful way. But he wondered if Jaime would ever see a distinction between that act and the fact that Finn was a wolf, too, making him equally capable of inflicting that kind of damage with his bare hands.

Would Jaime call him a monster, too?

Finn wanted to show Jaime that he wasn't alone; he wanted to tell Jaime about his own nightmares, the ones that still lingered years after their last mission had gone so horribly wrong. He wanted to tell Jaime that both he and Silas had battled their own mental health demons after being discharged, and about the six months of intensive therapy it took for them to be able to get a handle on their shifts and not hurt themselves or others when they were triggered.

Finn wanted to tell Jaime that strength lay in enduring it, but also in wanting to be better, in talking about it with others and taking small steps every day. He wanted to tell him that strength lay in those days when the setbacks seemed the greatest, and you still chose to get back up and take the same slow steps of progress all over again, anyway.

But that would lead to questions from Jaime that Finn wasn't ready to answer, and answers that were dangerously close to telling him that the monster prowling his nightmares wasn't so different from the one sitting at his kitchen table.

Jaime looked back down at his plate in the ensuing silence.

Say something. Anything!

But Finn was tongue tied, torn between sharing too much and not enough.

Jaime heaved a sigh. "I couldn't help then, and I'm terrified I won't be able to pull myself together enough to help now, by making people believe me." Jaime held his hands out in a helpless gesture, and dropped them onto his lap.

"I believe you," Finn finally said. Even if he couldn't, or wouldn't ever be able to show the beautiful, broken, healing man who smelled right the whole truth of who he was, he could at least give him that.

"I believe you, and they will too."

CHAPTER 9
JAIME

The next few days went by slowly, and all at once. Something had happened during their dinner conversation that first night in Jaime's dining nook. Finn was more distant now than he had been the first day, far more like the professional bodyguard and less the... whatever he had been to Jaime, before.

For a few moments, Jaime had seen glimpses of it—in the way that Finn had hungrily stared at him, in the tenderness of his hand on Jaime's when he helped him breathe, and told him that he believed him. It had felt like he was saying more; like what he really meant was that he believed in Jaime, believed in his ability to be strong for himself and for Vera, and to speak the truth during the trial without completely falling apart.

But after their conversation over that delicious meal— *who knew Shepherd's Pie could be so good*—it seemed that Finn saw just how broken Jaime had become; that he wouldn't ever be the naive and open-hearted boy from before.

That's who Finn had wanted.

But now he had Silas. Monstrously proportioned, gorgeous Silas, who in the short stops he made by the house to check on them could make Finn laugh and grumble in a way only born of two souls that deeply understood each other.

In the following days, there weren't any more moments between them like there had been in the kitchen, when Finn had looked at him with hunger and Jaime's pulse ratcheted up when he pictured Finn padding around in domestic softness, or when his hair stood on end like he was being watched.

Watched, because when Finn looked at him that way, eyes dark and focused, Jaime couldn't shake the sense that he would devour him entirely if given the chance.

And all Jaime could think was how divine it would be to be completely overcome by Finn.

It should have been a relief, but really it just made him sad. Another emotion to add to the shame, resentment, bitterness, and emptiness that he'd formed himself around in the last year.

Sad. He was sad that Finn didn't want him anymore.

He could vividly recall the moment he saw it click for Finn—the moment Jaime felt him recoil and withdraw his hand at his brokenness, weakness, and anxiety over the trial, over his inability to help Vera when she was killed by that man in such a brutal way. Finn must have already seen what it took Sam much longer to realize—that Jaime was a burden to those around him and he shouldn't get too close lest he become someone Jaime *needed*.

So, Jaime pulled back too. He let Finn keep his professional distance, and did his best to stay out of the way—especially when Silas stopped by to check on them.

The second day that Finn was staying with him, Silas and two others had come out to help install the cameras and motion detectors. Finn had found him that morning reading on the couch—Jaime had just started a new romance novel—and told him the team would be by in a few minutes to get everything set up.

He'd shuffled in the doorway for a minute, like there was something else he'd wanted to say, so Jaime set his book down to ask if there was anything he needed to do before they arrived.

"No, there's nothing. It will all be hard-wired in for privacy, so it won't run on your internet. They will take care of everything. Cameras are going to be set up in the entryway," Finn pointed at the top corner facing the door, "living area, kitchen, and hallways. All of your doors and windows will be monitored with motion detection and glass-breaking sensors."

He'd paused then, seemingly waiting for Jaime's input, so he nodded along. Finn's voice was different, like he was chewing on his words. Maybe he wore a retainer or something?

"Outside, I'll have them install enough cameras to capture the full perimeter of the home. Is there anywhere else you'd like us to monitor?"

Jaime shook his head. "No, thank you. That seems like more than enough. Hopefully none of it is necessary."

Finn nodded again, continuing to stare, and Jaime almost checked to make sure he didn't have something on his face, but then a knock on the door interrupted them, and Silas and the tech team were there.

It took them all day, but by dinner that evening Finn passed Jaime a tablet across the table, and showed him the various camera angles and features of his new security system. He'd poked around at it a little, but passed it back to Finn without much fuss. He'd said he would take care of monitoring everything while he was here, and that was that.

There hadn't been any more handholding or tender words over their crispy chicken and pasta that night, or in the following days.

FINN'S VOICE cut through the quiet, pulling Jaime away from his book. "I need to go and grab a few more changes of clothes from my place in Silver Rapids. I was thinking of running errands, too, and maybe grabbing lunch somewhere?"

They had settled into a routine over the last week, mostly keeping to themselves in-between meals. It was the first thing Finn had said to him that day. Already mid-morning, but still chilly, Jaime had tucked himself in by the gas fireplace to read his fourth romance novel in as many days while Finn tapped away on his laptop in the kitchen.

He was just getting to the part where the hot and

grumpy game warden was about to confess his deep and irrevocable love for the new wildlife veterinarian in town.

And then suck his dick.

It had been a slow and angsty buildup and Jaime was very invested in reading—*and then re-reading at a later time*—the payoff.

He blinked up at Finn, taking a few seconds to process his words. "Oh. Ok, sure. No worries, I'm sure I'll be fine here until you get back."

Finn stared, a muscle working in his jaw. He was very good at staring. And making as much noise as possible while clomping through the house at six o'clock in the morning.

Jaime hated how endearing it was.

"No." Finn cleared his throat, voice rough. He did that quite a lot. Maybe he was allergic to one of Jaime's house plants?

"Um, I wondered if you would go with me. To Silver Rapids. To lunch. With me? I know it's chilly, but it's a beautiful day. It would be nice to get outside for a bit. You should bring your coat, though. Or I have one you could borrow," Finn finished quickly, shuffling his feet.

Was he blushing?

"Oh." Jaime had not been expecting that.

The crease appeared between Finn's eyebrows. That, too, was irritatingly adorable. "Oh?"

"Yes, oh." Jaime blinked a few times. "I mean, yes, I'll go with you. If that's what you want? I figured you needed to get away for a few hours, I understand needing a break."

Finn was fully frowning at him now. "I don't need to get away from you, Jaime."

That stern timber of his voice made Jaime's stomach swoop and sent a pulse of arousal down the length of his cock. He was wearing his oldest and rattiest pair of sweatpants, and they were so threadbare they were practically seethrough. Which was exactly why he needed to rein in his train of thought now, before Finn saw just how affected Jaime was by that stern yet gentle tone.

With that tone, he could tell me to get on my knees like a good boy, feed me his cock, and I'd be the one thanking him afterwards.

He snapped shut the cover of his e-reader, and did his best to casually readjust his plumping cock while he sat up from his very comfortable, ego-destroying couch. Luckily, knowing that Finn was witnessing his struggle with the monstrosity helped settle his erection a little.

"Ok, then. If you don't want to be by yourself, I'll join you. Actually, I've never been to Silver Rapids, even though it's only fifteen or so minutes from here. Is that weird?"

Finn made a noncommittal hum. "It's not really on the tourist scene, it stays pretty quiet. But it's going to be a nice day, I thought we could go out for a walk. You've been cooped up in here for too long."

Jaime sighed, looking out toward the lupine meadow behind his house, on the cusp of blooming. "Yeah, I think I have. Let me go upstairs and get cleaned up and changed, I can be ready in a few minutes."

Their arms brushed lightly as he passed by, headed for the stairs, and Finn sucked in a quiet breath, shoulders stiffening.

Oh God, do I smell bad? Is that why he's always clearing his throat around me? I stink?

He hurried up the stairs and stripped his shirt off, taking a big whiff of the underarms before tossing it in the hamper. It just smelled like deodorant and fabric softener to him—he'd worn clean clothes and showered every day since Finn was there. He couldn't really smell that bad, could he?

Jaime needed to get out of this house. He was reading way too much into every minute reaction that happened between them.

Speaking of... well, not *minute* reactions, more like *average* reactions, thank you very much, Jaime stepped under the hot shower spray and took himself in hand to get rid of the semi he hadn't quite been able to tame in his flight from the couch.

I read entirely too many romance novels.

He really did read too many romance novels. That was where nearly all of his sexual knowledge and fantasies came from, and had fueled many nights of self-exploration with various toys and dildos—but Jaime's usual favorite scenes weren't what he thought of as he stroked himself with a firm, steady hand, thumb catching on the crown of his cock, the tip leaking precum.

No, his imagination was filled with thoughts of Finn using that stern voice on him, telling him to get on his hands and knees on the bed, maybe to stretch out and grab the headboard...

You're such a good boy for me, Jaime. Fuck, look at you. Are you going to let me inside of you, baby? Are you going to let me open you up with my thick fingers? Huh? Do you want to ride them? That's it, sit back on them and let me hear how much you fucking love how they feel inside of you...

Jaime's hand was flying over his cock, squeezing hard as his hips thrust erratically, and he imagined that it was Finn's calloused fist his length tunneled into, Finn's arm banded around his middle, pinning him down, holding him tight as he made Jaime take all of him...

He came with a gasp, eyes flying open wide, his forearm braced on the shower wall trembling with his climax. Jaime painted the tile with his cum, and watched it slide down along with the hot water dripping from his hair and off the tip of his nose, forehead resting against his arm.

Fucking hell. He'd never come that hard or fast in his life. None of his tried and true spank bank favorites could do what imagining Finn's voice had done. If that's how he reacted to just his imagination of Finn, what would the real thing be like?

Hastily washing his hair and scrubbing himself down with body wash, Jaime finished the rest of his shower quickly. He sped through his routine on rote memory, still in a daze from the explosive orgasm he'd just had, and threw on a pair of his nicer jeans and a long-sleeve henley.

He hadn't worn these jeans in a long time—definitely not since everything had happened last year. Turning in the mirror for a quick once-over, he noticed they still made his butt look good.

Would Finn look at his perky ass in these jeans?

Fuck, it's going to be a long day.

———

Jaime stood in Finn's living room, taking in the scarce furniture and even scarcer wall decor.

Finn and Silas's living room, he grumbled.

The giant wasn't there with them, but it was obvious the two men lived together. However, it wasn't the love nest he would have assumed it would be.

For one, he thought there'd be more pictures of them together. Or, well, just them. There were pictures that they were both in, but most of them were with two other men. One he vaguely recognized as Cameron Sheppard, head of the security team, but the other he hadn't ever seen before. The only other pictures of Silas and Finn together were of them as young men, an arm slung over each other's shoulder and outfitted in full military gear, and one where they appeared to be barely into high school, all knobby knees and lanky limbs.

He was secretly pleased to see that even Silas went through an awkward legs-too-long and feet-too-big phase.

Other than the pictures, the living area was relatively bare, with only a television and couch, separated by a plain coffee table. It certainly was not the same as his own cluttered style.

Hearing Finn tromping back downstairs from where he'd disappeared to a few minutes ago, Jaime hastily stepped away from the pictures he'd been snooping on, but Finn tipped up a smile and gestured to the picture of the four of them. "That was taken almost ten years ago, I think. Before one of our missions."

Jaime nodded. "I remember you said you were in the military, before moving to Silver Rapids."

"It's how I met Sheppard and Renner. After we got out, Sheppard started the security firm and Silas and I jumped on the chance. It was hard adjusting to... well, after." His smile faded, but his face and voice remained soft. "I think you understand that. Having an *after*."

Jaime nodded, unable to tear his eyes away from Finn's. "So the three of you work together; what about Renner?"

Finn didn't look away from him, but his face did some sort of crumpling thing, folding inwards. "He didn't make it out of our last mission. We were discharged immediately after he was killed." He did look away from Jaime then. "Si and I weren't well, for a long time after. We were in therapy for months. I still exchange messages with a therapist, and make appointments when I think it will help."

Jaime found himself striding across the room toward him. "Finn." He reached out but caught himself, letting his hand fall. "I'm sorry."

Finn stared at the hand he'd let fall, and then he reached out and took it, thumb rubbing across his knuckles like they had that very first day outside of his house, when Finn pulled Jaime back into himself.

They shouldn't be doing this, standing in the house he shared with Silas and holding hands, but Jaime couldn't help but squeeze back.

"We don't talk about Renner, really." Finn heaved a sigh, and looked back up, brown eyes soft. "Maybe someday, I'll tell you more about him. About who we all were, together as a team. But I wanted to tell you this, now, so that you'd know that I have an *after* too, Jaime. And it's terrible and overwhelming and draining and unfair. But there is also an *after* the *after*. And you're not alone. I know things aren't right with your brother, but that doesn't mean you're a burden, or weak, or too much. Not for me. Not for us. You're strong enough on your own—you've proved that over and over already by surviving and getting here. But you can lean on us, too. We aren't going anywhere."

Jaime didn't know what to say. Not about any of it. Finn had lost a friend; he knew what Jaime was feeling—what he had gone through, was still going through. Their circumstances weren't the same, but he could see the pain in Finn's eyes, now, and recognized it for what it was.

Grief. Shame.

His own pooled around him, but not in the familiar, tight, constricting way that made it difficult to breathe. No, it was like his mess saw Finn's, and wanted to soothe it, and thus, was soothed.

A beast taming a beast. Seeing and being seen.

He squeezed Finn's hand again. "Take me to lunch?"

Finn smiled, real and full, and Jaime thought it looked like the sun. "I know a spot."

CHAPTER 10
FINN

Finn might be tempting fate by taking Jaime to the place where they were meant to meet last year, but today was not going at all how he imagined it would.

So, fuck it. They were going to Andi's.

He hadn't planned on telling Jaime about Renner, or about his past struggles. He'd debated it over and over in his head for the past few days as he watched Jaime retreat into himself, and couldn't decide how to bring him back. They'd occupied space near each other, but hadn't really engaged since that first night at the dinner table.

He'd been ashamed of his response the next morning.

Of course, Jaime hadn't hurled that word at him in disgust or accusation. Bishop *was* a monster. He'd traumatized Jaime deeply, and Finn had made that about himself and his own insecurities. He knew that his response in the moment hadn't been the right one, but as he watched Jaime become more and more closed off over the next few days he couldn't decide whether he *should* try and make things better with him.

Because the truth was, regardless of insecurities and intentions and misunderstandings, Finn was also a monster, and he didn't want to bring Jaime even further into the danger he'd inadvertently walked into last spring.

A world he would run from as fast and far as he could, if he knew even half of the truth.

So, Finn did his best to stay professional—distant. That is, until he could smell Jaime reading one of those goddamn books all the way from the kitchen and found himself drawn in like a moth to a flame, that tug on his heart pulling him into the living room without realizing he'd even stood up from the table.

Scenting Jaime's arousal was overwhelming and unbearable—entirely too much, and never enough—and if they didn't get out of the house for a breath of fresh air soon, he'd do something rash, like beg on his knees for Jaime to marry him. Or maybe just to let Finn suck his cock.

He'd take either one.

Of course he knew that Jaime was reading romance books. The first time he'd smelled his arousal he'd nearly tripped down the stairs in his haste to see who'd breached the security alarms; who'd dared intrude on their space to make Jaime's scent heavy with desire and want, when Finn needed to be the one to make him feel that way.

He'd rounded the corner only to find Jaime splayed across the couch, a blanket casually draped across his lap, eyes glued to his e-reader. The light flush across the tops of his cheeks had told Finn enough—the boy was reading smut.

The realization nearly brought him to his knees.

Oh, but what if he could get Jaime to tell him about his favorite scenes whenever he finished a book? Maybe even explore them together? They could take a hot bath while he read, Finn's chin tucked over his shoulder and teasing Jaime with light touches and gentle strokes until he was panting in his arms and begging Finn to have his way with him. He'd figure out which books were Jaime's favorites, and read them himself so he'd know exactly what he liked, what he wanted to try...

"Well, look what the cat dragged in."

Finn surfaced from that hazy daydream, a warm blast of air on his face shocking him back to reality as they walked into the restaurant.

He smiled wide at the voice, and saw Andi striding through the swinging kitchen door, her tight, coiled curls braided in a protective style away from her face and whatever magical concoctions she'd cooked up in that kitchen. She'd dyed her hair again since he last saw her, now a bright teal against her medium tawny skin and dark freckles.

Silas and Finn had stumbled upon Andi's a few years ago when she'd first opened. The eatery used to be an old auto shop that she'd outfitted into a dining room, kitchen, and turned the bay above the garage into an apartment.

Sensing that they were paranormals like her, she'd introduced herself as a hearth witch, and said she moved to Alaska from somewhere in the lower forty-eight to get a new start in life. They knew better than to ask questions; unless you happened to be born in the area, most paranormals ended up in Silver Rapids via a story they'd rather not have made its way through the rumor mill.

Finn wasn't entirely sure what powers a hearth witch (or house witch, as some chose to be called) could wield, but he did know she made the best food he'd ever eaten—it was supernaturally good.

Since that first time they'd dined there—when her shrimp and grits changed his goddamn life—Silas and Finn ate at Andi's at least three times a week, and he'd pestered her until she had shared some of her recipes and techniques with him. The ones that didn't require magic, anyway. They'd become good friends.

"It's been, what, a whole week since you were here last? I was starting to think I needed to call a welfare check on you!" she said with a laugh. "Good to see you back and in one piece." Her smile turned softer when she looked toward Jaime.

Finn tipped his chin down toward him. "I should be embarrassed about how much I eat here, but the food is so damn good it's just a waste of time to try anywhere else. And when I can convince her to tell me her culinary secrets, it makes the incessant ribbing she gives me worth it."

She cackled. "I only tell you enough to get you out of my kitchen and to keep the giant one fed when I'm closed. Speaking of, I'm glad to see you brought someone else here with you, and not just that oafish brother of yours. I'm Andi." She stuck her hand out toward Jaime and he shook it, his face briefly scrunching up before going lax.

He smiled, eyes crinkling in the corners. "I'm Jaime. It's

nice to meet you. And I can't wait to try whatever smells so delicious in here."

She ushered them toward the back and into Finn and Silas's usual booth. The booth that he had sat in for over two hours last year, waiting for Jaime to arrive.

Seeing Jaime now, seated across from him and anxiously fussing with the silverware, Finn could only stare for a moment. It almost felt like some part of him had been stuck in this booth all year, waiting.

And now that he was here, now that they were here together, the part of him that had stood still shifted, and stretched.

It felt like waking up.

The whole front of the restaurant was artfully divided by partitions and screens for privacy, draped in twinkle lights and greenery. The lighting was soft, but not so low that you couldn't comfortably see the food in front of you, or your dining partner. This time of year, with spring's earliest blooms just beginning to push through the snow, she'd added pops of pink and purple in the usual ivy and garland. Dean Martin and Ella Fitzgerald were softly crooning through the speakers.

It was the coziest place Finn had ever seen aside from Jaime's cabin, and he adored it here.

Finn sat facing the exit, because as quiet and uneventful as the past few days had been, and no matter how familiar Andi's was, he couldn't let his guard down when they were out and about.

Andi didn't bother giving them menus. "I've got a pot of chicken lentil soup on with hot honey and jalapeño cornbread, fresh butternut squash ravioli, short ribs coming out of the oven in ten minutes that I can put over mashed potatoes, and a vegetable salad with an olive oil and dill dressing."

Heaven.

He finally looked up from Jaime's face. "We'll take one of everything you just said, for the table. And a couple of waters. Oh, and your peach tea for me, please. Jaime, do you like peach tea? Also, do you have any of those cinnamon butter dinner rolls? No, don't give me that look, I know you keep some ready to bake for when we come in. Jaime? Anything else you'd like to order?"

The younger man was staring at him like he'd never seen him before. "I'll try the peach tea, too, please. Nothing else for me, thanks." Still looking stunned, he brushed a stray auburn curl out of his eyes.

They sat in silence while Andi got their waters and tea, and then disappeared back into the kitchen. There were a few other couples in the restaurant, but the quiet atmosphere made their little corner seem private and cozy. Finn couldn't help but admire the way Jaime's eyes shone in the soft glow of the twinkle lights strung above them.

"It's been awhile since I've heard you talk that much," Jaime said, still fiddling with his napkin and silverware, voice hushed in the quiet.

It was Finn's turn to blush. "I like cooking and talking about food, and Andi has always welcomed me when I've pestered her about her recipes. She's taught me how to make pretty much everything I've made for you this week. Everything I can make that tastes good, anyway."

Jaime nodded, but was still fidgeting with the napkin.

Maybe he was nervous to be out in public after everything that had happened? They'd gotten a few glances from people on the street as they parked and walked inside, but no one had followed them. Finn knew there'd be less of that in Silver Rapids than in Monroe.

Or, maybe Jaime didn't like that Finn had brought him here, of all places. Maybe it was too much of a reminder of that night? Suddenly anxious, Finn asked, "Should I have brought you here? Or are you worried—"

"Silas is your brother?" Jaime blurted out, interrupting his question.

He looked wide-eyed, like he'd startled himself with the outburst. "I just, you never mentioned before that you had a brother. So I didn't think, I mean, I thought you two were, well. Not brothers." He blushed, the tips of his ears going pink, and Finn very much wanted to nibble them, just there.

Instead, he smiled and tipped his head in a yes and no gesture. "Not by blood, but in all the ways that matter, yes. He's the friend I told you about, the one I grew up with. We met in the 6th grade and became nearly inseparable. We've called each other brothers ever since; followed each other into the military and then moved in together once we were out and joined up with Sheppard at the security firm. "

In those early days of their friendship, they had claimed each other in some intrinsic way. Not in the way that Finn longed to claim a mate now—longed to claim *Jaime*, now— no, they'd known as teenagers that they weren't who each other wanted.

They hadn't smelled like they belonged together as mates or lovers, but as brothers—to Finn, Silas smelled like trust, and relaxed ears, and puppy-piling on each other after a long run through the woods.

He smelled like pack.

Jaime was blinking fast and looked scandalized. He stage-whispered, "But...I thought you were in love with each other! I thought you were a couple!"

Finn swallowed his drink of water wrong and choked, coughing and spluttering until he could get a breath.

Thankfully, Andi showed up just then with their plates and plates of food, giving him a few moments to collect himself. They'd have leftovers for at least a day or so, which was good, because Finn was running out of impressive meals to make Jaime. He didn't want to dip into his repertoire of *meh* dinners just yet.

Not until he'd shown Jaime just how impressive he could be in other ways, first. That is, if he ever let Finn touch him, after apparently thinking that he was in love with Silas. How absolutely fucking bizarre.

Once Andi refilled their water glasses and left, smirking at the two of them and wishing them a happy meal, he leaned over toward Jaime. Lowly, he asked, "What the fuck gave you the impression that I was *in love* with Silas?"

"You did!" Jaime was gesturing wildly now, ignoring the food steaming between them and voice pitching higher and higher, all attempts to stay quiet forgotten. "I heard you that first day, in my guest room! He told you that he loves you! He called you *Finny*! You said you felt the same way about him!"

It was Finn's turn to stare at Jaime like he'd just sprouted three heads.

Jesus Christ.

A slow smile spread across his face, wide and true and aching, and then he burst into laughter; deep, full, head thrown back, tears leaking out of the corners of his eyes, laughter.

Jaime's face pinched into a pout, and he made the most adorable little *huff* sound, which only made Finn laugh even harder.

Finally, he calmed down enough to speak. "Don't give me that face, baby. It's a damned weapon and I've done nothing to deserve it."

Jaime scowled even harder, blushing at the endearment.

Interesting.

Still sputtering with laughter, Finn calmed down enough to explain. "Of course I love him, he's my brother. And he's called me Finny since we were kids. Your case, the people involved, it's..." he shook his head, sobering more. "He's usually the one on point with a client, not me. But for reasons that are his to disclose, it's better that he stays in the background as much as possible. In your guest room, he was telling me to be careful. That's all."

Jaime blinked at him, owlish eyes wide and mossy and stunned. "Oh."

Is that what he would look like staring up at me from his knees, sucking on my cock?

Finn croaked out, "Oh?"

Jaime made that pouting face again. "Yes. Oh."

He chuckled, and picked up his fork. Finn tried, and failed, to shake off the image of Jaime, spit-messy and fucked-out, swallowing his cock. But, subtly, quietly, he felt a shift between them, in their dynamic, and he wondered...

"Can I ask you something?"

Jaime continued to blink at him, but nodded.

"First, eat," Finn said firmly, pointing with his fork at the food before them. Jaime blushed again. Didn't he have a similar reaction this morning when Finn had used the same tone with him? He'd chalked it up to all of the romance novels Jaime had been reading, but maybe Jaime enjoyed it when Finn told him what to do? Gave him orders?

His hand clutched the edge of the table, canines threatening to descend.

Focus. You are in public. You can't jump the boy in the middle of the goddamn restaurant.

His wolf prowled at the image that conjured.

Jaime squirmed in his seat at Finn's directive, but picked up his fork and stabbed at a ravioli. And fuck, the moan that came out of his mouth upon tasting the food made Finn hard as granite, length stiffening down the leg of his jeans.

Andi is giving me that butternut squash ravioli recipe before we leave, or I'll piss in her yard for a week.

Finn cleared his throat and dug into his own plate of short ribs. "Is that why you've been distant with me since the first day I was here? You thought I was with someone else? I know before, we were—" He cut himself off, unsure how to describe what they had almost been.

Jaime was quiet for a beat, sipping on the lentil soup. "Yes. Kind of." Still not looking at Finn, he set his spoon down and took a drink of water. "I'm not that same man you met a year ago, Finn. I can't laugh the way I used to, or meet an attractive stranger online and strike up a conversation with him. I can't be *him,* anymore."

The grief in his voice cut Finn to the bone.

"It made sense that you would be with someone strong and confident, like Silas. I can't be that. And I don't want to be someone you need to worry about. Stress over. Manage. I can't be work, for you."

A million things sprung to the tip of his tongue. Did Jaime really think that Finn would consider being with him a burden? Did he really think that Finn would only want something shallow and surface deep with him? Did he believe that Finn wouldn't want him because he had experienced something awful, and was working through it?

"Look at me."

The air thickened between them when Jaime did as he was told, everyone and everything else fading away. That tug on Finn's heart grew stronger, humming. "You are not now, nor have you ever been, a burden."

His voice was a quiet rumble, and he itched to reach across the table to hold Jaime's hand. "You are strong and resilient, and just because this hasn't been easy for you, that does not mean you are weak."

Jaime's eyes cast downward, and then Finn did reach across the table for his hand, gently pulling until he looked up. "You are allowed to let yourself respond to what has happened to you. And just because you can't find those old parts of you now, that doesn't mean they've left you. They can still be a part of you again, someday, if you want them. They might look a little different, that's all."

Jaime's voice was small in the hushed quiet between them. "What if I can't ever get them back?"

"Then you'll find new things that make you who you are. New things to love," Finn said.

Jaime's face fell, and Finn couldn't help but go on. "A year ago, you were a beautiful man that I saw on a dating app and wanted to know, but never got the chance." Jaime tried to tug his hand away, but Finn held on. "Today, I have that chance. And I will not let that chance go again, Jaime. You are still a beautiful man that I want to know more about, but that is because of who you are now, sitting in front of me. Not some imaginary, alternate, better version of yourself. This one, here. This is the real you. Please don't diminish that."

The hope brimming in Jaime's eyes nearly broke him, and he nodded in agreement, blinking away tears. "Okay."

Finn gently squeezed Jaime's hand and let go, picking up his fork. They shared a few moments of comfortable silence, eyes catching in the intimacy of their private little booth.

"So, this is Andi's." Jaime looked around, like he was finally relaxed enough to do so. "It's the perfect spot for a first date. Good choice."

His face turned grave, and words began to tumble from him. "I'm sorry. For ghosting you, for not explaining. I should have. I *wish* I had. But I was such a mess after everything happened, I couldn't handle anything other than reminding myself that I wasn't in that closet anymore. And then weeks went by and you didn't reach out, and I thought that was probably for the best because I was still so fucked up over everything, and—"

"Jaime."

He stopped, breathing quickly, and Finn wanted to hug him.

He's vulnerable.

Hold him.

Finn took a steadying breath. "You don't owe me an apology, or an explanation. I hate what happened to you. I *hate* it. I wish I could have done something. But we can't go back, either of us. And so I'm just... I'm glad we're here now. I'm really fucking glad you're sitting across from me right now."

Jaime nodded, eyes glassy and warm. "I'm very glad to be sitting across from you right now too, Finn."

They finished their meal in comfortable silence, legs brushing up against each other under the table until they both stopped pretending that it was an accident. Electricity shot through Finn where they stayed pressed together, a long line of shared heat.

Eventually he sat back, groaning at how full he was. Jaime mirrored him, complementing the food they had just shared and patting his belly. Finn had to look away, or else he'd never be able to stand without showing everyone in the building the raging erection he'd been trying, and failing, to tame.

Andi swung by with some boxes, and Finn grabbed the check before Jaime could as they got up and left, waving goodbye and saying they'd be back soon.

Finn ushered Jaime back to the truck with a hand on his lower back. It may have been his imagination, but he seemed to relax more into the touch than he had before. Swinging open the passenger door, Finn cast a quick glance around to make sure no one had followed them out of the restaurant before crowding Jaime inside the vehicle, putting an arm up to box him in.

But instead of stepping up into the truck, Jaime turned to face him—and Finn realized just how close they were in that moment. Jaime's head was tipped back to meet his eyes, exposing the long length of his neck, and he barely resisted the urge to run his lips and tongue and teeth along it.

Softly, Jaime said, "Can I ask you something now, too?"

Finn didn't move his arm or step away. "Of course."

Jaime fidgeted a bit with the hem of his henley, shyly glancing down to Finn's chest and back up. He swore he could feel the pull of that stare, like a magnet drawing them together.

"You said Silas is usually the one to stay with clients, but this time he couldn't. Is that the only reason why you're the one here with me? To protect him from whatever he can't be involved with?"

Finn raised his eyebrows, unsure how to answer that. It certainly was not the only reason—it hadn't even been the first reason—but Finn didn't want to spook Jaime with the full truth just yet. There were still so many things to consider before Finn allowed himself to be more open with him, about the level of danger he was in with the Salt Creek pack and everything else that Finn was.

So he gave Jaime some of the truth, fangs threatening to descend from the closeness between them, from breathing in his sweet lemon and vanilla scent. "No, that is not the only reason."

Finn took a step closer, and Jaime did not retreat. "When the news broke, I recognized who you were immediately. I wanted to make sure you were ok. I know that you did not invite me back into your life, Jaime. And I respected that for a whole fucking year. But when the contract came through, and I had a real, legitimate chance to see you, I couldn't stay away. I just couldn't. And if that's all you want this to be, me, hired to keep you safe while you prepare to testify in court, I'll try to respect that too."

He cupped Jaime's face, eyes flicking back and forth to gauge his reaction. "But I told you the truth in there. I want more, with you. If that's something you want, too."

Jaime's hands grasped Finn's sides, fingers tangling in the fabric of his sweater as he gently pulled him closer. "Yes, Finn."

Almost. Finn almost kissed him, when he saw Jaime's green eyes go hazy and soft, darting down to his mouth and back up, their lips the barest brush against each other. But the sound of loud voices cut through the moment as a group of deer shifters strode by, bringing Finn back to the world and reminding him of their surroundings.

Fuck, they couldn't afford to lose focus in public like that.

Sensing Finn's train of thought, Jaime let go of him and turned, hopping up into the passenger seat. He swung the door shut behind him, and as he walked around the truck to the driver's side, Finn tried to find the scraps of his remaining self control, because even the barest brush of Jaime's lips against his had unraveled him completely.

CHAPTER II
JAIME

K*iss me, kiss me, kiss me!*

He'd been silently begging Finn to close the distance between them, standing so close in the parking lot outside of Andi's, the place where they were always meant to start.

Where they should have started a year ago.

Jaime had really thought Finn was about to do it, but then the bubble they were in popped, and they realized that they shouldn't be starting this, whatever *this* was, out in the open.

Finn had been right about it being a gorgeous day outside; it seemed like everything was waking up from a long winter slumber. Jaime had remembered his own coat, even though he'd heavily debated "forgetting" it to see if Finn's offer to wear his was genuine, but he ended up setting it aside in the truck anyway to feel the fresh breeze on his skin.

They drove around Silver Rapids for a while, occasionally getting out to pop into a shop or two that Finn said he thought Jaime might like. He was always right.

The first they went into was a bookstore, and Jaime blushed when, after wandering around for a while, Finn found him scanning the back of a very smutty queer romance novel.

He smirked at Jaime, a knowing look in his eye. "Haven't read that one, yet?"

Jaime squawked, fumbling for something to say as Finn's rumbling laughter made his stomach do funny things.

Finn stepped up behind him, all heat and desire at Jaime's back, and leaned over to prop an arm up against the bookshelf. He whispered, "Do you think I haven't noticed what you're reading, baby? When you tuck yourself into that giant man-eating couch of yours by the fire? You'll have to tell me which ones you like best, and maybe I'll give it a try."

Finn winked, stepping back, and sauntered around the corner toward the mysteries and thrillers section, leaving Jaime gaping. And so fucking horny.

Finn had winked at him. And offered to read a romance novel with him. He'd called him *baby*—twice!

In a daze, Jaime picked up a few paperbacks that looked interesting, and took them to the front, smiling at the cashier who gave him a funny look. Was he one of those book snobs who turned their nose up at romances? Jaime ignored it until Finn stepped up to the counter with him.

"Jared, good to see you. This is Jaime." He was hovering close behind again, the warmth of his chest nearly touching

Jaime's back, teasing him. It was an effort not to lean further into him—he ached to feel Finn pressed up against him fully.

Jared merely nodded, dense white hair falling into his face as he did so. Actually, the man was sort of covered in white hair, his forearms thick with it. He almost seemed reassured at Finn's introduction, features softening as he bagged up Jaime's books. Odd. Jaime finished paying and noted that Finn had grabbed a couple of thrillers for himself.

After the bookshop, they walked a little ways until Finn turned them into another store. This one seemed to be some combination of a hardware store, grocery store, and a knick-knack stand, selling everything from ice-melt, cereal, and little handmade wooden figurines.

"Do you know that guy? Jared?" Jaime asked as they perused the aisles, unable to shake the odd feeling the interaction had given him.

It was like Finn had needed to make it known that they were there together. Not like, *together* together, even though the thought of Finn being territorial made him flush and his cock chub up, but more like he was vouching for Jaime's good intentions.

"Not really, not very well. He's been around Silver Rapids for a long time, longer than I have. You know how small towns can be, people don't like strangers."

The tense moment from earlier when Finn had crowded Jaime up against the truck had dissipated a little, but not entirely. There was still something charged between them—something that had stirred awake during their shared meal at Andi's, and Jaime couldn't shake the feeling.

While their conversation never veered into the heady

place it had in that adorable little booth over truly the best food of Jaime's life, it was still more open than it had been in the past few days. Jaime wasn't so afraid to reveal things about himself, and Finn seemed at ease knowing Jaime's distance had been out of respect for the miscommunication over Silas, and not out of a desire to be distant from him.

You're not now, nor have you ever been, a burden.

I want more with you, if that's what you want.

The real version of you, the one sitting in front of me. Please don't diminish that.

Jaime had been in a year's worth of therapy working through his feelings of self-loathing and unworthiness, and he still had a long way to go. One conversation with a man he had a crush on wasn't going to fix that.

But it sure fucking helped.

Parts of him whispered that Finn didn't mean it; that he just needed to wait until Jaime had another bout of anxiety, or someone came to hurt him and he needed Finn to protect him, and then Finn would see how much of a burden he really was.

But there was a lightness in him that wasn't there before today, and it helped as he used the exercises he'd learned in therapy to set those thoughts aside. To rationalize that they weren't real; it was just his own self-loathing and doubt at work.

Finn had only ever been honest with him—had only ever helped him, been kind to him, and pulled him back into himself. Not because he needed Finn to fix him, but because sometimes you needed someone you could count on, who saw you from the outside, and who could support you as you healed yourself.

Someone to tell you that you're worth healing.

Fuck, that was deep. How long had they known each other? In reality, only a few days. But they had been circling each other for weeks last year, and Finn hadn't ever fully left Jaime's thoughts. It seemed to be the same for Finn.

Finn grabbed a few items that he said he needed for the house, some caulking and a sander to patch up some of the work from the security tech install. As they paid and walked back to the truck together, idly chatting, Jaime had the fleeting thought that *this* was what he wanted.

How beautiful would it be, to spend his days running errands and finishing up domestic chores with a man who thought he was strong, and beautiful, and worth fighting for?

He wanted to find out.

THEIR DRIVE HOME was uneventful and quiet, but in the comforting way of two people who enjoyed being in one another's company. When they pulled into Jaime's driveway, Finn cut the engine and they sat there, listening to each other breathe.

Finn's profile was beautiful in the afternoon light, and when he turned toward Jaime that crease between his eyebrows relaxed, eyes going soft. Jaime couldn't help but glance down at his mouth again, couldn't help but imagine what Finn's lips would feel like on his.

Would Finn lead the kiss? Guide Jaime through it with

soft dominance and a demanding tongue, like that tone of voice he sometimes used would suggest? Or, would he melt under Jaime's touch?

Slowly, Jaime leaned toward Finn over the armrest and opened his mouth to say something—maybe to thank him for getting him out of the house today, or maybe to beg him to push Jaime into the back seat and take him right there in the goddamn truck cab—but Finn's eyes caught on something over his shoulder, and Jaime's words died in his throat at the look that came over his face.

Finn's lips pulled back almost like a snarl, and soil-brown eyes turned dark and molten, flickering in anger. Whipping his head around to see what Finn was looking at, he saw two men casually walking toward their vehicle, having circled around from behind his cabin.

"Call Silas."

Jaime didn't even recognize Finn's voice, rough and thick with anger. He handed Jaime his phone without taking his eyes off the two approaching men.

"Crawl into the driver's seat once I get out. Whatever happens, do not leave the truck. If this goes badly, drive to your brother's apartment, and call the police."

Finn stepped out and slammed the door behind him, headed straight for where the two men stood, smirking, having stopped their approach about ten feet away. Activating the door locks, Jaime crawled over to the driver's side and prayed he wouldn't need to follow through on Finn's orders.

He wouldn't leave him. He couldn't.

But he also wasn't stupid enough to believe that he'd be

able to do much if they were somehow able to overpower Finn. Watching as he stopped halfway between the truck and the two men, feet planted and arms crossed, Jaime found Silas's number saved in Finn's favorites and called him.

"Finny! You guys get back from Silver Rapids ok?"

"Silas? It's Jaime. Lamont. You've got to get over here, people are here. Finn said to call you. He's outside talking to them now."

"Fuck, ok. I'm on my way. Where are you?"

"My house. We just pulled into the drive. I'm inside the truck. He told me not to get out."

"Good. Do not get out of the truck, Jaime. Be ready to leave if you need to. How many of them are there? Is it the media, or someone else?"

"There's two of them, and I don't know. They were behind the house when we got here; Finn saw them walking up to the truck when we pulled in. They don't look like the media, but I can't hear what they are saying."

Please, don't let them hurt Finn.

He had to remind himself this was why Finn was here. He was good at this. Finn did this for a living. He was a professional, capable of handling two trespassers.

"I'm ten minutes away. Sheppard will be there in fifteen. Do not get out of the truck, Jaime. Leave, if you need to. Finn will be fine."

"I won't leave him." Jaime was shocked by his own conviction.

"Ten minutes, Jaime. It will be fine." Then Silas hung up.

Distantly, he thought Silas must have been on his way

over already if he was only ten minutes away. Finn and the two strangers were still standing there, and seemed to be having some kind of conversation. Not wanting to risk Silas or Sheppard arriving too late, Jaime pulled out his own phone and called the first person who came to mind.

Sam didn't pick up.

He tried several more times—no answer.

Furious at himself for reaching out again, and getting ignored *again*, Jaime gave up and dialed Detective Sutton's number.

She picked up on the second ring, and he explained the situation a little more steadily than he had with Silas. The detective said she was on her way, and she'd inform DA Rivera. Jaime briefly thought about calling Dana Chase, but decided that could wait. He wanted to know what they were saying to each other.

He hit the button to roll down the window just a crack, both so he could hear what they were saying to Finn and so he could get a bit of fresh air to calm his nerves.

"...want to know what he knows, that's all," said the stranger on the right.

Finn rumbled, "You were ordered here to fucking threaten him, dog. Let's all stop pretending otherwise. Tell Jeffrey to back the fuck off—he's under our protection, now."

Jeffrey? Jeffrey Dugan, Vera Novikova-Dugan's husband? How does Finn know him?

The stranger sneered. "For now, maybe. But if he tells his cop friend to back off Second Dugan, then maybe we can come to an agreement."

Suddenly, Silas strode out from the tree line, shirtless

and sweaty. Had he run all the way here? Where the hell was his car? In a few long strides he was shoulder to shoulder with Finn, both of them now standing between the intruders and Jaime.

"Hello, Silas. It's been awhile, how've you been?" the one on the left asked.

Silas only growled. *Growled.*

What the actual fuck is going on?

How did he end up with bodyguards who seemed to know Vera's husband? And why was he the one that was apparently threatening Jaime? Unless...

Oh.

Jaime's ears started ringing. Unless Jeffrey Dugan was the one threatening him, because he was the one who had ordered Vera's death. How stupid was he? Of course it was the husband, it's always the fucking husband.

But Jaime didn't know that, not in any way that mattered. He had no way of proving that in court—all he'd heard was the other end of a phone call. It must have been enough for Jeffrey Dugan to want him out of the picture, though. Or dead.

Still, that didn't explain why these two clearly knew Finn and Silas, and how his bodyguards knew that Jeffrey Dugan was involved.

Had this all been a setup?

Jaime slammed the lid shut on that train of thought, trying to slow his erratic breathing. No. Finn wouldn't do that. He wouldn't lie to him, not about that. He wanted Jaime to stay safe, he wanted to know Jaime—that's what he'd said.

Unless he's lying to you. You don't really know him that well at all.

He knows Jeffrey Dugan. What are the chances that you were meant to meet up with him on the same night Jeffrey's wife was murdered?

Before his thoughts could spiral anymore, or he did something rash like sprint out the other side of the truck and take off into the trees before any of them turned and noticed he was gone, two vehicles pulled into the drive, boxing everyone else in.

DA Rivera and Detective Sutton stepped out of the first, striding toward Finn and Silas where they were gathered around the trespassers.

Cameron Sheppard, all wiry muscle and a ball cap pulled low over his brow, stepped out of the other car, first looking to Jaime where he sat in the truck, and then locking eyes with DA Rivera, who'd halted his approach at Sheppard's appearance. Even though they weren't speaking to each other, something about the way they were staring made Jaime look away. Like it was too intimate for anyone else to witness.

Apparently, everybody knew everybody here except for him, and he was goddamn tired of it. He was tired of running, and being helpless, and kept out of everything.

Yanking open the door, he stepped outside as Finn whipped his head around. "Jaime, please. Get back in the truck until they leave."

Jaime didn't even look at him, just strode up to stand with the rest of them. "No."

Opening and closing his mouth before apparently

deciding that arguing would be fruitless, Finn sidled closer, partially blocking him from the now very outnumbered intruders.

"Ah, hello, Jaime Lamont."

"Don't speak to him," Finn snarled.

"Relax, and stop growling at us. He can speak to us if he wishes."

Detective Sutton bodied her way between them all, her short, round form cutting through the crowd of overly large men. "No, actually, he can't. Because I'm instating an emergency protective order, ceasing all contact between the two of you and Jaime Lamont. You'll be required to appear in court in a few days to finalize the order. Now, seeing as you're now both trespassing and violating a protective order, I'm required to escort you off the property. Get into the back of the car, now."

Jaime had never seen this side of Detective Sutton. Her blonde hair was pulled back into a ponytail at the base of her neck, and her blue eyes were piercing as she took control of the stand-off that seemed to be one wrong move away from turning into complete mayhem.

Jaime was suddenly very glad to have never been on the receiving end of the look she was now leveling at the two trespassers.

DA Rivera and Sheppard had apparently moved past their stare-off, because Sheppard was now pulling Silas off to the side, casting a wary glance around before handing him a bundle of cloth. Silas shook it out, and swung the offered shirt over his head.

Still unsettled by the whole exchange, and unsure what

to think regarding the way they all clearly knew each other, or that Finn had been keeping things from him, Jaime turned away from him and that confrontation for right now and found DA Rivera striding over. "Jaime. I'm sorry for the way all of this has happened. Are you ok?"

Jaime hadn't ever met DA Rivera in person, he'd only heard his voice over the phone. So he was absolutely not prepared for just how beautiful he was. If Jaime wasn't so caught up on Finn, he'd want to spend more time taking in this man's stunning hazel eyes, shockingly bright against his deep russet skin.

"I'm fine. I was in the truck for most of the conversation, anyway."

"Good, good." The DA cast a glance around at everyone else, eyes catching on Sheppard where he stood off to the side, speaking quietly with Silas and Finn. Detective Sutton was not quite shoving the two smirking trespassers into the back of the police vehicle. "Can I have a word with you, privately?"

Jaime nodded, and motioned the DA up toward his house, crossing his arms and waiting for him to speak. "Do you feel safe, Jaime? Here, with Cameron Sheppard's team?"

That set off the warning bells in his head even louder. "Is there a reason I shouldn't?"

The DA didn't answer his question, instead asking another of his own. "Have you had any contact at all with Jeffrey Dugan?"

So, they do think her husband had something to do with it.

"No. I haven't. But that's who sent those men, isn't it? I heard them speaking about him. Is that who Bishop was on the phone with? Is he the one who ordered Vera's murder?"

DA Rivera paused, and glanced back toward Sheppard. A muscle in his jaw clenched, and he seemed to come to some sort of decision. "We can't prove it yet, but yes. We think so. We are having him tailed, which is probably why he sent those two to scare you instead of coming himself. He's a very dangerous man, Jaime. If he or anyone claiming any affiliation with him approaches you, you need to get away from them immediately. I don't want you to be hurt because you've been caught up in all of this."

Jaime's breaths came faster, and he slowly counted backward from ten until he felt a bit steadier. "What does all of that have to do with me feeling safe with the security team?"

DA Rivera studied him. "I'm not sure. I was more wondering what your thoughts were on that."

Is he trying to get me to spy on them or something?

Apparently that thought was written all over Jaime's face, because DA Rivera waved his hands in a placating gesture. "I don't believe they had anything to do with Vera's murder, or that they would ever hurt you, Jaime. If I thought that, I would intervene immediately."

The DA's eyes were drawn back over to where Sheppard was standing, almost like he couldn't help it. "I knew Cameron Sheppard a very long time ago. And while I'm not sure how they are involved in all of this, I am confident that he wouldn't put someone like you in danger. I don't believe him or his team to be bad people, Jaime. But I want you to know you can call me, anytime."

DA Rivera focused back on him, and passed Jaime a

business card with a scribbled phone number on the back. "That's my personal phone. Please, if anything seems off to you, I'll make sure you're looked after. In the meantime, stay safe, yeah?"

Jaime didn't know what to say, so he just nodded. DA Rivera clapped him on the shoulder and stepped off the porch, heading back to where Finn, Silas, and Sheppard were all gathered together, three pairs of sharp eyes all focused on the two of them.

He wasn't sure why he hadn't told the DA that he'd overheard Finn and Silas confirm that they knew Jeffrey Dugan. Well, yes he was. He wanted to confront Finn about it himself, first. Maybe that was the stupidest, most reckless thing he'd ever considered, but he wanted to give Finn the chance to tell him what was going on.

He wanted to hear Finn explain everything, and for it all to make sense, and then they could continue whatever they had started today at Andi's—whatever had almost happened in the bookstore, and in the truck before Finn noticed the trespassers.

That all felt like a lifetime ago, already.

Detective Sutton was waiting in the cruiser with the two detained intruders inside, and after one last lingering look shared between them, DA Rivera and Sheppard each stepped into their own vehicles and departed one after the other, Silas piled into the passenger seat of the latter's SUV.

He watched them go, standing shoulder to shoulder with Finn.

Jaime turned toward him, looking him in the eye for the first time since they'd arrived. He wasn't sure what to make of what he saw. There was guilt and wariness in Finn's eyes, yes, but also longing and want. And tenderness, too.

It settled him.

Yes, Jaime would confront him about what he'd overheard. And whatever that led to, whatever lies it exposed, he was certain about one thing.

Finn would never hurt him.

CHAPTER 12

FINN

*J*aime knows that you know Jeffrey Dugan. He knows that you've kept things from him.

He knows.

He knows.

He didn't know all of it, though. And all of a sudden, confronted with the very real possibility that Jaime would reject him if he knew the truth—that Bishop was a wolf shifter, and so was Finn, and Finn wasn't that different from the man who'd hurt him so badly... fuck.

He'd thought that he wanted to be whole for Jaime, to be wholly wanted, but when it felt like everything between them was slipping through his fingers, he couldn't help but think that he'd take what he could get.

Finn would take Jaime wanting only half of him, if that's all he could ever have. It could be enough.

If their earlier almost-kiss had unraveled him, now he felt

frayed—pulled in both directions by his desire to show Jaime everything, and the fear that howled at him to hide.

Finn followed Jaime into the house and prayed that wherever this conversation led, it wouldn't end with him being thrown out of the house, forced to keep watch from the trees in his wolf shift. Silas may be just as comfortable, if not more so, as his wolf, but Finn very much appreciated hot showers, a bed, and eating food that had been cooked and seasoned.

He prayed it wouldn't end in Jaime deciding he didn't want Finn in his life, after all.

Jaime led them to the living room, mercifully taking the couch. Finn didn't think he could have this conversation if the furniture stole what was left of his dignity. Taking a seat in the armchair across from him, Finn held his breath, and waited.

"So. You know Jeffrey Dugan," Jaime said.

Straight to the point. Right. Good, okay. He could do this. He could navigate these questions without scaring Jaime away.

Sure, you can.

"Um, not really. Not in person. I know who he is. I know of him." Finn winced. He knew that wasn't the answer Jaime was looking for, nor was it the full truth. But he didn't know how to explain further without letting the wolf out of the bag, so to speak.

Still, the eyebrow Jaime raised said enough. He owed him more.

"He's part of an... organization. One we are familiar

with. Silas, Sheppard, and I, that is. We aren't associates of his! We just know what circles he runs in." He added the last part hastily, trying to sooth the shock blooming across Jaime's face.

"An *organization?* Like, what, the mafia? Is Jeffrey Dugan in the mafia, Finn? Wait, are *you* in the fucking mafia?"

Finn's eyes nearly bugged out. "No! No! I'm not in the mafia! And no, it's not like that. It's not, like, organized crime. More of a... club? Like, they all do business with each other."

This was not going well. Jaime was starting to panic, and that was the last thing he wanted. Holding his hands out, he pleaded. "Jaime. I had nothing to do with what happened to Vera. Neither did anyone else at the security firm. We only suspected that Jeffrey had something to do with it because of what we know about his... friends. How he does business."

Jaime slowed his breathing, and croaked, "Explain."

Finn took a deep breath. "It's sort of an understood rumor that Jeffrey Dugan married Vera for her father's business contacts in Monroe. He was a major developer in the area, and when he died, she inherited the firm and all the subsidiary holdings. When she was murdered, all of it went to Jeffrey. So it wasn't a stretch to believe that he had something to do with her murder."

All of that was true, Finn wouldn't lie to Jaime about that. But he was just not ready to tell him that the "club" he referred to was the Salt Creek pack, and Jeffrey Dugan was a high-ranking member who had frequent business dealings with their alpha. With Jeffrey as the sole decision maker of

Vera's substantial holdings, the Salt Creek business interests would greatly benefit, making them just as invested and likely culpable in Vera's murder as Jeffrey was personally.

But he couldn't tell Jaime any of that without addressing the giant, furry wolf in the room.

Jaime looked confused and angry. "Do the police know this? Surely, if they can prove that Jeffrey had a financial interest in Vera's murder they could arrest him, and his goons wouldn't be threatening me in my driveway. They'd have actual proof, not just the testimony of some guy who happened to overhear a fucking phone conversation!"

Finn tried to soothe him. "They do. The good ones, at least. Detective Sutton and DA Rivera. But Jeffrey's associates are well connected. They have a presence in Monroe PD. From what we've gathered, it's made prosecuting Vera's murder difficult, and now that there's someone to hold accountable, it's made rooting out Jeffrey's involvement even more difficult."

Jaime voiced pitched high in panic. "Are you saying you don't think that Bishop had anything to do with it? That he wasn't the one that was in her house that night?"

"No, that's not what I'm saying. He's definitely the guy, Jaime. He's the one who killed her and hurt you, and after he's convicted he's going to go to prison for a very long time for it. He can't hurt you anymore. But public pressure significantly eased once they arrested him. It may be easier for Jeffrey's contacts in Monroe PD to convince everyone to shelve the case after Bishop's trial and conviction."

They sat in silence for a long time while Jaime absorbed everything Finn had said. Somehow, he had found a way to tell Jaime just enough of the truth while hiding the rest. So then why did he feel like someone had carved out his chest with a shovel?

"Why didn't you tell me any of this before?" Jaime's voice was hollow, like it had been when he'd told Finn about his brother disappearing from his life.

Fuck. Fuck. Fuck.

Finn scrambled. "I didn't want to worry you anymore than you already were." He struggled to find the right words, the right thing to say so he didn't hurt Jaime and didn't let on that there was even more to all of this that he wasn't aware of. That there was more to Finn that he wasn't aware of.

"I wasn't sure if you would want to know how deep this goes. You were never meant to be caught up in any of it. You shouldn't have to worry about this, because it was never meant to affect you. I just thought we could keep you from having to be involved."

Wrong. Finn knew it was the wrong thing to say the moment it left his mouth, Jaime's face closing off completely.

He stood from the couch in an unfairly graceful rush. "But it did affect me, Finn. It did. I may not have been their target, but I was there. I saw what he did to her, and I couldn't help. And then he shoved me in a closet and I thought I was going to die. But I didn't. I survived, and now every fucking person around me wants to keep me from facing it!" He looked away, and Finn's chest went cold.

"I don't need you to protect me from the truth. That's not how this works. You can't... *manage* me, like that. I don't want that from you. Not you, too." Jaime's voice broke, and Finn felt like he'd been kicked in the stomach.

Fuck. Fuck. Fuck!

Jaime walked toward the stairs. "I'm going to bed."

Finn stood up quickly, following him. "Jaime, please. I'm sorry. Please, you haven't eaten dinner yet. Let's just... just, sit, and eat. And talk. I won't—"

Finn's plea caught in his throat, choking him. What could he say? He wouldn't lie to Jaime anymore? What a joke, when Finn was keeping so much from him still.

Jaime kept his back to him, voice pitched low. "You cannot tell me that you want to know me more, and then keep things like this from me. You cannot tell me that I'm not a burden to you and then treat me like someone you need to manage. You told me that I'm strong, but it makes me feel so weak when you and my brother don't give me a chance to decide for myself how to handle all of this."

He continued up the stairs. "I'm not hungry. Goodnight."

The click of Jaime's door closing might as well have been a bomb, shattering Finn's world.

FINN WAS A WRECK. He'd spent the entire night lying awake, tossing and turning, anxiously watching the monitors for signs of Salt Creek activity around the house, and ears strained for any hint of Jaime's movements. He'd locked himself in his room all evening and all through the night, and the only movement Finn heard was when he'd shuffle out of bed and pad to the bathroom and back.

Finn stumbled out of bed the next morning later than

usual, but Jaime still hadn't left his room. He whipped up some oatmeal for them both, topping Jaime's bowl with all of the things he knew he liked. He left a note telling him to warm it back up in the microwave, and that he needed to run a few errands and would be back soon.

What Finn really needed was a good hard run. The four-legged kind.

He needed to sink into that headspace where his emotions were muted, and it was easier to flip the switch on his anxious thoughts—where he could focus on the soft padding of his paws hitting the earth as he loped through the trees. He hadn't shifted all week, too afraid to go out of earshot of Jaime, and he was feeling it.

He texted Silas and asked him to come and watch the house for a few hours so that Finn could go blow off steam. Seeing as the two Salt Creek shifters had seen Silas yesterday, there wasn't any sense in him keeping his distance anymore.

Finn stepped outside when he heard Silas's truck pull up and met him in the driveway. Silas took one look at him and asked, "What happened?"

Finn shook his head. "Nothing. I just... explained that we had an idea about Jeffrey Dugan's involvement when we took the case, and hadn't told him about it. He was angry and hurt. Jaime doesn't like to feel like he's being kept in the dark about things. I should have told him sooner, but..." he shrugged.

Silas scanned his face. "It bothers you very much that he's angry at you. That you hurt him."

Finn locked eyes with Silas and nodded.

"But that's not what's driving your wolf to run, Finn. Talk to me."

It was an odd thing, when Silas gave him orders like that. Finn always thought that being half wolf made him immune to the more innate instincts—the desire to patrol and mark his territory, the urge to square up with other wolves and fight for dominance. But when Silas spoke in that way, when he gave him a direct order, Finn was all but compelled to obey. He didn't do it often, and almost always looked guilty after, especially when it interfered with the chain of command in their military years.

He didn't look guilty now, though. He just looked like a concerned friend. So, Finn didn't fight the order.

"I want to tell him."

The relief from speaking it aloud was devastating—all of his emotions swelled to the surface, and he couldn't stop the outpouring if he tried. "He smells right, Si. He smells like mine and he said he wanted this to be more, to try. He's curious and smart and unintentionally hilarious and *beautiful* and I want to hear him laugh every day and I want to be the one that makes him feel safe. But then I kept things from him, and he was hurt, and I—"

He heaved a sob, and Silas put a supporting hand on his shoulder. "What if I tell him and he hates me for lying about it? What if I tell him and he hates *me*? Looks at me like I'm a monster?"

Silas made a soothing rumble in his chest. "Come on brother, let's go sit in the truck." Finn cast a glance back toward the house, but Silas pushed him forward. "He will be fine inside, Finny. I've got an ear on the place, no one's nearby. Up, in the truck."

Finn shuffled in, and Silas followed on the driver's side. They both just sat together, deep breaths mirroring each other, and Finn basked in the ease of finally opening up his heart. Silas had always seen and known all of him, and had loved him like a brother even more for it.

"I knew it the moment we pulled into this driveway, you know. Sitting just like this. You shot out of the truck and went straight for him. The way you both looked at each other in that moment..." Silas nodded his head. "I knew."

"How? I don't think I even knew then."

Silas gave him a half smile. "You did, you just hadn't quite gotten there yet. I remember once when I was young, before we left the pack, I saw it happen. An alpha from a pack in Maine had come to visit for business, and he'd brought his children along with him. One of his sons saw a daughter of one of the higher ranking members, and—" Silas snapped his fingers, "just like that. They were only eighteen or nineteen at the time, but still, they were mated and wed within a week."

Silas chuckled at the wide-eyed look Finn gave him. "I'm not saying you have to bite and marry the man by tomorrow. I'm saying that for some of us, it's just like that. We know. And I can't imagine what it must feel like for you to know your mate, and want your mate, but to not be sure if your mate would want you in return. I know it has you all twisted up, Finn. But..."

Finn looked over at him. "But?"

"I think that fear is clouding your judgment. And you are

still doing what he's very explicitly asked you not to do. You are still hurting him by keeping him in the dark, managing what he knows because you think you know what he wants."

Finn made to argue. Jaime didn't want to be kept in the dark about the case—about things that affected him in that way—but Finn being a wolf shifter, Jaime being his mate, that was so much more. "It's different."

No, it's not.

"No, it's not." Silas raised his eyebrow at him. "You said he told you that he wanted to know you more. He wanted to try with you. Do you feel the same?"

Finn sighed heavily. "Yes. Obviously."

"Well, then. *Try.* If not for him, for your mate, then who? Who will be worth risking your heart for?"

Finn didn't have an answer to that.

"He's not your mother, Finn. I know she really did a number on you and your relationship with your wolf, but Jaime has never given me the impression that he would hate something just because he doesn't understand it."

Finn groaned. "Even if that thing he doesn't understand is the same thing that haunts his nightmares? That tore up a woman in front of him?"

Silas startled. "Seriously, Finn, is that what you think? You are not the same as Bishop. Just because he's a wolf and you are too, that doesn't make you the same. You are not bad just because of what you are. Would you say the same of me?"

"Of course, I wouldn't!"

"Well, then."

Finn digested that. Eventually, he sighed, and tipped his

head back against the seat as he looked up at the house. "How would I even go about telling him? He'd call me insane, kick me out, and call the cops before I could even finish explaining."

Silas hummed. "You could just show him. Rip the bandaid off, so to speak. It's what I would do."

Finn shot him an unamused glare, and Silas held his hands up in a surrender. "Fine. You and I are not the same in that approach, I get it. Think on it though, brother. Go for your run. I'll be here."

Silas paused, and reached over to clap Finn on the shoulder. "But don't deny yourself a lifetime of happiness and companionship out of fear. Please."

Finn nodded, holding back the fresh tears suddenly clouding his vision.

He reached for the door handle, but Silas stopped him. "Wait. Um, Finn." He cleared his throat, suddenly sounding nervous and looking like he'd rather be anywhere but here.

Confused, Finn asked, "What? Are you ok?"

Silas nodded, not making eye contact with him. "Yeah Finny, I'm fine. I just... I'm not sure if anyone's told you, or if you would have had a reason to know, or if it even would happen to you since you're half-shifter, but I should tell you something."

Now Finn was even more confused. Really, what could he want to talk about with him that would make him so nervous? The kind of porn he liked to watch? "Just say it, please. It cannot be as bad as I'm imagining."

Silas cleared his throat. "Have you ever had sex with someone in your partially shifted form?"

Maybe it can be as bad as I'm imagining.

"I'm sorry. What?"

Silas gave him a pained look and whined. "Christ Finny, I do not want to be having this conversation with you. But I can't be a good friend without making sure you're... prepared."

Finn raised his eyebrows, voice pitching high. "Are we seriously having a safe sex talk right now? You know we're both thirty-two years old? And that I have used a condom with every single person I've ever been with, despite our super-healing, disease-immune wolfyness?"

Silas pinched the bridge of his nose. "No, Finn, I'm not talking about using a fucking condom. I'm talking about sex while you are partially shifted. It's... different. Things are... different."

Finn waved his hands around wildly. "No, Silas. I have not had sex with someone while I'm partially shifted. That's actually been the furthest thing from my mind mid back-alley hookup!"

Some of the tension left Silas's face. "It won't be the furthest thing from your mind when you're with your mate."

That stopped Finn short. "Are you saying I'm going to want to shift if Jaime and I ever... become intimate?"

Silas moved his head in a yes and no gesture. "I'm saying your wolf will want to be right there with you when you're with him. All the time. Have you not noticed it?"

Blinking, he considered. He had noticed, actually. He'd barely been able to keep his shift in check whenever he was in the same room as Jaime, let alone... *with* him. "Oh, fuck."

Silas nodded. "So, for everyone's sake, it might be best to

tell him before you... you know." He made a lewd gesture with his hands, and Finn shot him an exasperated look.

"So that's what you meant by different? With my mate, I'll want to be partially shifted?"

Silas nodded, but then cleared his throat again. "Also. Um. This may not happen to you since you're only half wolf, but..." He looked like someone was forcing him to eat an entire plate of fish heads. Raw. Eyeballs and all.

"Just fucking spit it out Si, so I can get out of this truck and try and forget this conversation ever happened."

Silas whined again, and said something way too fast for Finn to believe he'd heard him correctly. "*Yourdickmightgetaknotwhenyoucome.*"

A beat of silence. Two. Three.

"I beg your pardon."

Silas tipped forward, resting his face against his crossed arms over the steering wheel, words muffled and resigned. "When you have sex in your partial shift, your dick might swell at the base forming a knot. It will get stuck inside... whatever your dick is inside. So maybe have a conversation about that, too. Before, you know. Surprise."

Surprise.

Surprise, Jaime. You're my mate and if you're cool with it I'm going to bite you to tie us together for life and then I'm going to fuck you when I'm all wolfy and hairy, and then my dick will swell and get stuck in your ass?

Of course Finn knew what knotting was, he was a grown man who'd been on the internet before. Sometimes you'd stumble across something you couldn't unlearn. But he'd thought that was just embellishment. An exaggeration from humans who had been with well-endowed shifters, and the truth got trickled down and mashed up with real wolf mating behavior, and then turned into lore and imagination due to most of the world still being in the dark about the whole 'paranormal creatures dwell among us' thing.

Although, he had to adjust himself at the thought of knotting Jaime—locking them together, pressing his cock deep, grinding against his prostate and making him squirm and whimper and beg beneath him, holding him down and making him take it.

Jaime would take it so well. He'd be such a good boy.

Well, it hadn't taken him long to get on board with that.

Silas groaned. "*Please* stop thinking about doing it! Fuck, this is already uncomfortable enough without you stinking up the truck."

"Hey, I'm not the one who brought it up!" He shouldn't complain, though. If Silas hadn't told him, this could have been a very bad situation where he truly scared or hurt Jaime.

If he ever decided to talk to Finn again.

"Why has no one told me about this before? Why didn't you tell me about this before? I knew about the whole 'biting your mate means forever' thing, but a knot? My dick will actually change? What the fuck?"

Silas sighed, resigned to his fate and probably wondering what he'd done to earn this particular level of hell. "I didn't tell you because it never came up. You never asked about shifting during sex, and you never indicated that you had met someone you thought might be your mate. And, shockingly, I wasn't particularly anxious to have this conversation!" He continued, "Wolves knot their mates to ensure pregnancy. It's a carryover."

Finn went pale. "Wait, you're not saying—"

Silas guffawed. "Christ, no, Finny. You can't get him pregnant. But on that note, condoms will be pretty useless if you knot him. Just so you know."

"Right. Well. Thanks for the information."

"Sure. Let's never do it again."

Finn couldn't get out of the truck fast enough, this time. "Yep. Never again. I'm going for a run to forget all of this."

Silas waved as he headed off.

———

He smells like ours.

Bite him and knot him, make him ours.

Finn bounded along the edge of the lake, through the trees, and made a giant circle in the Alaskan wilderness surrounding Jaime's cabin. The intense smells and sounds, along with the stretch and strain in his legs that had built up from staying too long in one form brought him some of the relief he was looking for, but that constant drum beat of want remained, always tugging him back to the cabin.

Back to Jaime.

Thump, thump, thump.

Don't deny yourself a lifetime of happiness and companionship out of fear.

Thump, thump, thump.

Claim him and knot him.

Now that it was there in his mind, he couldn't shake it. It

was like some innate, instinctual part in him had reared its head, sensing his arousal at the thought of knotting Jaime, and now it was a lingering, steady pulse that simmered low in his groin.

Thump, thump, thump.

Go back.

Thump, thump, thump.

His stride elongated, finally settling into four legs and a heart made for endurance.

Go back. Go back.

Thump, thump, thump.

Go back!

Without realizing it, he'd circled back already, nearly tearing through the tree line and into the clearing where Jaime's cabin stood before he halted, breaths coming in heavy puffs. He shook, but stilled when he sensed something was off.

Smell.

Silas wasn't in his truck. He could smell him nearby, but it wasn't his human form. Silas had shifted, which meant something was wrong.

Listen.

He could make out a low, rumbling growl—*Silas*—and a slightly whinier response. A wolf, but not someone he recognized. He was a split second away from circling around to the back of the house to help, when he saw it.

One of the Salt Creek wolves that had been there yesterday stepped out from the tree line across from where Finn was hiding, still fully shifted. The intruder remained on two legs, but his limbs were elongated, with talons extending from his fingers, and his lips were pulled back to show his prominent canines. A partial shift. In a few strides, the intruder was across the lawn and kicking down Jaime's front door.

Finn reacted without thought.

Leaping across the lawn, he threw himself inside the busted-open front door and tore through the living room. Shouts were coming from Jaime's bedroom, so he flew up the stairs, shifting as he climbed, and landed on the top step. Two elongated legs carried him down the hall and through Jaime's bedroom door in a blink, which had also been torn open ahead of him.

A howling shout left him at the sight of Jaime, eyes wide in terror and shock, backed up against the far wall as the intruder lunged across the bed, claws outstretched.

With speed he never knew he possessed before now, Finn hooked a clawed hand around the attacker's throat and yanked him back, hard, slamming him into the wall opposite Jaime, denting the drywall and pinning him with a snarl.

"I'll rip out your goddamn throat for this!" His words were thick through his canines, like he was chewing on them.

The shifter sneered at him. "Oh, so Silas's little half breed friend has a backbone, does he?"

Finn ignored him. Before he had time to consider how to get the other shifter away from Jaime, Silas thundered up the stairs and burst into the room.

If he was a mountain of a man in his human form, Silas was truly massive in his partial shift, nearly seven feet tall and thick as a tree trunk. Between his sheer size and the overwhelming anger and dominance that radiated off of him in this form, the wolf that Finn still had pinned to the wall cowered.

"I'll take care of him," Silas snarled. He reached a clawed hand over and grabbed the intruder by the scruff, pinning his hands behind his back.

Finn stepped back to block Jaime from the danger. "The other one?"

Silas snarled again. "Gone. He took off when you showed up. They must have followed me here and waited until you left."

"Are there any more of them?"

"None that I can smell in the area. Sheppard is on his way, he should be here in about ten minutes." Silas yanked the Salt Creek wolf out of the room, leaving only Finn and Jaime.

Waiting until the sound of their combined footsteps faded down the stairs and out the front door, Finn kept his back to Jaime, trying to slow his breathing and prepare himself for the fear and disgust and hate he would certainly see on his face.

But then Jaime made a small sound that had Finn's wolf whipping his head around, ears perked and zeroed in on the noise.

While he did see shock and fear, there was no disgust or hate in Jaime's eyes.

Instead, he saw wide-eyed wonder as he peered up at Finn, their height difference even more exaggerated in this form. Jaime remained plastered against the wall, palms splayed at his sides, but his shoulders relaxed when Finn turned toward him fully.

He had two shallow scratch marks running from the base of his throat and down his chest from when the Salt Creek shifter had tried to grab him.

Finn let out a high-pitched whine at the sight, and he stepped toward Jaime before halting at the sound of his voice.

"Finn?"

CHAPTER 13
JAIME

"Finn?"

Of course he knew it was Finn. While the man standing before him looked, well, not human, he still looked like *Finn*. He still had the same shaggy blonde hair, and rich brown eyes, and he still looked at Jaime with tenderness and care. Except now, his eyes held something so vulnerable and poignant that Jaime nearly had to look away.

But he didn't, because he had a feeling that if he looked away from Finn right now, in this moment, they would never come back from it.

"I won't hurt you, Jaime." Finn's voice was thick and raw, and the fluffy, pointed ears now perched on his head were drooping. But Jaime could understand his words just fine like this, even through all of those teeth.

Am I hallucinating?

Blinking a few times, Jaime unglued himself from the

wall and took a step toward Finn. "I know you won't, Finn. I know that."

The words rang true. He had absolutely no idea what was going on, or how his infuriatingly attractive bodyguard was currently standing in his room, naked, covered in hair, with enormous claws and fangs and fluffy ears, but he did know that even with all of that, Finn wouldn't hurt him.

Oh.

Oh.

Finn was naked. Very naked. And this *version* of him was absolutely massive in more ways than just height. Unless Finn's cock was that huge all the time, in which case, unfair.

But not really, though, if I'm the one lucky enough to feel it rearranging my insides later.

A large and hairy fanged man is standing in your room, naked, and you're thinking about fucking him?

Yes, he was.

Finn took a step toward him and Jaime couldn't help but glance back down—his cock was truly massive. Even soft, it hung heavy between his thighs, and shifted as he walked in a way that implied heft.

Jaime felt his face go hot, and he hoped the semi he was now sporting would go unnoticed among all of the other things that were happening right now. But then Finn's ears canted forward in interest and his nostrils flared, nose still shaped like a human's, and he looked down toward where Jaime's own cock was lengthening in his pants.

So, not unnoticed, then.

"You're naked." Jaime thought that should explain things well enough.

Finn looked back up at his face and studied him in a way he knew he'd never been looked at before. Jaime took another step closer, just because he wanted to. The tension left Finn's shoulders, and he finally stopped looking at him like Jaime had just kicked his puppy.

Puppy. Heh.

Jaime chuckled to himself, and considered that he might be in shock. Finn, the man he'd stood up a year ago and who'd walked back into his life in the most unexpected way could turn into a giant, hairy, fanged man? He had to be close to a foot taller than Jaime like this, and while most of his face remained unchanged, his ears were now furry and nestled in his golden hair, like a... wolf.

He had prominent canines that dropped down and framed his bottom lip, and the rest of his teeth seemed sharper and longer. His arms and legs were elongated too, making his current attempt to look smaller than he was even more obvious.

His fingers and toes were tipped in sharp, dark claws, and his thighs and lower torso were covered in thick, soft-looking fur, a shade darker than the sandy golden blonde of his hair. It thinned the further up it went, not entirely covering his ass and groin area, peaking in an exaggerated happy trail between his pecs where it spread back out, covering his chest.

Jaime looked back up from his appraisal, noting the cautious look was back on Finn's face. His voice was thick when he asked, "Are you ok, Jaime? Is there someone you want me to call for you? Someone you feel safe with?"

I feel safe with you.

Finn was still reading him closely, and may have seen that sentiment on his face, but still, Jaime answered. "I think I'm ok. I'm not hurt. I may be in shock. You know, given everything." He waved his hands in Finn's general direction, who nodded his head as if he understood.

"You do—I mean, you are, like, huge. Right? And covered in hair? And very naked? And your teeth are pointy? That's real, right? Because if it's not, then no, I am not ok and should probably go to the hospital."

Finn's mouth tipped up in a half smile, revealing more of one fang.

That should not be cute. It should not.

"Yes, that's all real. I know it's... I know you may be frightened of me, like this. But I promise you, I'm still in full control of myself. I would never hurt you. Neither would Silas or Sheppard."

His eyes were back to that earnest, vulnerable softness that made Jaime want to curl up in his arms and squeeze him for being too cute while he simultaneously figured out who hurt Finn so badly that he thought Jaime would scream and cry and hate him just for looking like this.

"There's a lot to explain," Finn went on. "And I will tell you everything, Jaime. Everything." He sighed. "I need to go outside to check on Silas and talk with Sheppard when he arrives. But we will not decide anything without your input. I won't keep you out of this, not anymore. After we've settled everything and found a safe place for you to stay tonight, I'll tell you everything. If you still want to hear it."

Jaime looked at him, all of him. He took in Finn's claws,

teeth, elongated limbs, and all of his earnest, tender words. "Yes, Finn. I want you to tell me. I want to listen."

A shudder passed through Finn, and right before Jaime's eyes, as if the weight of the moment had finally lifted off his shoulders, big, furry, growly Finn shifted and bunched and adjusted back into the Finn that looked like a human.

But he was still naked.

"Thank you, Jaime." Even in his human form, his fangs remained enlarged.

Cute.

He didn't think he was in shock anymore.

Just then, Sheppard hollered out and made his way up the stairs. Upon seeing Jaime and a very naked Finn standing so close to each other, he let out a resigned sigh. "Right, well. He knows?"

Finn said, "I'm explaining the rest to him later, but he knows the important bits. He saw both Silas and I shifted."

Sheppard glanced down and smirked. "I don't think that's the only important *bit* he's gotten an eyeful of."

Seeming to remember that he was naked, Finn blushed and covered his cock with his hand. Well, *gathered* his cock in his hand was more like it, because even though it was soft, it was certainly big enough to not fit behind his palm.

Also, that did nothing to hide the amazing view Jaime had of his ass.

Damn.

Finn cleared his throat. "Um. Right. Let me put some clothes on, and I'll meet you both downstairs."

Still smirking, Sheppard walked out.

Finn shyly glanced back at Jaime. "Later. I'll tell you everything later."

Jaime smiled at him, a real one. "Later. I promise."

———

THE NEXT COUPLE of hours were complete chaos, and Jaime did his best to stay out of the way, tucked into the background.

The security team had reported the attack, but left out the *hairier* details when making their official statements. Jaime saw Sheppard talking quietly with a few of the officers who had shown up, though, and he wondered if some of them were like Finn and Silas. And Sheppard, too, apparently.

Since there was an official protective order on file between Jaime and the two men, whose names he still didn't care to know, they completed a full investigation of the break in. A couple of the officers raised their eyebrows at the level of damage that had been done to the doors and the wall in Jaime's bedroom, but no one argued when Silas claimed he was the one to throw the guy around in the struggle.

Hell, Jaime had no doubt he could put a man through a wall even without all the extra mass in his other form.

Dana and DA Rivera also came, both seeming genuinely concerned for Jaime's safety and well-being, fussing over the scratches on his neck. He assured them both that he was fine, he wasn't hurt, just a bit shaken up, but they'd still insisted that he was looked at by paramedics.

He obliged, and sat in the back of the ambulance while

the medic put a couple of bandaids on him and answered the DA's questions, Dana hovering protectively.

She had dark, sleek black hair speckled with gray that framed her prominent features in a way that reminded Jaime of a raven, and when she stared down DA Rivera for asking questions she deemed unnecessary, Jaime was again grateful that she was on his side.

But she did let a few questions get by. Yes, the security team had done their job well. Yes, he felt safe with them.

It wasn't until after they left, promising to be in touch and reminding him they were only a phone call away, that Jaime realized—all of that was absolutely true.

He *was* fine. He did feel safe.

It was such a stark shift from the last time he'd parted ways with the detectives after being patched up by a medic, tucked under Sam's arm in a daze and feeling like his life had been ripped from him.

He'd seen three men who he had thought were just normal people turn giant, hairy, and growly right in front of him, but he was ok. And it didn't feel like shock. It felt more like, before, nothing had made sense. The way that Vera had died so quickly and violently hadn't made sense. But now, he had a rational explanation for it. Or well, maybe not rational, but an explanation, nevertheless.

There were things going on that Jaime had been kept in the dark about, which were making him feel lost, confused, weak, and afraid. But somehow, facing the reality of who was after him made him less afraid.

Or maybe that was the three giant, growly men on his side, protecting him.

Now that he knew what to look for, it seemed obvious that Finn, Silas, and Sheppard were different. The way the three of them moved in tandem, somehow communicating without speaking, making sure that at least one of them was never out of reach from Jaime the entire time the house was swarmed by police, showed him how serious they were in doing their job well. So yes, he did feel safe with them.

He felt safe with Finn.

Finn, who wouldn't stop staring at him every chance he got. It didn't bother Jaime, most of the time he stared right back, giving him a reassuring smile. Jaime wasn't sure what came next—he had no idea what he was in store for *later*, when Finn explained everything that was going on—but he knew he would listen. He wanted to listen.

Last night, holed up in his room, throwing his own pity party had shown him that. Yes, Finn had hurt him by not sharing what he knew about Jeffrey Dugan, but it wasn't the same as the way Sam had made him feel this past year. And Jaime knew that Finn's words earlier were true—he wouldn't keep things from him anymore.

I know you may be frightened of me like this, but I'm in control. I won't hurt you.

Oh, Finn. Of course he had kept so much from him at the start. He honestly couldn't say what his reaction would have been if Finn had tried to tell him. Finding out this way, while jarring, may have been best all around. And no matter what Jaime found out, no matter what Finn shared with him, he was very certain about one thing.

He wanted all of Finn.

This Finn, standing protectively in front of him with his

arms crossed, a plaid flannel stretching across his broad shoulders. And he wanted the other one, too, the fanged and clawed and hairy one that he met upstairs. The one who'd protected him and snarled and growled at the man who tried to hurt Jaime, and then turned those big, chocolate, puppy dog eyes on him that pleaded with him not to turn away.

Yes, he wanted them both.

Jaime stood in his living room with Finn, Silas, and Sheppard, and watched as the last police cruiser trundled back down his driveway. Finn was still staring, like he expected to see the moment the shock wore off and Jaime finally realized that he was alone with three giant predators.

He'd better fix that.

"I don't mind your staring, Finn. I actually quite like it. But please stop looking at me like you expect me to lose my marbles and bolt for the trees at any minute." He turned to see Finn blush and shuffle on his feet, sheepishly rubbing the back of his neck.

Silas smirked. "I told you to rip the bandaid off. See?" he gestured at Jaime and gave him a winning smile. "Everything worked out."

Finn growled at him.

Sheppard gave a long-suffering sigh, and made a face at Jaime like he'd dealt with their brotherly shit for too long and had no patience for it left. "I'm glad you are alright, Jaime, and I'm sorry if we gave you a shock. Our background doesn't usually come up in most cases. This is a unique situation. I know that Finn has offered to fill you in on everything, but I want you to know that I will keep you fully informed from this point forward, too. Now that you know about us, there's no sense in keeping you in the dark anymore."

Jaime heaved his own sigh, this time in relief, and listened as Sheppard continued.

"However, regarding your brother," Sheppard looked between him and Finn, "it isn't in our usual practice to disclose more than is absolutely necessary with people who aren't directly involved in our lives. I'll leave it up to you and Finn to make a final decision, but my recommendation would be to refrain from sharing certain details with him, at least for now."

"Thank you. For now, let's stick with what we've told the police," Jaime said.

Sheppard nodded. "Good. Well, I've got paperwork coming out of my ears back at the office, so I'm headed out. I'll work on sorting out the safe house. Jaime, if rooming with these two idiots gets to be too much, let me know, and I'll get you a hotel room."

They all chuckled, and Sheppard waved before he also got in his truck and disappeared down the end of the driveway.

The damage to Jaime's front door was extensive enough that he would have to stay somewhere else for a few days before they could get someone out to fix it. Plus, Dana, DA Rivera, and Sheppard had all agreed that it would be better if Jaime stayed in an unknown location until the trial.

Sheppard had told him he would ready one of the security team's safe houses that they used for clients when necessary, but it would be better if he stayed in a hotel or with Finn and Silas for tonight so the safe house could be opened up and stocked before they arrived.

Through a blush, Jaime had mumbled that he would be fine at Finn's if he was ok with that, and then he'd laughed out loud when Finn nodded his head in agreement so vigorously it looked like it might pop off.

Silas turned to Jaime, grinning ear to ear. "Sleepover time. This is going to be so much fun!"

Finn growled again.

Finn and Silas did have a guest room, but the bed was currently covered in piles and piles of laundry.

"It's all clean, I swear," Silas assured him. "Let me clear it off and you'll have somewhere to sleep."

Finn growled some more. Had he always done that, and Jaime was just now noticing? Or had he stopped trying to control it? "Jaime can take my bed, I'll sleep in here."

He turned to Finn. "Are you sure? I don't mind sleeping in the guest room. I don't want to kick you out of your own bed."

Finn scowled at the pile of Silas's laundry as though it had personally offended him. "I'm sure."

Silas smirked. Clearly, Jaime was missing something in this exchange, but he wouldn't argue about it because he secretly liked the idea of sleeping in Finn's bed.

Jaime dropped his overnight bag off in Finn's room and scurried back out, lest he be caught snooping, or worse, sniffing Finn's sheets, and found the two men in the kitchen.

The three of them fumbled their way through making dinner in the small room, and every light brush or accidental touch from Finn—or not so accidental, on Jaime's part—made his nerves light up and heat pool in his groin. He felt drawn to Finn in a way he'd never wanted anyone else, ever.

By the fourth time Jaime casually leaned back so that Finn's chest brushed up against him as he passed by, causing them both to inhale sharply and Finn to firmly grab his hip with one hand, Silas had clearly had enough.

Throwing his hands up, he turned and gave a pointed look to them both. "Seriously, you two. It smells like a goddamn brothel in here, not a kitchen. Let me eat my dinner, and I'll leave you alone for the rest of the night. But until then, please cool it, because I cannot breathe."

Finn growled again.

Jaime blushed, and mumbled an apology.

Silas waved him off, and pointed at Finn. "You. Stop it with the growling. I know you can't really help it, but I'm not trying to steal your... Jaime. I live here, too, in case you've forgotten since your brain has apparently turned to soup splashing around in that hard head of yours. I can't help it if the guest room smells like me. *Because I live here.*"

Finn looked sheepish, and gave Silas those sappy puppy dog eyes that should be illegal. "I'm sorry. You're right, it's hard to control. But I will try. We will be gone by the morning."

Silas nodded. "And stop it with those eyes, too. A guy can't ever be mad at you when you look like that. It's unfair."

Jaime was only understanding about half of this conversation, but it was enough to gather that the tension between him and Finn was detectable among the... giant and hairy.

"Oh my God!" Jaime slapped his hand over his mouth in sudden realization.

Two pairs of alert eyes whipped toward him. "What?"

Jaime pointed an accusatory finger at Finn. "You knew! The whole time! That's how you knew what I was reading! Oh my God!"

Finn's face was a mixture of smug guilt.

Silas asked, "Knew what? Wait, no, never mind. I do not want to know. Let's just finish dinner so I can leave as soon as possible, please."

Jaime was sure he was red all the way to the tips of his ears, and he shot Finn a glare as he turned back to his chopping, but it lacked any heat.

For an entire week, Finn knew that Jaime was reading smutty romance. And lusting after him nearly every chance he got.

God, how embarrassing.

Mercifully, dinner was ready a few minutes later, and they ate in companionable silence, sprinkled with small talk and familial bickering between Finn and Silas. It was so achingly domestic and wonderful, it only magnified the simmering heat pooling low in his belly. This snapshot of companionship and ease made Jaime *want*, and at the center of it all was the arrestingly gorgeous man sitting across from him.

After their plates were in the dishwasher and the kitchen was cleaned up, Silas stood from his seat and stretched.

"Well, I'm headed out for a run, and then I'll keep watch out there for the night. I can't imagine that they'd try something again so soon, but after this afternoon, we can't be too careful."

At Jaime's confused look, Finn clarified. "He prefers to do surveillance in his, uh, other form. It's more comfortable for him." He turned toward Silas. "Please, be careful. Don't stay out all night if you get tired—come and get me, and we can trade off. I mean that."

Silas gave him a knowing look. "I'll be fine, brother."

Something in Jaime's chest ached from watching them, and he had to look away. It was too similar to the way he and Sam used to look out for each other. Or the way he'd thought they had, anyway.

Before the thought could drag him too far down, though, Silas strode over and clapped him on the shoulder. "I'm glad you're safe here with us, Jaime, and I'm glad you're in the know. I know Finn has told you this already, but we will protect you."

Jaime smiled, and patted Silas on his other shoulder. "Thank you, Silas."

Finn growled, and then looked guilty about it.

Silas wished them goodnight with a knowing smirk, and strode for the back door, tossing off his shirt and pants in the process before walking out into the night only wearing his boxer briefs.

After a moment of stunned silence, Jaime said, "Ok. First question. Do you always have to get naked before you turn into whatever it is you turn into?"

Finn threw his head back and roared with laughter.

CHAPTER 14
FINN

J aime was taking the revelation that supernatural
beings exist so remarkably well that Finn was certain
he was still in some prolonged state of shock.

Surely, he should take him to the hospital for a
check-up? No one could handle what had happened in the
past eight hours as well as Jaime was.

However, another *very insistent* part of Finn was begging
him to take the man upstairs to his bed and claim him, to bite
him and fuck him and come deep inside of him so that the
world would know that Jaime was his.

"You're staring again." Jaime said it like an observation,
not a complaint.

"I'm sorry. I keep wondering if maybe you're still in
shock and I should take you somewhere. I just, uh, never
expected you, or anyone really, to be so casual about learning
all of this. Also you're the most beautiful man I've ever seen,

and it's going to take me quite a while to get used to being in the same room as you."

The last part sort of fell out, but, well. They were being honest, right?

Jaime blinked, mossy green eyes processing. He cocked his head at Finn. "How many people have you told? About, you know." He waved his hands at him in the gesture he made when he was referring to Finn's wolf.

"My shift."

"Huh?"

Finn gave him a half smile. "We call it a shift. I'm a wolf shifter. So are Silas and Sheppard. We have a partial shift, the one you saw today, and a full one, where we look like very large wolves. But there are other shifters like us who take other forms. Foxes, bears, deer. Some other things. So, we call it a shift."

Now it was Jaime's turn to stare. Finn took a step toward him, bringing their chests close enough to meet with each inhale. "And, to answer your first question—no one, Jaime. I've told no one, because there's never been anyone I wanted to tell. Not until you."

"Oh."

Finn felt Jaime's exhale puff against his neck, and he fought to hide the canines that had refused to go away since dinner, when he'd had to rein himself in from growling at Silas to get out before bending Jaime over the kitchen counter. "Oh?"

Jaime narrowed his eyes in playful exasperation. "Yes. Oh."

Finn laughed, but Jaime's blink of surprise at his exposed canines had Finn snapping his mouth shut and stepping back.

But a cool, freckled hand cupped his face and halted his retreat. Jaime's eyes were soft like new grass, and he did not look away. "Will you show me again? Your shift?"

"Jaime, you don't have to—"

"You don't need to take me to the hospital, Finn. I'm not in shock. I'm not sure I have the words to explain why, or how, but I feel *free*. I feel like I can see things more clearly now, like I understand more of what I have found myself involved in, and that makes me feel better. I feel more like myself than I have in a very long time."

He shuffled closer, closing the distance between them—a long line of warmth where they were pressed chest to chest and hip to hip. "Yes, I was scared today. But not of you. I've never been scared of you. And yes, I am overwhelmed, but you are helping to make that better. Whatever you have to tell me, or show me, it's not going to scare me off. I want you, I want to see—"

Finn kissed him.

It was hard and all consuming, his entire world centering on the softness of Jaime's lips and the press of him every-where, *everywhere*.

He cupped the nape of Jaime's neck and leaned in, tilting the shorter man's head back and angling his jaw, devouring his soft gasp of surprise. Finn's lips parted, tongue searching until Jaime opened up for him. At first, he tried to keep his teeth restrained so he didn't frighten him, not now that they were *here*, but then Jaime was cupping his face in return, and darted his tongue out to lap at the tip of one of Finn's canines.

He nearly came in his pants.

The groan that left him was not human, and Jaime's responding moan had him harder than he'd ever been in his life. Keeping his hand wrapped around the soft skin at Jaime's nape, tongues still searching and claiming and Jaime's hands dancing up and down Finn's back and chest like he didn't know where he wanted to feel, to hold, Finn grabbed Jaime by the hip and walked him backwards until he was pressed up against the wall, caged in.

Finn ground his hips into Jaime's, rocking their hard lengths together until Jaime broke the kiss with a gasp, head thrown back. He loosed himself upon the freckled planes of exposed skin, nipping and sucking, reveling in the slightly salty tang of Jaime's sweat mixed with his lemon and vanilla taste as he made his way down his long neck.

Finn stopped when he reached the spot where Jaime's shoulder and neck connected—where his scent concentrated, beckoning. Right where he'd bite and claim him.

And then I can knot him and he will be mine forever.
Soon.

Jaime mewled and squirmed beneath his lips and teeth, gasping his name in breathy exhales, his fingers tangled in Finn's hair, tugging lightly. "Finn. Finn. Please, touch me. I want you. So long, I've wanted this for so long. *Please.*"

Jaime's trembling hand took hold of Finn's where it was pressing fingerprints into his hip and moved it to his front, grinding the hard bulge in his pants against Finn's palm.

They both gasped. "Fuck, yes, Jaime. Yes. I'll give you what you want, I'll give it to you baby."

Finn fumbled with Jaime's zipper, pushing his pants and briefs down just enough to pull his hot, hard cock out and take him in hand. Halting the love bites he'd been nipping along Jaime's collarbone, Finn panted and looked down to where he slowly pumped Jaime's cock.

It fit perfectly in his hand, with the flushed head peeking out of his closed fist, leaking already. He wanted to taste it, to lap at Jaime's precum and choke on his cockhead after lodging it down the back of his throat.

He wanted to swallow Jaime whole.

"Fuck, you're perfect Jaime. Perfect." Finn started to pull away, made to get on his knees, but Jaime's grip in his hair and around his shoulders tightened, halting him.

"I want to feel you, Finn." Jaime hooked a leg around his hip and thrust himself into the cradle of Finn's hand, yanking him back in close and rocking against his prominent erection.

A broken groan left Finn as he began fumbling with his own zipper and dropping his pants just low enough for his cock to spring free.

"Fuck," Jaime grunted, breaths heavy as they both looked down, foreheads pressed together and taking in the size difference between them. Finn wanted to howl with how perfect his mate was.

"Can I touch you?" Jaime asked.

Finn had never wanted anything more in his life than to feel Jaime's hands on him in this moment, and couldn't bring himself to be ashamed of the way his voice cracked when he begged, "*Please*, Jaime. Yes. Touch me, baby."

He claimed Jaime's mouth again, and the tentative, unsure touch ghosting up and down his shaft nearly sent him through the roof. Breaking the kiss but staying close, lips brushing up against each other as they moved, Finn released his hold on Jaime's cock and gripped his hand instead, so that they were both wrapped around Finn.

"Like this," he guided, and squeezed the younger man's hand around his length, setting a hard, steady pace. Feeling Jaime's soft, cool palm pumping him had him throbbing in pleasure, head dropping to rest on Jaime's shoulder as his balls pulled tight in impending release.

Jaime began thrusting up against their knuckles and whining for more friction. "F-Finn. I'm going to come s-soon," he hiccuped.

"Fuck, baby, me too. I've got you. I'll get you there."

Finn released his hold over Jaime's fist and batted his hand away. Looking directly into his eyes, wide and hazy with pleasure, Finn ran his tongue several times along his palm. When it was slick enough, he reached back down and took both of their cocks in hand. He stroked them together in long, hard pulls that had Jaime mewling and gasping and clinging onto Finn's shoulders like he couldn't hold himself up anymore.

Jaime's leg tightened around Finn's waist, hips thrusting up into his fist where he pumped them in rhythmic slides that were driving them both mad with pleasure, Finn's wolf surging up and wanting to take over.

He forced the shift back, not ready to deal with the

particulars of that right now. But, Silas had been right. In the past, his wolf had been nearly dormant during his various hookups. Now, with Jaime, it was clawing for release.

His wolf grumbled, successfully tucked away for now, and Finn grasped the nape of Jaime's neck again, fingers tangling in his hair as he held him close. Driving the most beautiful sounds from Jaime with each tug and flick of his wrist around their crowns, slipping against each other in their combined precum, he brought them both hurtling toward the edge. "Come, Jaime. Come for m-me."

Jaime inhaled sharply, and Finn couldn't look away as the boy's mouth dropped open in a silent scream. He felt the hot splash of cum coat his hand as he continued to pump them both through Jaime's orgasm, who was trembling as his cock kicked in Finn's fist, hands clutching and grappling on his shoulders.

It was the scent of Jaime's release that punched Finn over the edge, too, and he continued to pump them both, now slick with Jaime's cum, for a few more pulls until he cried out, shouting Jaime's name and pressing him into the wall as Finn thrust and ground his release into the cradle of Jaime's hips.

Cock throbbing and shooting long ribbons of cum between them, pleasure simmered at the base of Finn's spine as he buried his face in Jaime's hair and pulled his sex-heavy scent deep into his lungs.

For long moments they stood there, breathing each other in, with Finn's weight holding Jaime up. Eventually, Jaime's leg released its tight hold on his hip and slid down, and he committed to memory the breathy, hitched murmurs Jaime made while still floating in a post-climax state. Their soft, over-sensitive cocks hung nestled against each other, and both of their shirts were streaked with cum.

Some of Finn's release had landed all the way up on Jaime's chin, and he watched Jaime slowly uncurl his tight grip on Finn's shoulder and swipe at it. Green eyes flicked up and met his, as if making sure Finn was watching, before the tip of Jaime's pink tongue darted out from his swollen lips and lapped Finn's spill off the pad of his thumb.

If he could come again so soon, he would have.

"*Jaime.*" Finn's voice was low and gravelly, words thick between his still descended canines.

Jaime lifted a hand up to his cheek and ran the pad of his thumb along Finn's lips, exposing the tip of a fang. "So that's why you sometimes sound like you swallowed a bit."

Finn stared, enthralled as he explored his sharp teeth like they weren't dangerous, or frightening, or all of the other things that Finn feared he was.

Hand falling away, Jaime began to fidget with the hem of his t-shirt as he peeked up through cinnamon lashes and gave him a shy smile. "Um, so. That was... nice. Good. It was good. Was it good for you?"

The earnest hope and vulnerability shining in his eyes dashed any fears Finn had that Jaime would regret what they had done together. He nodded, and leaned back in for a slower, tender kiss. It was gentle in a way their kisses hadn't been before, but still devastating. Finn wanted to luxuriate in Jaime's lips and tongue forever.

Long moments later, Finn broke the kiss and wrapped

his arms around Jaime in a tight hold, pressing sweet words into his hair. "I've never come so hard in my life."

He exhaled, unable to find the words for how axis-shifting and revelatory it was to hold Jaime in his arms, to kiss him and hear his sounds of pleasure and know that he was the one responsible. All he could say was his name, over and over. "Jaime. My Jaime."

Jaime shuddered in Finn's arms, and he realized they were both still streaked with drying come, pants undone. So gently, he reached down and tucked Jaime away, righting his clothes, and then did the same for himself. Taking off his shirt, he swiped at the cum covering them both. "We should go clean up. I can give you a change of clothes, if you like."

Finn pretended to forget that Jaime had brought his own overnight bag—he wanted him in his shirt.

Apparently, Jaime was also willing to pretend. "I'd like that."

The moment still felt too tender for conversation, so Finn took Jaime's hand and led him up the stairs to his bathroom. After finding an old t-shirt and a pair of sweats with a drawstring, he set them on the counter for Jaime to change into when he was done. "Leave your dirty clothes on the counter and I'll put them in the wash. If you need anything, just holler."

Jaime smiled and nodded, and Finn shut the door behind him before promptly face-planting onto his giant bed, star-fishing his legs and arms. He luxuriated in the sounds of Jaime padding around his bathroom and stepping into the shower.

Jaime knows that I turn into a giant animal, and he's not afraid.

Jaime just came in my hand, pressed up against me, and he said it was good.

If this was a dream, he never wanted to wake up.

Still, there was a lot to be said between them. Finn needed to fill him in on the rest of the mess with Jeffrey Dugan, and before anything else happened between them he needed to tell Jaime everything about what it would mean for them to be together.

He needed to tell Jaime that he was Finn's mate, and what that meant for them if they decided to make the bond, or reject it. It wasn't fair to keep that from him any longer. So he got up, snagged Jaime's dirty clothes from the bathroom counter, and threw them in the wash.

And he did *not* smell them. Even though he wanted to. Very much.

When Jaime stepped out from the bathroom Finn was again sitting on his bed, albeit with a little more dignity than before in preparation for this conversation.

However, upon noticing that Jaime was wearing Finn's t-shirt, and *only* his t-shirt, all of Finn's rational thoughts and plans were forgotten. While it covered the swell of his ass, landing somewhere mid-thigh, the sight of Jaime's long, bare legs would have brought him to his knees if he weren't already sitting.

All of those freckles leading up, up, up... he needed to follow them and bury his face in the soft swell of Jaime's thighs—needed to know if they tasted as delicious as they looked, dusting him all over.

And then the fucking scent of him; he still smelled like *Jaime*, all lemony sweetness, but also like Finn's soap and his shirt and the faint musk of his cum still lingering... devastating.

Absolutely devastating.

"Come here," Finn rumbled, holding out a hand. He wondered if his teeth would ever look human again now that the taste and scent of Jaime was permanently branded on his senses.

Jaime, already pink and flushed from the hot water, shyly made his way over and braced his hands on Finn's shoulders. He grabbed Jaime's hips, hands spreading wide so that his pinky tips teased the bare skin of Jaime's thighs as he slid them up, and down, up, and down.

Jaime made a throaty noise, eyes hooded, and stepped further into Finn's hold. "Finn... Is it always like this?"

He looked into Jaime's eyes, and saw the answer to a question he'd wondered about since he felt Jaime's tentative, inexperienced touch on his cock downstairs. Still, he needed to hear Jaime say it. "No. Never. It's never been like this for me with anyone else."

Finn exhaled hard, and tugged Jaime down until he was curled up next to him, arms wrapped around each other. "I have had sex with other men, but it's been a long time. There was never anyone I wanted to be serious with, and casual flings just made me feel tired." At Jaime's glance, he clarified. "I don't think there's anything wrong with casual, it's just not for me."

Jaime tucked his chin back in, nuzzling further into Finn's side. "So this isn't casual, for you?"

"No. No Jaime, this is not casual. It never has been. This, what's between you and I... there are things I still need to tell you about me, about what I am. It will help all of this make sense, why this feels so intense. But before we do that, I want to make sure you're ok with what we did together downstairs."

Jaime sat up and looked at him in surprise. "I—yes! That was amazing, Finn. I wanted that. I want you." He blushed and pulled back, sitting up fully. "I've, um. I've never done that. With anyone. Ever." He cast his eyes around, twisting the hem of Finn's t-shirt so that it was riding even further up the soft swell of his thighs.

Focus.

Finn reached out and took Jaime's hand in his, thumbs soothing along the tops of his knuckles. Jaime's eyes found his again and some of the tension left his body. "I've exchanged exactly two handjobs with a guy I met in college, but it never went further before school got out for the summer and he moved back home. We hadn't really been seeing each other, so when he left we just stopped talking, it wasn't like a breakup or anything."

Finn nodded, and Jaime continued. "So I've never, you know, had sex. Or, anything else. What we did, for me, was everything. It felt like everything."

He pulled Jaime back into him. "It was everything for me, too. And I definitely want to do it again, and more, if that's what you want. Soon. *Very soon,*" Finn growled. "But I really do need to tell you some things first, so that you know what being with me would entail."

"I know. Thank you. And I do understand why you've

kept this from me. It's not exactly the kind of thing you can just go around telling people. I still think you should have told me about Jeffrey Dugan's involvement from the start, but I understand why you kept this part from me," Jaime said.

Finn palmed the back of his neck. "Right, about that... let me shower first, and then I'll tell you everything."

Jaime raised an eyebrow at him, but agreed. "Fine."

JAIME

Jaime was physically and emotionally exhausted from everything that had already happened that day, but he kept himself awake while Finn showered by snooping through his room and then moving his clothes to the dryer. He threw on a pair of his old, ratty sweats, and when he stepped back into the room, Finn was already dressed in a soft t-shirt and white boxer briefs.

Yum.

The apprehensive look on Finn's face pulled him from marveling that he'd felt that prominent bulge in Finn's underwear come all over him just an hour or so ago, and he pushed aside thoughts of heated touches and slick tongues so that they could *talk*.

Ugh, fine.

He took Finn's hand as they settled back onto the king-sized bed and sat cross-legged, knee to knee, while Finn filled him in on, well, everything.

Ok, not *everything*.

He hadn't explained what he was implying about them being *together* together, yet. But what he had told Jaime was quite enough to process, for now, thank you very much. It was still true, though, that he felt better after knowing the full scope of the mess he'd found himself in, that he felt more grounded and present than he had in a very long time.

And not all of that was due to Finn tugging his soul out through his dick a few hours ago.

Fuck, that had been the absolute hottest thing he'd ever experienced in his life, and he'd read enough smut and experimented with enough sex toys to know a thing or two about intense orgasms, even if they had been at his own hand. Or his own vibrating dildo.

The way they had come together was completely overwhelming, leaving Jaime feeling spent and unmoored until he looked into Finn's eyes and swore he felt a warm *pull* snap between them, tethering him.

And Finn hadn't let him flounder.

No, he'd held him through it all, and then opened up to Jaime about his past sex life in a way that made Jaime feel like he could talk about his, or the lack thereof, in a way that wasn't embarrassing. It had been perfect, and Jaime very much wanted to do it again. He wanted more.

But right now, he needed to process the fact that a very large and powerful wolf pack was actively trying to kill him because of the vague possibility that he had incriminating information on one of their high ranking members.

"If they are this intense over someone who *might* be able

to cause trouble for them, what do they do to someone who is actually a threat?"

Finn reached out and took hold of one of his hands, stopping him from fiddling with the hem of his t-shirt. Finn's t-shirt. That had been a spontaneous moment of bravery, and Jaime was very glad he'd ridden the wave of confidence, because walking out of the bathroom and seeing the lust glaze Finn's eyes had been very fun.

"They kill them."

Jaime whipped his head up. "Wait, are you saying you think Vera was a threat to them? And that's why they killed her?"

Finn shrugged. "I don't know. The part I told you about before is true; if I had to bet, she died so that Jeffrey has control over the Novikov fortune. But, maybe she was."

"Then what were you referring to?"

Finn continued to stroke his thumb over Jaime's knuckles. "Silas's family used to be a part of the Salt Creek pack. His family fled in the dead of night when he was just a boy because the alpha threatened to kill him. That's when he started going to the same school that I did in Monroe."

"The alpha threatened to kill a child? Why?" Jaime couldn't mask the disgust in his voice.

Finn shook his head. "I don't know. Silas has never told me the reasons they fled, just that it had something to do with him and an ultimatum the alpha made. I'm not even sure he knows the full story, his parents were always very tight-lipped about it. They said it was for his safety."

Finn shifted, their knees bumping as the mattress

bounced them against each other. "We left for the military right out of high school and moved to Silver Rapids when we got out. The people there, paranormals, don't like the Salt Creek pack. Their violent and old-school reputation draws too much attention, and paranormals move to Silver Rapids to get away, not to have the police showing up on their doorstep every other week. But that means we've never really had to interact with them until now."

Jaime cocked his head. "Old-school?"

Finn waved a hand. "Traditional pack way of living. It's very hierarchical, they all live together in compounds and what the alpha says is law and all that. If an investigative reporter discovered their home den without the paranormal context, I'm sure they would think it was some ultra-conservative cult or something."

Jaime shuddered, flipping Finn's hand to trace patterns along his palm. "So that's why you were the one to stay with me in the beginning, and not Silas—because he didn't want to be on Salt Creek's radar."

Finn closed his hand around Jaime's. "It's the reason we all agreed for it to be that way, yes. But it was not my first reason, Jaime. I told you, I couldn't stay away after I heard about the leak. I was planning to find you on my own, before I found out about the contract. My being here was inevitable —I just had the lucky excuse of your brother hiring us to make it official."

He squeezed Jaime's hand again. "And if you had told me that you didn't want to see me, that you didn't want me in your life..."

Finn looked up, eyes nearly feral with intensity. "I would

have stayed in the woods outside of your house in my wolf form every single night until I knew that you were safe again."

Jaime blinked, mouth slightly open. Finn's eyes were piercing, almost challenging him to look away, to turn away from him. "Does that scare you? Was that too much?"

Determined to rise to that challenge in Finn's eyes, Jaime just shook his head and tugged on the hand in his until Finn was leaning over him, one hand supporting his weight at Jaime's hip.

This close, Jaime's gaze darted back and forth between Finn's. "I asked you before. Will you show me your shift, again? The one from earlier?"

Finn exhaled hard and broke eye contact, as if surprised that Jaime did not shrink away from him. "It's late, and you've had a very long day. We should get some sleep and we can talk about the rest in the morning, yeah?"

Jaime looked down, but nodded. He was disappointed that Finn had dodged his question a second time, but he was right. It was late, and it wouldn't do to have any more serious conversations until they'd both had a good night's rest.

"Um, so I'll just go to the guest—*oof*."

Suddenly finding himself flat on his back and staring up at Finn looming over him, goosebumps shot up his arms as Finn spoke. "You will not sleep in a bed that smells like another man, Jaime."

Wide-eyed, Jaime nodded, but knew the second Finn felt the evidence of what that goddamn tone did to him, his already chubbed-up cock hardening and tenting his threadbare sweatpants.

A predatory gleam flashed in Finn's eyes, and he shot him a wolfish grin as he pressed his own hardening erection down against Jaime's. "*Nngh.* Finn, if you keep doing th-that, I'll have to go to the guest room just to get some sleep."

Finn growled, and began rocking as he pressed, the pressure of his cock grinding into Jaime's and making him go hazy and loose. "You'll sleep here with me tonight."

Jaime's dick throbbed at his words, the glans catching on the fabric of his pants, tacky with precum. "Fuck!"

Finn chuckled, and the bass note rumbled low in his belly. "Do you like it when I tell you what to do, Jaime?"

He whined, but the fog of lust and desire made it easy to tell the truth. "Yes."

Finn chuckled again, and began nipping his canines along Jaime's neck and exposed collar bone. "I thought so, baby. I knew it wasn't just those filthy romances you read that had you smelling like dessert all day. Like a goddamn four course meal, Jaime. *Fuck.* Do you have any idea how hard it was to resist you? Hmm?"

Instead of letting him answer, Finn pulled back from his nips and licks along his jawline and propped himself up on his forearms by Jaime's head. He widened his knees, caging Jaime in and giving himself more leverage to press his hips down even more insistently, making Jaime cry out.

Finn continued like that, steadily rocking and grinding into him. "If just the scent of you was enough to drive me wild, I bet your taste will ruin me. Should we find out, Jaime? Would you like it if I use my mouth on you? If I suck you?"

By now the shirt Jaime was wearing had ridden halfway

up his stomach, and Finn moved a hand to palm at his soft belly while staring at his stiff cock tenting his pants like it was indeed a delicacy. If what they had done earlier downstairs had been intense, Jaime thought that having Finn's mouth around him would shake him to his core.

And fuck, his imagination of Finn using that commanding tone on him was nothing compared to the real thing. So he let himself slip further into that hazy place of pleasure, reveling in the press and grind of Finn's body atop his. "Yes. Yes. Please, Finn. I want that."

Finn growled in answer, yanking both of their shirts off, and slid down the length of Jaime's body, kissing and nipping and sucking and licking as he went. He stopped and teased his tongue over one of Jaime's nipples, and then the other, and *that* was certainly something they were going to investigate more later. But Finn seemed just as impatient as Jaime was, so he quickly continued his downward slide until he was propped between Jaime's thighs.

Finn pulled Jaime's pants down until his knees were free, gently guiding one foot out, and then the other, before hooking one leg over his shoulder, opening Jaime up in a way he'd never been before another. Finn watched Jaime's cock bob against his stomach, eyes dark with lust, and then he looked up through sandy lashes.

"Are you sure?"

There was a hint of vulnerability there, and it settled Jaime's nerves at being so exposed, making his heart ache to think that Finn thought he would reject him, that he thought Jaime could ever be frightened of him. So he propped himself up on his elbows, and did not look away.

"I'm sure. I want you, Finn. I want to feel your teeth on me. Don't hold back. Please."

Finn let out a broken whine, and he threw one arm across Jaime's belly, his claw-tipped hand splayed wide to pin him down, while the other palmed the inside of the thigh not slung over his shoulder, spreading him open. Finn settled further into the cradle of his hips and nuzzled and nipped all around Jaime's leaking cock, teasing the soft skin of his thighs.

It seemed like Finn was everywhere except for where Jaime needed him the most. He mewled, wriggling under the hand pinning his belly and hips to the bed. Propped up on his elbows, spread wide beneath Finn, Jaime watched as he finally took mercy on him, his kisses and nips circling in until he flashed predatory eyes up at Jaime and swallowed his length down in one go.

"*Unnf!*" Unable to form words, Jaime's eyes rolled back as he felt himself tap the back of Finn's throat. The sounds coming from Finn were fucking lurid as he swallowed through a gag, seating Jaime firmly in the hot slide of his throat.

"Oh God, oh God, Finn—" Jaime hiccuped a breath, hips involuntarily rocking up to bury himself further into the wet heat. "S-slow down, or I'm going to—going to come already," he choked out, voice cracking.

Finn pulled his mouth from the base of him all the way to the sensitive head and lightly suckled there, tongue circling his slit and lapping up the steady stream of precum. He repeated the motion several times, and Jaime sobbed at the gentle pressure, which was somehow just as intense as being swallowed wholly.

Jaime peered down again to find Finn staring up at him, eyes focused and lips shiny. He pulled his mouth off Jaime's cock before he could come, the wet *pop* sounding lewd in the quiet of the night between them.

"Keep looking at me, Jaime." Finn's words were gruff and thick through his descended canines, a strand of spit and precum connecting his mouth to Jaime's dripping tip.

Seeing himself spread open and pinned, those fangs so close to the most vulnerable parts of him, made Jaime even harder, and his shaft bobbed as they stared at each other, each taking great heaving breaths.

Finn's focus shifted from Jaime's face back to his cock, head tilting like a fox who'd just pinned the rabbit—a predatory gleam in his eye as he watched even more precum slip out and create sticky trails along his stomach.

Without looking away from Jaime's length, Finn said, "Watch me swallow you, baby. Do you like seeing my fangs around your cock? Do you like feeling them cradle you, knowing that you've surrendered yourself to me, that you've allowed me to bring you so much pleasure with something so dangerous?"

His warm breath puffed against Jaime's shaft as he spoke.

"Please, Finn," Jaime keened, adjusting his leg over Finn's shoulder so he could thrust up, begging.

His wet tip tapped along Finn's plush lips, and they widened in a feral grin. "Say it, baby. Say you love my fangs, and I'll give you what you want. What you need."

"Fuck," Jaime ground out. "Yes. Please. Show me. I want to watch my cock disappear into your mouth. I want to see your fangs around me while you do it. I love it. I want to feel them. Please, Finn."

Finn snarled, "Eyes on me, Jaime. Don't look away."

It was a command, and Jaime's body responded accordingly—flushing even further and sinking into the mattress. But Jaime also heard the vulnerability in his voice. Finn needed Jaime to watch; he needed to know that Jaime saw all of him, and was not afraid.

He opened his mouth to voice his reassurance that he trusted Finn wholly—that there was never anyone or anything else he could look at when Finn was in the room—but all that came out was a shout as Finn adjusted his hold on Jaime's thigh and stomach, anchoring him down, and opened his mouth.

The flat of his tongue cradled the underside of Jaime's cock, wet and warm, and Finn closed his lips around his sensitive head and started that gentle suckling thing he did again, and— "*Oh, oh, ooh*, Finn—*nnnngh!*"

Finn's canines sat flush on either side of his cock. Jaime had never seen or felt anything more erotic in his life, and his hands scrambled for purchase before finally landing on the back of Finn's head and tangling in his hair. Not to guide, but to ground himself, needing the connection to keep from being completely lost to the pleasure of Finn's mouth and teeth.

Finn began slow, sucking pulls up and down his cock. Jaime could feel his teeth bumping along his shaft, but they never hurt him, never pricked or pressed too hard. He couldn't help the noises coming from him, plaintive cries and breathy hiccups as he lost himself in the steady rhythm of Finn's teeth and tongue, hurtling closer and closer to a climax that he knew he'd never recover from.

The wet heat of Finn's mouth disappeared, making him cry out in protest, but there was no time for Jaime to complain further as it was quickly replaced with a huge calloused fist closing around him, nearly engulfing his cock and leaving just the reddened tip exposed. Elongated claws extended from his thick fingers, but Finn held them carefully away as he began stroking Jaime in short, fast pulls.

"Do you want my tongue, Jaime? Do you want my tongue on you?"

Holy shit, Finn was actually going to kill him with that tongue. "Ye-es," he whined, unable to stop himself from thrusting into Finn's closed fist, hands back to grappling in the sheets. "*Please*, Finn!"

"Shh, I've got you baby." He gently scraped his fangs along the meat of Jaime's ass, soothing the sensitive flesh with a kiss afterwards. "My Jaime, I'll give you what you need. I want to watch you come all over yourself."

Finn's hand abandoned Jaime's cock, leaving him reeling, and gripped onto his ass, thumb pulling a cheek to the side. He swore, "*Fucking beautiful*," before lapping the flat of his tongue over Jaime's hole, over and over, dragging all the way up his taint and balls.

Jaime saw stars. "*Fuck!*" he sobbed, "I'm—Finn, I'm s-so c-close—close. *Ah!*"

Finn's fist was tight on Jaime's cock again, working him

hard, before he fit his lips and tongue and teeth back over his tip, just peeking out from Finn's grip, and *sucked*.

Jaime's orgasm hit him like a freight train. He jerked under Finn's heavy arm still pinning his belly to the bed as cum pulsed from him in steady spurts down Finn's throat, mouth open in a silent, breathy shout.

He closed a trembling hand over Finn's to halt the fast pulls on his sensitive shaft, showing him how he liked to be held through it with a steady, firm squeeze. Finn continued to nurse his crown, swallowing everything Jaime gave him.

Finally, Finn pulled off and peered up at him, face messy with cum and spit. "Fuck, Jaime, watching you fall apart is the hottest thing I've ever seen." His voice was gruff and shaky, like he was barely holding himself back from devouring him entirely.

Jaime couldn't manage more than a hiccup.

Finn released Jaime's sensitive cock and swiped at the cum and spit covering him. Hand suitably slicked, he sat up, dropping Jaime's knee off his shoulder, and moved his anchoring hold to Jaime's inner thigh, pinning him open for Finn's devouring gaze. Feasting on the sight of Jaime wrecked and hazy, he took hold of his own thick length and began tugging roughly.

Finn's cock was a work of art. Jaime was unable to look away, and with piercing clarity, he knew he would paint this moment. His legs canted to the side, the meat of one thigh bunching in Finn's clawed hold while the other hand worked himself over Jaime's soft and spent cock, resting against his abdomen.

Yeah, he'd fucking frame this.

The shaft was a shade darker than the rest of him and the head was flushed a pinkish-red. It was truly large, girthier and longer than any of the dildos he'd ever used, with a fat head that Jaime wanted to wrap his lips around *now*.

He couldn't wait to feel it pressed inside of him, stretching and making room in Jaime's belly like Finn had in every other facet of his life.

Finn's breathing grew labored, and his hard pulls fell out of rhythm before he shouted and jerked forward, still holding Jaime spread wide, and came all over his spent cock and belly. Jaime watched in rapt fascination as Finn kicked and pulsed through his orgasm, wishing he could feel that inside of him.

When the last of his cum dribbled down his fist, Finn tipped forward and sprawled on top of Jaime. He threw his arms around Finn's shoulders, pulling him close and holding him through it as they both came down from the high.

When the rushing in his ears receded, Jaime could hear his own hiccuping breaths and soft mewls alongside Finn's slow, deep inhales.

If someone had told Jaime yesterday that just the very next day he would have the two most intense orgasms of his life with Finn, pressed up against him with their hands and mouths on each other, he would have laughed in their face.

And yet here they were, chests synced and softly nuzzling each other's hair in post-climax bliss. But even through the lingering fog of lust, it was the feeling of rightness, of complete comfort and safety that he'd been chasing for so long that had tears running down Jaime's face.

When Finn looked up from where he cradled him and

saw his tears, he scrambled back in a panic, hands reaching out to hover as if to check if he was hurt.

"Jaime—Jaime—what, I mean, are you ok? Did I hurt you? Christ, I shouldn't have... I used my *teeth*, fuck, Jaime I'm so sorry!"

"Finn!" Jaime reached out to catch one of his hands, but Finn was still frantically scanning him up and down, looking for where he was hurt.

"I'm sorry Jaime, please let me help, I can—"

Jaime sat up on his knees, braced his hands on Finn's shoulders, and pushed him backwards until he was the one looming. Jaime caught his face between his palms. "Finn. Stop."

Finn stilled, staring up at him with those wounded puppy dog eyes. "Tell me how to fix it, Jaime."

Jaime's tone was firm. "Stop freaking out, and listen to me."

Finn just blinked wide, chocolate eyes at him.

It really should be illegal to look at someone like that.

"I am not hurt." Finn opened his mouth to interrupt him, but Jaime pressed the tips of his fingers over his soft lips to stop him, feeling the catch of a canine. "I am not hurt, Finn. That was... I thought coming in your hand downstairs was intense. But what we just did was so much more. You make me feel whole, and seen, and wanted. And when we were done..." he huffed, searching for the words.

He lifted his fingers from Finn's mouth and gently pressed the pad of his thumb against the tip of his right fang, a small noise coming from Finn. "You make me feel safe. Not managed, or controlled. Being here with you, feeling you on top of me—it feels right, Finn. And I've never felt that way before. It just hit me all at once."

Pulling his thumb back, he leaned down and caught Finn's lips in a soft kiss. Sliding his tongue along Finn's mouth, he tentatively opened for him. It was so gentle, and somehow astonishing and new all over again.

It seemed that every time they came together, Jaime was pleasantly overwhelmed by just how much there was to learn and explore with Finn. Some of that was because it was new to Jaime, outside of his own touches, but mostly it was because he was sharing it with Finn.

And he wanted all of it to be with Finn, forever.

Finn broke the kiss first before coming back for heated, lingering brushes of their lips. But when he opened his mouth to deepen their kiss once again, Jaime flicked his tongue over the tip of his canine like he had before, since it seemed to drive Finn wild.

This time didn't disappoint, because now it was Finn who was mewling and whining beneath Jaime.

He was such a beautiful paradox; capable of fierce protectiveness when Jaime was in danger, and steady dominance when Jaime asked for it, but beneath his exploring tongue and lips, Finn melted. They'd have to explore this version of him later, too.

Jaime would start a list of all the things he wanted to try.

Between gentle laps at each fang, Jaime spoke. "I love these. I love seeing them, and kissing them. I love feeling them on my skin and the way you used them while you sucked my cock." He knew the tips of his ears were red from being so forward, but this was too important to hold back.

He pulled away enough so he could see Finn's face. "I'll tell you if there's ever something I don't like, but I wanted that. Your teeth, and… when you told me what to do."

He fiddled with the sheets beside Finn's head, squirming on top of him, and the worry finally lifted from his eyes, leaving only the soft pleasure from their kiss.

Finn's mouth tipped up in a crooked grin. "You did, didn't you?"

Jaime gave him a look. "You know I did."

Finn smiled wide, fangs on full display. It made Jaime's chest ache. He continued, only because he wanted to keep that smile on Finn's face forever and ever, "I like when you take control. Like that." Softer, he said, "It makes me feel like you want me."

He let himself be flipped back around, legs coming up to cradle Finn's hips as he hovered over Jaime and looked at him with such soft reverence, it nearly made him cry again. "You are safe with me. Always, Jaime."

Finn shifted so they both lay on their sides facing each other, and pulled him further into the cradle of his arms. He kissed Jaime's hair, and spoke softly into his ear. "And I will always want you. More than I've ever wanted anything." His voice grew heated, "And I liked that too, what we did. There's a lot I'd like to try with you, Jaime. If you want that."

Jaime rubbed his cheek on Finn's chest. "Yes, Finn. Always yes."

Finn stood long enough to grab a wet cloth to clean them both up, before he lay back down, shifting them so that Jaime was comfortably spooned in front of him, both exhausted from the long and tumultuous day.

"Get some sleep, baby. We'll need to head out early in the morning."

Jaime shimmied deeper into Finn's embrace, and let the worries and questions of what tomorrow might bring float away from him. For now, he felt cherished and warm in Finn's arms, and drifted into a sleep better than he'd had in a very long time.

CHAPTER 16
FINN

"What the *fuck* is going on?"

Finn woke up with a start, registering a loud bang followed by shouting. The soft, sleep-warm scent of Jaime hit him, along with the steady thrum of *mate, mate, mate,* nestled deep in his chest. But an unknown, yet slightly familiar scent was also there.

Too close!

His instincts kicked in, and before he was even fully awake he shifted and uncurled his body from around Jaime, thundering across the room, and pinned the stranger to the wall—claws at his throat.

Mate is vulnerable.

Protect, protect, protect!

"Hey! What the—Jesus Christ, what the fuck are you?" The stranger cried.

Jaime stirred awake behind them. "Huh?" he snuffled, and rubbed the sleep from his eyes, blinking in the harsh morning light. When Jaime finally focused on them, he leapt out of bed and across the room, also shouting, "Finn, don't!"

Jaime yanked at his wrist, pulling him away. Confused and stunned, Finn finally registered the stranger's face. And then understood why the scent seemed familiar.

He was shorter than Jaime, and sturdier. Not quite stocky, but built more like a swimmer than Jaime's long faerie-like nothing-but-legs profile. They had the same eyes and hair; maybe Jaime's were a murkier green, and his hair was a shade darker, but they shared the same pale, freckled complexion, and the same ruddy cheeks.

There was absolutely no doubt about who this was. *Sam Lamont.*

Finn felt his stomach drop to the floor. He had just threatened Jaime's brother. A brother he very clearly loved and cared for deeply, despite their current falling out and the hurt that was palpable between them. And then Finn realized that not only had he just threatened Jaime's brother, but he had done it shifted. And *naked.*

Oh God.

"What the fuck is going on?" Sam shouted again, rubbing at his neck where he'd gone red from Finn's hold. If he didn't know from experience that Jaime's skin—and Sam's too, probably—marked at even the gentlest hold, he'd be even more worried.

"Sam," Jaime croaked.

Sam's face hardened, and the look he gave Finn would have scorched his fur had he not already shifted back into his human form. Self conscious, he grabbed a pillow from the bed to cover his dick.

"Jaime. Get your things, we are leaving. You're coming to live with me. I don't know what the fuck this *thing* was doing to you in his bed, but it stops now. I can't believe I trusted them to look after you."

Sam pointed his finger at him, and Finn knew this was it. He had just threatened Jaime's brother's life, had his claws at his throat, and Jaime would finally see that he was capable of doing just as much damage as the monsters that haunted his dreams. Clenching his teeth, he kept his head down.

He couldn't bear to see the shock and fear on Jaime's face.

Sam continued, "You, whatever the fuck you are, stay away from my brother. I'll be filing a police report. You'll never touch him again, you monster."

Finn winced, but looked up, needing to say something, needing to say he was *sorry*, but before he could, two things happened.

Silas walked through the door, harried and shaken, a look on his face that Finn had never seen before. He took in Finn's nakedness with raised eyebrows, and then Jaime's before quickly averting his eyes to the ceiling.

And then Jaime punched his brother in the face.

"*Owe*, shit!" he cried, shaking his hand as he took a step back from Sam.

Finn dropped the pillow and darted forward to check if Jaime's hand was hurt, and Silas moved toward Sam who was bent over his knees, holding his nose. Pulling him up, Silas cupped the back of Sam's head and tilted his face up toward him, moving it this way and that before releasing him.

Then Silas moved so that he was positioned nearly between the two brothers, which only seemed to irritate Sam because he elbowed his way around him and gave him a look that made Silas go sheepish and shuffle his feet. Given their height difference, all of that would have been hilarious if he wasn't currently cradling Jaime's injured hand.

Or meeting his brother for the first time, balls and claws out.

"You'll be fine," Silas said gruffly to Sam, eyes still intense. "That probably hurt Jaime's hand more than it did your nose."

Indeed, Jaime's hand was red and would probably be sore for a few days, but Finn didn't detect anything broken. Still cradling it before him, he gently rumbled, "We should put some ice on it, Jaime."

Jaime was shaking with rage, and hadn't seemed to hear him. Finn grabbed a blanket from the bed and draped it around him, so he wouldn't feel so exposed, while Sam glanced back and forth between them, wide-eyed and shocked.

Jaime's voice shook, but he straightened his spine. "Don't *ever* call him that again. And you have no right, *no right*, to tell me where to go, or who to be with, or how to stay safe."

He stepped toward Sam. "You can't just ignore me for a whole fucking year because I'm such a burden to you and then storm in here demanding I follow your orders on a whim. You can't say shitty things about the people I care for just because you haven't been around enough to understand what's going on!"

"Jaime—" Sam began, voice breaking, but Jaime kept going.

"Where have you been, Sammy? I called you. Many times over the last year, and you ignored me. I know I've been a lot. I know I've needed too much from you. But I just — fuck, Sammy, I just needed my brother! That's all! Forget about the money and the lawyer and everything else. I wanted my brother. *And you weren't there.*"

Finn's heart broke all over again at the pain in Jaime's voice. He wanted to tell him that he'd never been too much, he'd never been a burden. But only Jaime could heal the parts of him that felt that way. Only Jaime could decide when he was ready to confront those feelings with his brother for them to work through together. All Finn could do was make sure Jaime knew every day how much he wanted him and cared for him.

How much he loved him.

Suddenly, he desperately wanted to tell Jaime how much he loved him. That he'd fallen in love with him sometime in the last week, swiftly and deeply and irrevocably. Maybe even before that, when Jaime was only a face and a voice through his phone.

He knew how crazy that sounded, but even then, he'd known Jaime was *right*. He'd known he'd never be able to walk away, not fully. But that could wait. It wasn't the right moment, and there were still things he needed to share first.

He also refused to confess his love in front of Silas and Sam, naked, hiding his cock behind a pillow.

Sam looked like Jaime had hit him again, and Jaime's

anger had clearly burned too bright and quick, sucking all the energy from him and leaving only the hurt and pain.

Jaime turned away from Sam. "It's fine. I am capable of making my own decisions and looking after myself. I'll be fine. You don't have to worry about me anymore. Please, just go."

"Jaime, that's not what I want. I didn't—I can't—please, come home with me. Alone. I'll explain everything, and we can—"

"No." Jaime's voice was thick with tears, but resolute.

Sam was crying now, too. "Jaime, please."

He shook his head. "No, Sam. I'm not coming with you. I survived the last year without you. Alone. I was never helpless—I don't need anyone else to *manage* me. I hate feeling like that. I want to be around someone who wants to be around me, too."

He looked up at Finn, hope in his eyes. "And I think I've found that, now. A choice. A chance to be with someone who wants to be with me, not someone who thinks of me as a burden."

He turned back to Sam, squaring his shoulders. "So you can go. There's a safe house that the security team is preparing for us. I'll stay there until the trial."

Sam cast a glance at Finn, still wary. "You'll be there with him."

"Yes." Jaime's voice turned hard again. "And you cannot go to the police about what you just saw. There's nothing to report. Finn is my—Finn is with me. And I'm with him. What you saw, just forget about it. It has nothing to do with you."

Sam, incredulous, waved his hands at Finn in a gesture nearly identical to one he'd seen Jaime make. "Jaime, you can't seriously expect me to just forget about *Big and Hairy* over there, nearly ripping my throat out!"

Silas choked a laugh into a cough, and Finn knew he'd hear that nickname again.

Still, Finn winced at the mention of threatening Sam, but Jaime snapped back, "Don't be fucking dramatic. He did not."

Finn made eye contact with Silas over the brothers' heads, and grimaced. He kind of had, but he wasn't going to argue that point.

Jaime continued. "Besides, you stormed in here, unannounced, screaming like a banshee. I know how grouchy you can be in the mornings. Now, I'm tired, and cold, and naked, and I want to go back to bed. Leave."

Sam was looking at him like he'd never seen his brother before. Like they were strangers, and this was the first time they'd ever met. Maybe it was, in a way. From what Jaime had said, Sam had always taken care of Jaime, even when they were little, and again when Jaime was first attacked. And Jaime kept reaching and reaching for him this last year, only for Sam to retreat further.

Until now. Until Jaime stood up for himself and chose his own path forward. "Fire the lawyer if you want. End the contract with the security team, if you want. I don't give a fuck. I'll figure it out."

Finn had a moment of internal panic before he relaxed. His decision to take Jaime's case had never been about the contract—it was merely an excuse to justify shoving his way back into Jaime's life when he'd walked away last year.

But Jaime hadn't walked away willingly; he'd been forced to drop contact due to some terrible circumstances, and now that they were together, there wasn't a force on Earth that would keep Finn from him.

So, fuck the contract. He'd quit and hole up with Jaime in a safe house somewhere indefinitely for all he cared. He had the savings. And he'd show Jaime just how wanted and loved and safe he was, for as long as Jaime wanted him back.

Sam looked utterly defeated, like a completely different man from the one who had stormed in demanding answers. "Jaime, don't do this."

Jaime sighed heavily. "We are both responsible for breaking this, Sam. I needed too much from you, and you pushed me away because of it. Maybe someday we can mend that. But I cannot continue having this conversation with you right now. I really need you to leave."

Sam stared at his brother for another long moment, then at Finn and Silas, before he turned and left.

Silas watched Sam leave with that same intensity. He glanced back, pointedly not looking at Jaime covered only by the blanket. "I'll follow him, and make sure he doesn't go to the police."

He stepped out the door, and tossed over his shoulder, "Sheppard called, the safe house is ready."

THE QUIET IN the truck was tense as Finn drove them north from Jaime's cabin past Silver Rapids, taking the only real highway this far into the Alaskan interior until they hit Fairbanks just over five hours away.

They wouldn't be going that far, though; the coordinates Sheppard had sent him through a secured device directed that he turn east off the highway in two hours before another two hours of backroads finally got them to the safe house.

This place truly was tucked away in the Alaskan wilderness.

Sheppard warned him that the cabin's water supply came from a giant tank out back, so while they did have a tiny shower stall and running water in the kitchen sink, there was no indoor plumbing, and they'd have to conserve water. But, their overnight delay had allowed him to get people out to clean and open everything up, heat the stove, and stock the fridge and pantry and other amenities.

They'd just be shitting in an outhouse for the next week until Bishop's trial.

Jaime hadn't said much after Sam left; all of the courage and bravado had left him, so that he just looked hurt and worn. They'd packed quickly and silently, leaving their personal phones on the coffee table for Silas to hold onto. It wasn't safe to take anything that could be tracked, and Jaime didn't seem inclined to bring his phone along anyway. The only times Finn had ever seen him use it were to try and call Sam or his lawyer, and they both knew he'd be at a safe house and could get ahold of him through the secured phone the security team provided.

Not that Finn thought that Jaime would answer, if he knew it was Sam calling.

So they drove, with Jaime staring out the window and Finn stewing over whether he should say something. He stewed for the next four hours, in fact, all the way down the rough and jarring dirt road that was barely passable this time of year. If Sheppard used this house year round, he'd have to fly or snow mobile clients in.

By the time they pulled up to the cabin, the ground in front of the door cleared by whoever opened and stocked the place, Finn had worried and spiraled himself so far into worst-case-scenario territory that he didn't know which way was up.

Jaime still wasn't speaking.

Was he angry with Finn about threatening his brother, and he just hadn't said anything in the aftermath of their argument? He'd told Sam that they were together, but did he regret that? Should Finn have double checked that Jaime wanted to be all the way out here with him? Was he afraid of being this isolated and alone with a guy who could turn into a wolf? Did he regret being intimate with him?

"Finn."

Snapping out of his anxious thoughts, he looked over toward Jaime, who had already opened the truck door and stepped out, stretching his legs. Finn was still sitting in his seat, hands clutching the steering wheel, engine idling. "Sorry. Right, I'll get our bags."

Jaime turned to take in the cabin. It was small, longer than it was wide with a steeply pitched roof. The walls went up five or six feet before meeting the roofline, so it wasn't quite an A-frame, and several steps led to a porch spanning the front of the cabin.

There were three large windows framing the roof peak, but the windows along the ground level were small, and Finn had no doubt they were reinforced, both for security purposes and because of wildlife.

He grabbed their bags out of the back seat. "Stay by the truck, I'm going to go check that everything is clear inside. This time of year bears can be unpredictable and aggressive, and they'll break in if they smell food."

Jaime paled and shuffled back to sit in the truck and wait. Finn entered and did an initial sweep, noting the lower level was all one open space with a kitchen, living area, and a wood stove for heating. He fed it a few pieces of kindling to get the room warmed up, as it had clearly been some hours since the people who had opened the cabin had left.

Opposite the stove, sat a couch and chair flanked by large shelves filled with books and board games and puzzles, and then a narrow set of steps led to a loft area which contained one large bed. A matching set of windows framed the peak that sat over the space, and someone had strung up fairy lights all along the loft area, making it feel soft and warm.

Had those always been there, or were they a special touch that Sheppard had requested, knowing the two of them would be there for a while together?

Right. Well, this would be cozy.

He set their bags down by the bed and stepped back out onto the porch to wave Jaime in, and while he was heading inside Finn paced around the side of the cabin to check that the outhouse was clean. He fiddled with the stash of toilet paper a little before making his way back around to the front porch where he pulled out their secured line and fired off a quick message to Sheppard and Silas, letting them know they'd arrived, before pocketing the phone again.

And then he just stood there, staring out at the scenery.

The view was breathtaking; true wilderness with a vista of the interior's taiga that Finn knew would showcase stunning sunsets over the distant mountain range. He couldn't take it in though, couldn't relish in the soft sounds of animals moving through the brush or the creek trickling nearby, because he was too worried that he'd already fucked up this thing with Jaime before it began.

Again.

Taking a final, deep breath, he turned away from their beautiful view. Enough was enough; if Jaime was going to reject him, he'd better just go face it instead of hiding in a fucking outhouse like a coward.

Walking back inside, he locked the door before turning to see Jaime standing in the middle of the living area, fiddling with the hem of his shirt and avoiding eye contact.

Even when he was nervous, he was nearly otherworldly enchanting in the way he moved—Finn could stare for hours and hours and still not completely take him in. Stepping toward him, he gathered his courage to speak, but as usual, Jaime beat him to it.

"If you've decided that you don't want me, just tell me. I'm sorry about what my brother said. What he called you. It's not true. You're not a monster. Or, you're not the kind of monster that Bishop is."

Finn felt like someone had kicked him in the gut. So,

Jaime did think he was a monster? Just a different kind of monster than the ones he already knew?

Seeming to sense his downward spiral, Jaime looked up at him, intense and focused and in the way that Finn had always imagined he looked at a subject before he painted them. All-seeing. It gave him goosebumps to feel the full weight of Jaime's attention. It was overwhelming, but not dissecting. He was being seen entirely, but not judged.

And because Jaime always saw Finn, his face shifted from wary hurt to sharp determination. "I've asked you several times now to show me your shift. All of you. But you've avoided me, and I think it's because you don't want me to see you for those things. You want me to see you for *you*."

Jaime stepped forward and cupped his jaw, running his finger along the blunt end of a normal human canine. "But I already do. And I ask to see those other parts because I want all of you. I want everything. I love your teeth, and I love what you look like, all big and hairy and growly."

He turned red, and Finn remembered that fleeting moment in Jaime's bedroom after he'd pulled the attacker off of him, and had smelled Jaime's arousal at seeing Finn shifted for the first time.

Jaime continued, "I ask to see you because those are parts of you, too, Finn. I don't separate them from the man standing in front of me. And you use the word monster like it's a bad thing, but it's not. Not when it's about you, about all the wolfy sides of you. I want those parts, too. Now. Always. I don't want you to hide from me, Finn."

He doesn't really mean that. You haven't told him every-

thing. You haven't told him you want to have sex with him when you look like that.

Finn exhaled hard, leaning into Jaime's palm. "I keep thinking that the next thing I show you, the next thing I tell you, will be the thing that scares you off. Please. I don't want to see that in your eyes. If this is all we can ever be, it can be enough for me. This can be enough."

Jaime's face sharpened in anger, a flash of what Finn had seen directed at his brother this morning. He placed a hand on Finn's chest and pushed, knocking him back against the kitchen counter. "Do you think so little of me? Do you really think that I only want some of you, Finn?"

Tears pooled in Jaime's eyes, his anger making his face ruddy. "If this is your way of telling me that you do not want anything more with me, then just say so, and I won't ask again. But I have asked, Finn, because I want to know you. From the very fucking beginning I have wanted to know all of you. If you aren't ready for that yet, then tell me, and I will wait. I will wait as long as you need me to wait. But stop pushing me away out of your own fear of rejection and then telling me it's my fault."

Finn whined at the sight of Jaime's tears, all of his fear and doubt bubbling up, up, up—needing out, needing absolution. Silas's words came back to him, then.

Try. If not for him, for your mate, then who? Who will be worth risking your heart for?

Jaime was. Of course he was.

"You're my mate," Finn blurted out, words tumbling over each other in a rush. "My person. I've known it from the moment we met in your driveway. Maybe even before.

You're my mate and I love you very much and I want to claim you as mine, if you want that too. But you should know it's not like marriage. It binds us together, here." He laid a hand over Jaime's heart, right where he felt a matching tug on his own, it's beat frantic under Finn's palm.

He'd planned how he would tell Jaime. About being his mate, about the bite, about the 'maybe-balooning-dick' thing —all of it. As he'd held a sleeping Jaime in his arms last night, Finn lay awake and planned to sit him down, maybe with some space between them so that Jaime didn't feel overwhelmed.

He'd start from the beginning, and explain that he'd felt a connection right away, even when they hadn't met in person yet. How when they had finally been face-to-face, he'd *known*, and done his best to respect Jaime and not push.

But now that Jaime knew about him, maybe someday he'd be comfortable letting Finn claim him, bite him. If he had a knot, they'd talk about it, try having sex without him shifting. Surely he could just not put the knot in? He could keep himself in check, so he wouldn't hurt Jaime.

He'd thought through everything, planned everything to be nice, and safe, and as normal as that kind of conversation could be.

But Jaime had never asked for any of that. All Jaime had ever asked of him was to be honest, to not withhold important things from him. Even before he knew about Finn being a shifter, he'd wanted to be included in Finn's thoughts.

And now that he did know, all he ever told him was how much he liked the wolfy parts of Finn. *Loved* them. Jaime didn't just tolerate them or ignore them, he sought them out when they came together. He climaxed at the sight and feel of Finn's teeth wrapped around his cock, and moaned and writhed beneath him as he nipped and teased him. He'd been aroused by Finn when he was partially shifted, and repeatedly asked Finn to show himself that way, again.

Jaime wanted all of Finn, in the way he had always needed to be wanted. And as Jaime blinked up at him, eyes wide but not fearful, he brought a hand up to cover Finn's where it rested over his heart.

Yes, he could give Jaime what he'd been asking for this whole time—what Finn had desperately *wanted* to give him this whole time.

It had just taken him a little while to work up the courage.

Twisting them so that Jaime was now the one pinned between his body and the counter, Finn shifted. His claws caught in the material of Jaime's shirt and his descended canines ached to sink into the soft flesh where his neck and shoulder connected.

Finn met Jaime's wide-eyed gaze, voice trembling now, and continued. "It's forever. No matter if we are together or apart, you'll feel me. You'll be mine, and I'll be yours. It can't be undone. And if you decide you want that, you should know it means that I will bite you, here."

He moved his other hand up to cradle the place he would claim Jaime, the soft skin warm and inviting. "I don't know if it will hurt, I've never asked. It's a private moment between people and not something you really ask questions about. Which I know seems ridiculous given the gravity of the act, but, well."

Finn shuffled, and then added softly, like a question, "I'll try to make it good for you?"

Jaime still hadn't said anything, but he kept his hand over Finn's resting on his heart, and wrapped the other around his waist to pull him close, their hips slotting together. Jaime gave him a soft smile, eyes glassy and tender, so Finn figured, what the hell.

Might as well rip the bandaid off, as Silas would say.

"Also, if I bite and claim you, it will be very difficult for me to have sex with you without shifting into this form. My wolf wants you, just as much as I do. Maybe because I do. I'm not really sure how it works, but it feels like a mutual decision. Anyway, Silas says that when I have sex in this form I'll get a knot, and I'll want to put it in you and it will get stuck. A knot is—"

"I know what a knot is," Jaime blurted.

Now it was Finn's turn to blink down at him, finally stunned to silence after his emotional outburst. Jaime turned bright red and didn't continue, making Finn wonder...

"Jaime, how do you know what a knot is?" He felt the side of his mouth tip up.

Jaime squirmed beneath him where he was pinned against the counter, avoiding eye contact now and shifting his hold on Finn so that his fingers absently stroked through the fur on his forearms. "Keep going. You were telling me that you want to make me yours and have hot wolfy sex with me and that you love me."

Finn's mouth split into a wide grin. "You read werewolf smut, don't you?"

Jaime cast him a haughty look, nose up in the air. "I may

have stumbled on one or two novellas. Short ones. Accidentally. A while back. Not recently."

Finn leaned in, pressing his smile, teeth and all, into the soft skin behind Jaime's ear. And licked.

"*Unnf*, Finn! We are having a moment, and I want to tell you that I love you back!"

His protests were all for show though, because Finn could smell that he was *very* into this unexpected turn in their conversation. Also, Jaime was still clinging to him, fingers buried in his fur, and Finn could feel him hardening in his pants.

Interesting.

He nuzzled and chuffed in Jaime's hair, his scent sweet and strong. "You'll have to tell me about your favorite parts from those novellas that you've maybe read a long time ago."

Jaime huffed, still stroking Finn's forearms, and pouted, "I don't know how I'm the one that knows what a knot is and not you, when you're the wolfy one."

Finn blushed. "I know what it is, I just didn't know that I had one. It's never... made itself known, before. I don't even know if it will happen since I'm only half shifter, but Silas warned me that being with my mate will be different. He didn't want us to be surprised."

Jaime giggled, green eyes dancing, and Finn needed the sound branded on him. He needed it direct in his vein—he needed to hear it forever. "I would pay to hear how he explained that to you."

Finn grimaced. "It was horrific. I wanted to pour bleach into my ears. I'm still not sure I can look him in the eye."

Jaime continued to giggle, and Finn tucked his nose back into his hair, needing the closeness. "You love me?"

He felt Jaime swallow, laughter turning into a soft hum as Jaime pressed his lips into Finn's neck. "I love you. I'm not sure when it happened... I knew I loved you yesterday, when I saw you shifted in my room and you looked at me like you needed to be scooped up out of the rain and kept warm. I knew when you made me oatmeal with all of my favorite things, even though I was avoiding you. And I think I knew when you hounded Andi for the butternut squash ravioli recipe so much that she nearly threw you out of the restaurant, just because I said I liked it."

Finn chuckled. "And because I need to hear the sounds you made while eating it again. That wasn't purely altruistic."

He felt Jaime's beaming smile against his skin, felt the catch of his human teeth at the base of his neck, miming the bite he'd make when he claimed Jaime. "I knew when you were ready to protect me this morning from someone barging into our room. And I knew I loved you when you listened to me when I asked you to stop. When you let me stand up for myself, and tell Sam how I felt."

Jaime took a deep, shaky breath, and pulled back just enough to look up at him. "I want everything you said—I want all of it, with you. And I don't ever want to lose you again. I want to be yours in every way that is meaningful to us both."

He placed his hand over Finn's heart, eyes intense. "And I want you to be mine, too. Bite me, claim me, knot me, but I'll make you mine, just as much as you make me yours."

CHAPTER 17
JAIME

J aime saw his words land, easing the remaining tension in Finn's shoulders until they settled in his heart, right where Jaime felt a tug on his own.

His head was tipped back, looking up into Finn's eyes darting back and forth between his, and he was ready to say *yes, I'm sure, yes, I want you,* all over again, every day if that's what Finn needed. But he gave a small nod, as if he'd finally heard everything he needed to be sure that Jaime wasn't going to run from him.

Not again, not ever.

Finn caught Jaime up in a wet, filthy kiss, his tongue sweeping in to taste and take and plunder, teeth clacking as Jaime opened up for him. Finn lifted Jaime up onto the counter to bring him closer, their height difference significant with Finn in this form, and pushed Jaime's thighs open wide as he slotted his hips between them.

Finn pressed kisses and tender words into his cheekbones and along his jaw. "Yes, Jaime. I love you, I love you, I love you. My Jaime. Make me yours. Please."

His teeth caught and tugged on the reddened tip of Jaime's ear, and claw-tipped fingers trailed lightly down his belly in teasing passes that made Jaime cry out in want.

Finn's hands grasped Jaime's waist and held him in place while he kneed his legs open wider and ground his bulging erection into Jaime's own. He scrambled for purchase along Finn's shoulders, even broader now, and if they went on any longer like this he'd come like that first time—throbbing and pulsing, pressed up against Finn.

But he wanted more, he wanted all of it—Finn on top of him, stuffed inside of him, all around him. So he reached for Finn's waist, fingers bunching in the bottom of his shirt. "Off. Off. Take this off."

Finn leaned back just far enough to do as he asked, before diving back in to take his mouth again. And because he could, Jaime trailed his tongue along one canine, letting it catch there before moving to the next one. Finn whimpered and melted into Jaime, hands banding around his shoulders and back as he bent forward and tucked his face into his neck, mouthing along it. "Jaime. Please."

Pushing gently, Jaime backed Finn up until he could hop down from the counter, and continued guiding him backwards until the backs of Finn's knees hit the couch, and he was sitting down.

Long legs bent askew, Finn peered up at Jaime with wide, wondering eyes, ears perked up toward him. He was so beautiful, Jaime could only stand there for a moment, taking him in.

The soft, sandy blonde hair dusting his chest flickered in the firelight and caught in the soft glow coming from the loft. Finn reached claw-tipped hands out to wrap around Jaime's hips, thumbs pressing into his belly and pulling Jaime forward until he was straddling his lap, sprawled on top of him.

Leaning in to capture Finn's mouth, Jaime ground down against his hard length, which was even larger now than in his human form. Mewling and wriggling on top of Finn at the memory of him pumping his release all over him last night, Jaime thought about what it would be like to wrap his lips around the fat, slick head, how it would feel to choke down as much of him as possible, Finn's fingers in his hair, encouraging him to take more...

Fuck, I need that right now.

Jaime's thoughts had him grinding and rocking their cocks together, the catch and chafe of their clothes restricting his movements just enough to keep him from coming, even with Finn's hands cupping his ass, encouraging his movements. Breaking the kiss before he completely lost himself to the pleasure that only Finn could show him, Jaime gently rested his forehead against Finn's, both of them breathing heavily.

"I want to suck your cock. Can we do that?"

Finn's mouth was slightly open, fangs fully out and flashing. "Fuck. Yes, Jaime. Whatever you want. I'll give you whatever you want."

Jaime grinned. "Right now, I want to taste you. And then I want you to open me up on your fingers and fuck me. You know that I've never been with anyone before, but I do have several large toys that I'm very fond of, so I know how to prep myself. They aren't as big as you are even in your human form, though, so we'll need to work up to *that*."

He pointedly looked down at Finn's massive cock and grinned, feeling freer and lighter than he ever had in his life. "And I don't think you should knot me the first time, but we'll get there."

Finn made some sort of whine-growl noise that was so hot, and so adorable, before nodding his head vigorously in agreement. "Lube? Condoms?"

Jaime blushed. "Oh, um. I brought both. You know, just in case. I mean I *hoped*—"

Finn cut him off with another searing kiss, before pulling back and looking at Jaime with a serious expression. "One more thing you should know, first."

Jaime gave a playfully exasperated sigh, letting his weight tip back and rest against Finn's knees. In return, Finn gave him an equally playful slap on his ass—*why the hell do I still have my jeans on?*—and growled, "Be a good boy, and listen."

Oh.

The list. That is going on the list.

Reading his face, Finn chuckled, "Later, baby. First, I'm happy to use a condom this time and every time, if that's what you want. But you should know that when I knot you, it's not going to work as intended."

Jaime let that image shimmer before him; his ass tipped up, legs spread open with Finn seated inside as far as he could go. His fat cock and knot pressing up against Jaime's prostate, creating the most delicious pressure as cum spilled out everywhere, overflowing around Finn's knot while he pumped load after load inside him...

Fuck.

Pleasure zipped up Jaime's spine. Had he always had a fluid kink, or was this a sudden-onset type of a situation?

He cleared his throat and croaked, "That won't be a problem with me. You know I've never been with anyone, and when they checked me out after the attack a year ago they gave me a full panel of everything. I'm negative."

Finn nodded. "Me too, we get tested regularly as part of the physicals for work. But the other part that I need to tell you is that all of those health exams are mostly for show, to share with our clients who aren't in-the-know."

At Jaime's confused head tilt, Finn explained, "We heal at an exceptionally fast rate. It's why we went on so many missions in the military—even the most serious injuries only took a few days to fully mend. And we can't get or pass on any infections or diseases."

Jaime blinked. "So... are you saying that we don't need to use a condom?"

Finn tucked him in closer. "Yes, that's what I'm saying. If you don't want to, that is. If you do, I will. I always have, every other time I've been with someone. It's never bothered me."

Hot, unwarranted jealousy flushed Jaime's cheeks, and he squirmed back on Finn's lap, fingers finding their way to the fur on his forearms. Looking down, he muttered, "Thank you for telling me."

With the tip of a claw, Finn brought his chin back up, widening his legs so that Jaime was forced to adjust and slide back down, further into his hold. "Everything about this—about you—is different, Jaime. And not just because you're my mate, but because I'm in love with you."

He lightly scratched up and down Jaime's back, and he wanted to purr at how good that felt. Finn went on, "So much of this will be a first for me, too. When we come together while I'm in this form, the knotting, that will all be new for me. But also..."

Finn looked at Jaime with such tenderness, such reverence, he found he wanted to paint that, too. He'd have a studio full of Finn's soil rich eyes and thick forearms and the furry happy trail that led from between his pecs all the way down to his beautiful cock. He'd paint it all.

"...Also, I've never made love. I've never wanted someone the way I want you, I've never shared myself this way with anyone. I want to feel you fully, I want us to be as close as we can ever be. There is no one else for me but you—there never has been."

He danced his lips over Jaime's in a featherlight kiss. "I only mentioned it so that you would know, but also so you wouldn't feel pressured to go bare if you don't want to. Especially this first time."

Jaime smiled softly, feeling silly now for his jealousy, and grateful that Finn was so open to options. Still...

"I want to feel you, all of you. No condom, please." He grinned again and rocked on Finn's lap, eager to get back to where they were before, now that the important bits had been discussed.

Finn seemed inclined to agree, because he moved to

stand up with Jaime in his arms, but instead Jaime leaned back and placed a hand on his chest to stop him.

"Wait. I said I want to taste you first, like this."

He palmed Finn's overlarge cock through his pants, and felt him shudder. "*Jaime.*"

Teasing a barely-there kiss to Finn's mouth, Jaime began sliding off his lap, kissing and scraping his teeth down Finn's pecs and belly, running his fingers through the fur dusting his chest and thighs. He whined and twisted beneath Jaime's soft, teasing touch, hands grasping wherever he could reach, claws the gentlest drag on Jaime's sensitive skin. Finn's knees made room as he knelt on the rug, and Jaime had to pause to take in the sight.

Staring down at him, Finn already looked wrecked.

He was panting hard, mouth slightly open, showing off his extended canines. His ears were angled forward, eyes warm and intense and wholly focused, like nothing else existed except for Jaime kneeling before him. Finn widened his legs even more, and Jaime couldn't look away from where the crotch of his pants pulled tight over his straining erection. He kept rocking his hips up in aborted little motions, seeking some kind of friction.

Jaime needed to help with that. Now.

Reaching up to brush his fingers along the waistband of Finn's pants, blunt nails lightly scratching through the soft hair on his belly, Jaime asked, "Can I take these off?"

Finn gave a helpless whine and nodded his head quickly. "Yes. Yes. But, you first."

Jaime gave him a playful smirk and used both arms to pull his shirt up and over his head, tossing it off to the side.

Finn's gaze honed in on his bare chest and belly with a predator's intensity, and goosebumps rose along Jaime's skin from the attention, nipples peaked and hard.

A low rumble came from Finn. "I'm going to taste every single freckle on your body. Every single one of them, Jaime."

He shivered beneath the weight of that gaze, the heavy promise in his words. "Me first."

Reaching forward, he fumbled with Finn's zipper before grabbing hold of his pants and boxer briefs and gingerly lifting them up and over his straining erection. Finn tipped his hips up to help, and Jaime got them down just far enough for his cock to spring free before he stopped.

And stared.

Finn's erection was beautiful last night. Long and thick, Jaime will never forget the image of it straining above him, pumping his release all over Jaime's belly. But like this, seeing the full effect of it, Jaime could only marvel at its heft, and how the weight of it bobbed against his stomach, tipping slightly to the side, too heavy to stand straight when fully hard. The shape of it remained the same; his long shaft swelling to its full thickness in the middle before tapering slightly, the head crowning large and round on top.

The same as before, yes, except like this it was just... more. He was also slightly swollen at the base, right where his shaft jutted out from his balls. And oh, fuck, the size of his balls...

Struck by the sight of Finn's cock, Jaime was hard as granite.

Realizing he was still staring, blinking owlishly and

unmoving, Jaime peered up at Finn through his lashes. He looked sheepish, shuffling in his seat and ears laid down to the sides while his large hands flailed like he wasn't sure where to put them.

Cute.

"I know it's a lot. I know I'm a lot. You don't have to—*Oh!*" Finn's sentence was clipped in a breathy shout as Jaime leaned forward, both hands braced on Finn's thighs, and sucked his wet tip in all at once. "Fuck! Jaime!"

Finn was trembling now, hands still flailing until Jaime found them, lacing his fingers through one and guiding the other into his hair. He moaned at the tug and scrape of it, and bent forward to take more of Finn's cock down his throat, as much as he possibly could before he was gagging and pulling off, gasping.

He knew he was being sloppy and inexperienced, but Finn didn't seem to mind, going by the look of shock and pleasure on his face.

"Show me, Finn. Show me what you like." Jaime leaned forward and took the fat head back into his mouth, suckling there like Finn had done to him.

Finn hiccuped, "Yes, like that." His hand twisted further into Jaime's hair and gently guided him down, encouraging him to swallow more. "Take a little more, just like that. There you go, baby."

The soft dominance of it had Jaime whining and thrusting his hips forward, seeking friction, relief, grinding into the sofa cushion.

Through heavy breaths and fangs, Finn choked out, "Use your other hand, yeah. Harder. *Mmmph. Oh*—fuck.

Yes. S-such a good fucking boy—boy. Already so good at this, Jaime. *Jaime!*"

Jaime sunk into a hazy pleasure, Finn's words casting a spell over him, making him feel liquid and warm. He used a hand to twist and tug along Finn's cock where he couldn't fit it into his mouth, before dropping down to gently massage and tug on his balls while dragging his tongue along the sensitive underside of Finn's tip.

His slurping hums and wet gasping breaths were lewd in the quiet of the cabin, but seemed to be driving Finn's pleasure even higher. Grasping his shaft again, Jaime tried alternating between gentle pressure and a more firm hold, tightening even further at Finn's encouragement.

Eventually, Jaime wanted to work up to taking him all the way into his throat and swallowing, like Finn had done, but his jaw was already aching from the size and, well, he didn't think Finn was going to last long enough anyway.

Finn widened his knees further and released his tight grip on Jaime's hand, now tangling both in his hair and guiding Jaime's sucking pulls as he made little involuntary thrusts up. Finn was whining now, breathy *uh, uh, uh,* sounds coming out every time Jaime took him further.

With both hands free, Jaime used the saliva and precum leaking all over to glide his hands up and down the base of Finn's cock, one on top of the other.

Finn tugged gently on Jaime's hair. "Baby—baby—baby, I'm going to come s-soon—soon, if you don't stop—"

Jaime hummed and fit his mouth back over the thick crown. He could feel the root of Finn's dick swelling, and when he paused, both hands a firm squeeze around the rapidly expanding base as he continued to suck and lap at the tip, Finn gasped.

"*Ooh—oh, Jaimejaimejaimejaime.* Look at me. L-look at me—me. There. Good boy. Keep it right—there. *Hmmph.* Take it. Yeah, just like that. Take it—it!"

Finn's voice pitched even lower as he grunted and hiccuped out jumbled praise and commands between aborted thrusts up, up, up, and Jaime could feel the rumble of it in his chest.

He was floating now, a pleasure-induced fog had blanketed his senses as he peered up at Finn through his lashes, wet tears leaking while he held his breath between gasps. Eyes locked, all he could do was listen to Finn's words, let his firm hold at the nape of his neck guide him as he continued his two-handed grip at the base of Finn's cock.

"Harder, Jaime. Squeeze. Yes. Such a good boy. Yes! Fuck! *Ooh—ooh!* I don't—I don't know—Jaime. I'm going to—*Ah!*" Finn cried out, and the base of his cock swelled large in Jaime's grip.

His knot.

It was such a surreal experience to hold Finn's knot in his hands, to feel it pulse and throb as he sucked down as much of his cock as he could, tongue teasing his slit. Jaime may have read more than a *little* werewolf smut in his day, but experiencing the real thing was revelatory. He had a feeling that sex with Finn would continue to be that way for a long while, yet.

God, he loved this man. He was so damn lucky.

Jaime continued his steady, firm hold the way that Finn liked, and then he was coming down Jaime's throat in deep, heavy pulses. He swallowed through it all—cum tasting salty and slightly bitter, and entirely of *Finn*.

Intoxicating.

Finn's hold on the nape of Jaime's neck was firm as he fed Jaime as much of his cock as he could take, and he groaned when Finn's hips jerked and thrust with each spill, cock kicking in his mouth.

Jaime tried swallowing all of it, but there was so *much*. Finn just kept coming, pumping more and more down his throat, a tiny *hnnf* sound coming from him each time. Some dribbled down Jaime's chin, creating even more mess.

When Finn's grip finally relented, Jaime pulled off with a wet gasp. Breathing hard, he rested his cheek on Finn's thigh for a few seconds, or maybe minutes, until he caught his breath.

Dazedly, he patted his hand around on the ground without looking until he found his discarded shirt, and swiped at his wet face. So gently, he cleaned up the mess they'd both made of Finn's spent cock, resting heavily on his thigh.

Knees stiff and erection aching, Jaime flicked his gaze up to find Finn staring at him, flushed, eyes pleasure-bright and shocky, and so very loving.

"Jaime. Baby. Come here," he panted, reaching out with one taloned hand before it flopped back on to the couch.

Jaime smirked, and finished removing Finn's shoes and pants, discarding everything to the side before he crawled his way up into his lap again. Finn listed to the side, groaning, and rolled them until Jaime was laying half on top, all pressed up against each other on the narrow couch.

Still breathing like a freight train, Finn wrapped a hairy arm around him, idly scratching up and down his back, giving him the most delicious goosebumps. Jaime arched into it, sighing in pleasure.

They laid like that for several minutes while Finn's breathing slowed, and even though he was still hard and aching, Jaime thought that he could live in this moment forever. He'd been on his knees for Finn, had let him feed his cock down his throat, and yet he had never felt more powerful, more erotic and sexy as he had in that moment.

Eventually, he realized the rumbling he felt wasn't Finn's breathing at all, but a steady hum coming from his chest. And it seemed to be getting louder.

"Are you *purring?*" Jaime asked into the quiet, lips moving against Finn's neck as he spoke.

With monumental effort, Finn propped his chin up on his hand and shot a confused look down at his chest. "I don't know."

At Jaime's raised eyebrows, Finn gave a sleepy chuckle. "Truly. This has never happened before."

Jaime giggled, "Oh."

Finn's smile was small and as warm as the midnight sun. "Oh?"

Jaime threw an arm across his eyes. "Yes, oh," he got out between giggles.

Finn was laughing too, the moment infectious. "What is so funny?"

Full on belly laughing now, Jaime turned into Finn's chest. Between gasps, he explained, "You're a giant, hairy, wolf man. An apex predator. And you purr like a kitten."

They both laughed at Jaime's explanation, tumbling against each other. Finally quieting, Jaime pressed his hand against Finn's chest, fingers lightly scratching through the hair there. He loved how it felt against his skin.

The purring picked up again.

Finn wiped at the laughing tears on his face and laid his head back down on Jaime's shoulder. "Fuck. I think you might have actually killed me. Sucked the life straight out of my cock."

Jaime gave an amused hum, and turned to place a trail of kisses along Finn's temple.

Turning his head so their lips brushed as he spoke, Finn sobered. "Was that ok? I've never... I mean—I've never reacted that way. I didn't even mean to come, but as soon as we started, fuck, Jaime. I just, I mean, did I hurt you? Make you take too much? I should have asked first, if you wanted me to—"

Jaime pressed his lips lightly against Finn's to stop the nervous ramble. "I've literally jacked off to nearly that exact scenario, Finn. Starring you. The knot was a fucking amazing bonus, by the way. I'm glad we cleared that mystery up."

He stroked his fingers through Finn's chest hair. "Yes, I'm ok. No, you didn't hurt me. Yes, I want to do it again, and yes, I want you to keep telling me what to do during sex. I'm still hard from it." To prove his point, he rocked his stiff erection into Finn's thigh where it was slotted between his legs.

Somehow, he still had his jeans on.

Finn's eyes darkened, and to Jaime's surprise, he turned his body more fully into him and ground his re-hardening cock against his. "Good. I'm glad. But I'll always check in, Jaime. And if there's ever anything you don't want to do—"

"I'll tell you," Jaime said, cutting him off and reaching down to take Finn back in hand. "Now, I vividly recall saying exactly what I *do* want you to do to me after I sucked your dick."

Finn pounced.

CHAPTER 18
FINN

"Finn! Don't drop me!"

Jaime clung to him as he carried him up the stairs, thrown over one shoulder.

Finn chuckled. "As if I'd ever drop you. I'm very strong, Jaime. But you should stop squirming if you want us to make it to the bed before I fuck you."

Finn lightly smacked his ass to emphasize his point.

Jaime squawked, "Hey!"

It lacked real heat, though, and Finn could smell that carrying him up to their loft cave-man style and bouncing him on the heavily blanketed bed turned him on.

Somehow, even after being face-fucked, tossed over Finn's shoulder, and then dropped onto the bed only in his jeans, Jaime managed to land gracefully.

His hair was all askew, and his eyes were still watery and hooded, limbs sprawling and stretched out, and Finn couldn't look away from him. He needed to study him. Thoroughly. Right now.

He'd never been able to look away from Jaime. How had he gotten so lucky? His mate was perfect.

Jaime smirked up at him. "You're staring again."

Finn chuffed and crawled his way up until he was hovering over Jaime, eyes dancing over long limbs and the expansive freckled planes of skin below him. "You're beautiful. I told you. It's going to take some time for me to get used to being able to look at you like you're mine."

Jaime's smile softened, soothing Finn in ways he didn't know he needed soothed. "I am yours."

Jaime hooked his hands around Finn and yanked him down so that his full weight was pressed into him. "Now I want you to fuck me like I'm yours."

Finn shuddered and growled into Jaime's neck, lapping kisses and nips there, tasting his freckled collarbone, and felt a pulse and throb at the base of his cock intensify. His knot.

Fuck.

When had he forgotten that he was shifted? How was it possible that he was already so comfortable like this around Jaime?

The sight of his mate gripping his knot tight with both hands while he slurped down his cockhead, taking everything Finn gave him until he was pumping his load down his throat, will be seared into his memory forever. And his knot... he would never get used to the pulsing need for intense pressure and heat, the overwhelming urge to push his way in, and down, to stuff his cock so far into Jaime's belly and *press* while came.

Jaime had utterly destroyed him with that blowjob, and he didn't think he had the strength to hold himself back again today.

"Yes. Yes. But I need to shift back, first."

Jaime released his grip on Finn's shoulders, allowing him to sit up a bit. He squirmed beneath him and gave an over-exaggerated pout. "But I like the purring."

Finn chuckled, but said with gravity, "We'll work up to it, baby. I do not want to hurt you. Let's leave the knotting for another day." As he said it, he shifted into his human form and settled back into the cradle of Jaime's hips, adjusting to their far more normal height difference.

Jaime smirked and drifted his hands down from Finn's shoulders to grab his ass. "I don't think working up to it is going to be a hardship."

Finn gave him a wolfish grin, still hard even after that earth-shattering climax he had downstairs, and rocked his hips. He dropped his voice low, the way he knew that Jaime liked. "I'll do my best. Now, turn over."

Jaime scrambled to obey, a tiny whimper escaping him and that soft, hooded look back in place with Finn's command. Thankfully his jeans had been unbuttoned at some point, so all he had to do was hook his fingers and pull, taking his boxer briefs off too.

Finn shucked them all the way down and tossed them off the bed before leaning back over Jaime, sucking in a breath at all the beautiful, exposed skin presented to him.

Jaime's back was one long, graceful line down to his narrow hips, freckled constellations guiding Finn to the dimples sitting just above his soft cheeks that were begging to have his thumbs pressed into them.

So he did just that, tipping Jaime's ass up for a better view. Ruined.

He was absolutely ruined by the sight of Jaime's round, freckled cheeks, all cream and cinnamon-dusted, his dusky hole begging to be fucked. Finn's cock thickened fully and throbbed at the sight. Canines still fully descended, he leaned down and placed light, reverent kisses to each of those dimples, thumbs digging into the meat of Jaime's thighs to hold him in place as he shivered beneath him.

"Finn, please. Don't tease me," Jaime begged.

Peering up at all that skin he hadn't tasted yet, Jaime's head propped on his crossed arms and turned to the side so he could watch, Finn debated it.

Taste all of him later.

Take him, now.

He needed to reel himself in. "Ok, baby. Ok. I'll give you what you want."

He reached a hand up to lace his fingers through Jaime's while he continued to pepper kisses all along his lower back, watching him twitch and squirm as soft, involuntary *mmph* noises slipped out. He must be ticklish.

Interesting... Finn could—

Later.

Right. Later. Squeezing Jaime's hand before letting go, Finn trailed his kisses and nips down the meat of one cheek, using both hands to angle his ass up just right. "Stop me if there's anything you don't like."

Jaime made a petulant *huff*. "I will. But if you do not put your fingers inside of me soon, I swear I will—*Ooh Finn!*" he sobbed, effectively cutting off his threat.

It wasn't his fingers, not yet, but Finn's taste of Jaime last night had been far too brief. He decided to rectify that.

Finn had never actually done this before with anyone— the act was far too intimate—but some instinctual part of him that had woken up when he found Jaime demanded it.

Finn *needed* to taste him everywhere.

Dragging his tongue from Jaime's balls to his hole, Finn tasted the heart of his mate's scent and unraveled—surrendering to him completely. He felt Jaime unraveling too, shuddering and moaning beneath him as he softened and fluttered while Finn lapped there, readying Jaime for his fingers and fat cock.

Coming up for air, Finn gasped down at the sight beneath him. Jaime was sprawled out, wrecked, ass and thighs red from where he'd been holding too tightly. Leaning over him, Finn ran two fingers along his plush lips. "Open up for me."

Jaime's eyes were so hooded and hazy that he wasn't sure he was even really seeing anything, but his sweet boy obeyed, and wrapped his lips around Finn's fingers, sucking. "Get them nice and slick for me, baby. Good boy. There you go."

Jaime keened when Finn pulled out of his mouth and slid back down his body, angling his ass up with one hand. Making sure his claws were safely sheathed, he massaged over Jaime's hole, relaxing it further. Using his opposite thumb to pull one cheek aside, Finn eased a finger into the first knuckle, slowing when he met resistance.

Jaime made a breathy *ah* noise and twitched in his hold, but Finn felt him flex and then relax around his finger nearly immediately. "Shh, look at you, baby. You're taking my finger so well, already."

His balls tightened at the sight of Jaime's rim fluttering around his thick digit, and Finn tried thinking of deeply unsexy things to back himself off of that ledge he was already dangerously close to.

Like taxes. Or Silas's dirty laundry.

Slowly, so slowly, Finn opened him up with one, then two, and then three fingers, all the while trying desperately not to come or shift at the sight of Jaime, *his* Jaime, soft and pliant beneath him, listening to his pleasured cries and moans for *more, more, more!*

"S'enough, Finn. Please. M'ready." Jaime was all liquid, sleek planes of freckles beneath Finn.

Panting heavily, he ground out, "Lube?"

Jaime raised a shaky hand, gesturing somewhere near the loft stairs before it fell back on the bed. "Bag," was all he managed to hiccup out.

Swiping at the duffle with one hand, loath to leave Jaime even for a second, Finn dug until he found the bottle. Leaning back over him, Finn pressed kisses up Jaime's spine, into his shoulder blades, nipping and sucking at that soft spot on his neck.

Helping him along, because Finn was fairly certain Jaime was all fluffy cumulus clouds by now, he whispered into his ear, "Turn back over for me, baby."

After some shuffling and adjusting of long sleek limbs and his own thick, hairy ones, and many heated kisses between them, Finn had Jaime straddling his lap while he was sitting up, supported by the headboard at his back.

They were both breathing heavily, and a sheen of sweat coated Jaime's brow, a flush spreading down his shoulders and chest. His cheeks were red, too, but his eyes were bright with wonder and anticipation. And maybe a little trepidation.

"Finn. I don't know, like this. I mean—I don't know how—"

"Shh, Jaime. My Jaime. We'll go slow. At your pace. Whatever you like, whatever feels good, yeah?"

Jaime bobbed his head, features softening again.

Uncapping the lube, Finn drizzled a generous amount onto his cock, slicking himself up with a few pumps. "Lift up for me baby, there you go."

Jaime braced a hand on Finn's shoulder and the other on the headboard. Finn used the leftover lube on his fingers to coat his hole, sliding two inside and hooking them *just so*...

Jaime keened. "Finn! Now. Now, I need you now."

Pulling out, Finn hastily wiped his fingers on the sheets and grabbed Jaime's hips to steady him.

To steady them both.

Finn's voice shook. "Ok, baby. I've got you."

Jaime, one hand still braced on Finn's shoulder, reached down between his spread thighs and held Finn's cock steady as he slowly lowered himself down, snugging the fat tip right up to his rim. Pink mouth open on a silent gasp, eyes wide and locked on Finn's, he sank down just enough for the crown to enter with a catch and *pop* they both felt.

Groaning together, the resistance gave way to the most delicious tight heat Finn had ever known.

Both hands now scrabbling along the headboard, Jaime whined, "Finn—*nnngh!*"

Trembling, Finn held tight to his hips and fought the urge to thrust up and come immediately from the snug, hot hold of Jaime's ass around him. "I've got you, I've got you, I've got you baby... go nice and s-slow.... So slow for me... there we go."

Jaime began shifting his hips back and forth slowly, slowly, taking a little more of Finn inside him each time. Unable to concentrate enough to actually kiss him, Finn just pressed his forehead against Jaime's as he moved, looking down between their bodies to watch where they were joined, entranced at the sight of his cock disappearing into Jaime's pink hole.

"Baby, my Jaime. Look at you, look at us. Such a good-d boy—*Guhh!*"

All at once, Jaime sank down, taking him to the root, his ass nestled in Finn's lap. He tore his eyes up to Jaime's, who's brows were pinched together, mouth forming a soft *oh.*

Finn nearly scrambled to lift him off before Jaime placed a hand on his shoulder, shifting back and forth. "Just—give me a minute, *ah!*"

So Finn did his best to hold still, aside from his trembling, fighting the urge to punch up into Jaime as he felt his ass clench around his cock. He petted up and down Jaime's arms and back, whispering sweet praise into his ear as he adjusted to Finn's girth.

Slowly, Jaime began rocking forward and back again, and

then he was riding Finn properly, his flushed and pink tip dragging along Finn's stomach, creating wet trails of precum. "Finn—*hiccup*—*Ooh*, so g-good. This is—*hiccup*—good!"

Being fully seated inside of Jaime stripped Finn bare, leaving nothing but the parts of him that now belonged to Jaime, irrevocably. It was a good thing he'd already come once today while shifted, had already knotted in Jaime's hands, because Finn wasn't sure he'd be able to hold his shift back right now otherwise.

He leaned forward and slanted their mouths together, tongue seeking refuge and connection, needing them to be fully one everywhere, everywhere, everywhere.

Jaime was lost in pleasure, whining as his rhythm faltered. "Finn, please. I can't—I need—please!"

Finn knew what he needed.

Gathering his strength, he gripped Jaime's hips hard enough to bruise, already having left angry red prints all over his ass and thighs, and began lifting him and dropping him back down on his cock, hard, while he simultaneously thrust up into his downward motions.

Jaime broke their kiss with a gasp and sobbed, throwing his head back and locking his arms around Finn's shoulders. He wrapped his legs around Finn's waist tightly and pressed his face into Finn's neck, surrendering completely to his hold.

They were both beyond words at this point, and Finn lost himself in the steady rhythm of his cock tunneling through Jaime's tight heat and the breathy *uh, uh, uh,* sounds he made with each of Finn's thrusts up as he pulled Jaime down. That, paired with feeling his mate pressed everywhere, sweat-slick skin hot and his scent rich and drugging, had him throbbing for release.

Nails dragging along Finn's back, Jaime latched onto his shoulder with blunt human teeth, right where he ached to bite him in return, and Finn lost himself.

Barely aware of the rumbling growl coming from him, Finn hastily pulled Jaime off his cock and tipped him backward. Rising up over him and hooking his arms under Jaime's knees to fold him nearly in half, he sank back inside that perfect pink hole, as deep as he could in one go.

Jaime cried out, his voice breaking and hitching higher with each thrust.

Finn began to pound into Jaime, grinding on each press inside, seeking that spot that would drive him through the roof by angling his cock up, up, *up* into Jaime's belly with each pump.

"*Ooh*—F-Finn*nnggh*. What—what is—*hiccup*. So deep. Deep. It's—it's—there! Don't—stop!"

There it is.

Continuing his merciless pounding, Finn ran his teeth along Jaime's neck, teasing right where he wanted to bite. Pulling back, he licked and sucked his way up to Jaime's ear, and tugged on the tip.

"Tell—me. Tell me. What does my—*fuck*—my cock f-feel like inside you, hmm? How does it feel—feel?"

Hands scrabbling along his back, yanking Finn impossibly closer as his feet tipped up and gave him even more room to pound him into the mattress, Jaime caught his breath enough to answer. "S'good—good. I'm s-so full. Finn. I'm full. *Please!*"

Finn's balls tightened with his impending release, Jaime's hiccuped words driving him even higher, so he canted his hips just enough to continue to hit that spot, again and again and again, making Jaime cry out and sob in pleasure, driving him right to the edge.

Finn's climax was bearing down on him, and he was sure he wouldn't last but another handful of thrusts. "Touch yourself, J-Jaime. *Mmmph*, grab that beautiful—*oh, fuck*—cock and make yourself come. Come, baby. You're such a good—boy."

Jaime keened, writhing beneath him as he slid one hand down and grabbed hold of his shaft, tugging hard and fast. Finn continued his frantic pace, thrusting in and angling Jaime's hips *just so*, hitting his prostate as he continued to whisper filthy words until Jaime shouted his release, cum splattering all over himself.

Jaime's other hand made its way into Finn's hair, and between the pull of it as he came and watching his release splash all over his soft belly, Finn's orgasm slammed into him. Punching his hips up into Jaime's ass as deep as he possibly could, over and over and over with each kick, Finn roared his release.

Dropping his hold on Jaime's legs, Finn tipped forward until he was laying over him, just the barest hint of his weight supported on his forearms to keep from squashing the boy completely.

Jaime didn't seem to mind, because through Finn's great heaving breaths he could hear Jaime's soft, pleasure-shocked mewls and little *ah*'s as they shifted, arms banded tight around each other, both completely spent.

The aftershocks continued to move through them, causing Finn's hips to jerk forward as his oversensitive shaft kicked a few final times before he gently pulled out. Finn caught the wince that Jaime tried to hide, and gathered him close to press gentle kisses all over his face, telling him how good he'd been, how well he'd done, how much he loved him, that he was his.

Only his.

Finn could scent the mess of cum and lube that dribbled out of Jaime's loose hole, and told himself to get up and go find a washcloth to clean them both up, but he just couldn't move yet.

There was some deeply rooted part of him that preened at the thought that Jaime smelled like him, now.

Keep him full. Make him smell like ours, always.

Well.

Finally feeling strong enough, he rolled off of Jaime and whispered that he'd be right back, extracting himself from Jaime's grasping arms and adorable pout, stumbling down the stairs.

Apparently, his mate was clingy after sex.

Good.

He hastily cleaned himself off and wetted down a cloth, grabbing their water bottles before heading back up to the loft. Finn found Jaime just as he had left him; long, cinnamon-sprinkled limbs tangled in mussed sheets that smelled like sex and *them.*

He'd dreamed of this, and emotion swelled in him to find that the reality was even better.

Jaime opened one eye to peek up at him, and smirked.

Blushing at being caught staring, again, Finn crawled back over him and gently cleaned Jaime off, nudging him this way and that until he was no longer sticky and back in Finn's arms. Running his hands up and down Jaime's back, he noted the sensitive skin of his soft thighs and ass was still red, and there were light finger-shaped bruises forming on his hips.

"Are you ok?" Finn asked, gently caressing over those areas. Jaime peered down at himself and flushed.

Looking back up at Finn, his eyes were clear. "That was perfect, Finn. So much more than I could have ever thought. You were perfect." He took hold of Finn's hand and placed it right back over where he'd held him firm enough to bruise.

Finn exhaled and breathed in the scent of Jaime's hair.

"So, was it good for you, too?" Finn could tell that Jaime's question was meant to be cheeky, but his voice came out softer, smaller.

Propping his head up so they could really see each other, Finn said, "Earth shatteringly good. Being inside of you and feeling you come on my cock..." he shuddered. "Every time we are together, I think I can't possibly experience more pleasure than that, and yet, every time, I feel made new by you."

Jaime hummed in agreement, tucking his nose into the soft bend in Finn's arm. "We've got plenty of time to reach that peak."

Finn traced the freckled constellations across Jaime's nose and cheeks, scattered along the curve of his ear, and down his shoulders as the deepest sense of peace he'd ever known settled inside him.

"We have forever, if you want it?"

Finn heard the hope in his voice, the achingly tender love and devastating vulnerability offered in those words.

And when Jaime placed a hand on Finn's heart, all of it was reflected back at him, shining so bright. "Forever. I want it."

———

THEY WERE both exhausted from their emotional morning, the long drive, and their marathon sex, but it wasn't late enough yet to go to bed. So, they laid there in each other's arms, feet tangled in the sheets, and spoke of everything and nothing—filling in the details of things only briefly shared before they were split apart a year prior.

Finn told Jaime about his childhood; how he never knew his father, and that his mother's disdain and slaps had made him hide his wolf from her as best he could, but that the time he'd spent with Silas's family taught him to embrace the wildness inside of him. He told Jaime about following Silas into the military, and how grateful he was for the chance to fully be himself for the first time in his life with people who accepted him, but that he still grappled with the things they had seen and done. Finn told Jaime about his deep resentment for those in power, who had found two young shifters trying to find their place in the world and had used them for their own gain, before spitting them back out at their lowest.

Jaime told Finn about losing his mom to cancer when he was eight, and about his father's drunken indifference after she passed and how Sam took care of him and moved them both out of Anchorage to a small apartment in Monroe right when he'd turned eighteen. He talked about how losing their childhood dog, Alfie, had prompted him to start painting pet memorials.

Softly, he told Finn about how much he wanted to be able to do that again, someday.

Tentatively, Jaime asked him about losing Renner. He explained that it had been their last mission, how Renner and Sheppard had split up from Finn and Silas, both pairs tasked with different objectives, but something had gone horribly wrong. Finn explained that Sheppard hadn't ever fully talked about what had happened, but the three of them were discharged immediately afterwards. They were all put in therapy and then released into the civilian world again, where they joined Sheppard at the security firm.

Finn shuffled further into Jaime's embrace, carding his talons through his hair. "Are you ok? I mean, after seeing Sam, and after the attack and everything?"

He ran the pad of his thumb lightly over the faint scratch mark on Jaime's neck. He knew it was a stupid question—of course Jaime wasn't ok. The entire course of his life was all thrown off the rails, and that fight this morning had been awful.

Jaime shrugged his shoulders. "Yes and no. I feel better, after finally telling Sam how I feel. How much his absence has hurt. How much I wish that all the other stuff hadn't gotten in the way. And I feel safer with you, and Silas and Sheppard, than I have for the last year."

Jaime sighed. "But the trial is less than a week away. I'm still so afraid that I'll get up on the stand and freeze. I'm afraid that all of this is going to come boiling up at the exact wrong time and I'll fall apart in front of everyone. I'm afraid that I won't be able to do this, for Vera. I couldn't do anything for her, before. I should at least be able to do this, now."

Finn wrapped his arms around Jaime's shoulders, holding him close and pressing his words into his hair. "You are so strong, Jaime. I have no doubt that you'll get through it. But even if you don't, even if you need help, there's strength in that too. And I will always be here. You are never too much for me."

Jaime sighed, and buried into Finn's hold. "Thank you."

Finn knew it didn't fix Jaime's pain, or set aside his fear. But it would be the honor of his life to stand beside him as he battled those things for himself.

Just as he was thinking it was time to head downstairs and feed the fire, maybe start dinner, Jaime asked another question. "If none of this had happened—Vera's murder, Sam hiring you all... If you and I had been able to go on our date last year, what do you think would have happened?"

Finn shifted. "What do you mean?"

Entwining their fingers in the air between them, Jaime pulled Finn's hand down to press a light kiss to the tip of each clawed finger. "Say our first date really happened. Would you have told me about your shift? Would we have gotten here?"

Finn sat with the question for a long time. Jaime let him, exchanging shared breaths. Finally, he said, "I don't know. I still would have known right away that you are my mate. I think a part of me already knew, even before we met. But..."

he sighed. "I truly don't know if I would have had the courage to show you, without all of the other circumstances involved. Without needing to protect you."

Jaime nodded, understanding. "I wouldn't take it back, you know."

At Finn's cocked head, Jaime continued. "I hate that we lost a year that we otherwise could have had together. I wish that Vera hadn't been murdered, and that you and Silas and Sheppard weren't wrapped up in this mess with the Salt Creek pack. But I do not regret that this year of pain brought me back to you. That it gave us a second chance. And I'm so thankful that it landed you on my doorstep that day. I'm so thankful you found me, that you would have come for me, regardless of whether Sam had hired you."

Finn found Jaime's lips in a desperate kiss, salty and hot from his tears as he put every ounce of love he felt into the press of their mouths, and tried to convey how much he had needed to hear that. "Oh, my Jaime. Me too."

After a long while of slow, tender kisses, Jaime pulled back and stretched, giving Finn a languid smile. He watched Jaime's muscles bunch and contract with a predator's focus, but blinked up in surprise at his next words.

"I'm hungry. Also, can't you turn into a giant wolf? I'd like to see that, please."

CHAPTER 19
JAIME

"**S**o, you *do* always take your clothes off before you turn into a giant wolf."

Jaime was seated on the couch before the fire, naked except for the blanket draped around his waist. Finn had fussed over him when they ventured downstairs, tucking him in before he made dinner, but Jaime had batted him away.

He'd be lying if he said he didn't cherish the attention, but there really was no need. Yes, he was a little sore from the deep pounding Finn had just given him, but he secretly loved it—loved seeing and feeling the evidence of Finn's desire, his loss of control. Finally coming together with him, feeling Finn so deep inside of him, was pure ecstasy.

He couldn't wait to do it again.

Jaime slurped down the best chicken and dumplings he'd ever had, and eyed Finn as he finished his dinner first and set the empty bowl on the coffee table.

"Ok, you ate. Now will you show me?"

Finn huffed, and Jaime beamed as he stood.

Finn gave him a look. "You would take your clothes off too, if you'd ripped through as many good shirts as I have over the years. Also, I'm still not convinced that we shouldn't have you checked for a concussion or sleep deprivation. You're handling the fact that I turn into an animal entirely too well."

Jaime shrugged. "The government basically told us that aliens are real a few years ago. This is not that much more of a stretch."

At Finn's disbelieving look, Jaime asked, "What? Would you have preferred it if I panicked and flung holy water at you or something?"

"That's vampires."

Jaime choked on a dumpling, coughing. "Holy fuck, are vampires real? Are aliens real? Witches? Bigfoot? Oh my God, is the Megalodon real?"

Finn smirked, and shook his head as if to say, *I'm standing in front of my mate, naked, about to turn into a giant wolf, and he's more concerned about Sasquatch?*

Ticking his answers off on his fingers, Finn replied, "Yes, fuck if I know, yes, I've heard he's an asshole, and baby, please do not go into the ocean alone. Ever. I don't know if there's a giant shark swimming around out there or not, but you definitely should not mess with the merfolk."

Jaime gaped at him, spoon frozen halfway up to his mouth. Processing.

Mermaids.

"You're fucking with me."

Finn grinned. "No, I'm not. But if you'd like, we can take this upstairs for another go."

A matching smile stretched across Jaime's face, so wide it ached. "I fucking love you. We're talking about this more later. Please, show me your wolf now." He gestured with his spoon for Finn to continue, who just shook his head in fond exasperation.

And then he turned into a wolf the size of a horse.

As with his partial shift, a tremor passed through Finn's body before he bunched and stretched into this form. Landing on four feet, the wolf shook his head before lifting great, big, soil brown eyes up to peer right at Jaime, and huffed.

Jaime blinked, setting down his now empty bowl. Logically, he knew that it was Finn looking back at him, but still, some part of his brain was very aware that he was now trapped in a small cabin with a giant predator.

He swallowed, and swore the great wolf tracked the movement. "Right. Yes, I see. You're a wolf. Very... wolfy. Are real wolves actually this large? Your paws are the size of my head. Or, well, I guess you are a real wolf too, obviously. But like, the ones everyone else knows about."

Finn took one large step forward and butted his head against Jaime's chest, stopping his rambling. Reflexively, Jaime reached up and dug his fingers into the fur around Finn's ears, scratching there. He listened as a deep rumble came from Finn, and all of his nervousness left him.

Giggling, he crooned, "My wolf who purrs."

Finn chuffed, the purring growing louder as he nuzzled his head all along Jaime's neck and chest. He felt Finn's body begin to rock back and forth, and looked up to see Finn's tail. Wagging.

Finn, the giant wolf who purred, was wagging his tail at Jaime.

"Oh my God, you're adorable." He stood up, taking the blanket with him wrapped around his shoulders like a cape, and ran his hands along Finn's side and down to his tail, walking along his great big body. With his head raised, Finn was tall enough to look Jaime right in the eye.

"You have a tail, and you can purr. Really, Finn, why are you so *cute?*"

Finn huffed at that, but Jaime swore he held his head a little higher. He moved up and around his body and sat down on the couch again, where Finn promptly pressed his face back into Jaime's chest. "Do you want me to scratch your ears again?"

Finn chuffed and pressed harder.

"Ok, yes, I get it." He began scratching, using both hands to rub the base of Finn's ears. Jaime could feel the tension leaving his heavily-muscled shoulders, and Finn's eyes started drooping.

Jaime smiled, and softly asked, "How could I ever be afraid of you?"

Finn pulled his head back to look at Jaime fully, his brown eyes the same, still loving and earnest. He whined, and without warning lapped his tongue up the side of Jaime's face in one great big kiss.

Laughing, Jaime shrieked when Finn did it again and again, batting at him as he fell back into the couch.

Eventually, Finn relented and padded back, a large

tremor going through him before he was standing back on two legs, staring at Jaime in wide-eyed adoration.

Wiping at his face, Jaime groused, "*Ugh*, great. Now I need to go and wash off again."

Finn tackled him back into the couch and began landing wet, smacking kisses all over him while Jaime cackled.

THE NEXT TWO days were some of the best of Jaime's life, even with the looming threat of the trial, Jeffrey Dugan and the Salt Creek pack, and Jaime's argument with Sam hanging over him.

Yes, he was still terrified that he would panic and be unable to give his testimony in front of everyone, and yes, a part of him did wonder what Sam could have possibly said to explain his actions this past year, but it was hard to focus too much on either when he was so fucking happy.

And *safe*.

They were out in the middle of nowhere, completely untraceable, hidden from the Salt Creek wolves. Even though he was terrified to testify and to face the possibility of losing Sam forever, he knew those were his battles to fight— his fears to confront. And he was so damn grateful that he had Finn to help with the rest, to protect him from the threats he couldn't face alone.

Like giant, vengeful wolves.

Also, Finn was a sex god, wringing climax after climax out of Jaime until he was all cotton candy soft thoughts and loose limbs draped over Finn. He always had a look of pure male satisfaction and smugness on his face after he fucked Jaime so good he couldn't move, and Jaime would have teased him about it, but, well, he usually wasn't even able to say his own name, let alone form whole sentences.

They'd fucked all over the cabin. In the loft, obviously, on the couch, out on the porch while watching the sunset, and once they'd even tried to shower together in the tiny stall, Finn pressing Jaime up against the wall and grunting filthy praise into his ear as he fucked him in short, deep thrusts that ground against his prostate every time, making his balls tighten right from the start.

Jaime came in record time, panting open mouthed kisses along Finn's chest and shoulders, cock untouched except for the hot slide and grind between them.

The sex had been incredible, but seeing as Finn had to step out once Jaime's knees stopped trembling so he had room to actually clean himself off before trading places, they'd kept their showers short and solo, purely for washing after that.

Jaime's favorite, though, was when he'd stumbled down the loft steps, having just swallowed Finn's cock until his knot popped in Jaime's tight hold and he poured his hot release down his throat with a broken whine.

Finn had stepped back inside the cabin after using the outhouse, took one look at Jaime where he stood, naked and flushed, gulping down a glass of water, and crowded him back against the counter, spun him around by the hips, and urged him to bend over with a hand on his back.

"Hold on to something, baby."

Doing as he was told, Jaime stayed bent over and gripped

the edge of the counter as he heard the *snick* of the lube bottle from somewhere behind him, then the lewd, wet noises of Finn slicking himself up.

Jaime was still prepped from that morning, and they had discovered together that he *really* liked how the initial stretch felt—the near too-much edge just as pain tipped into pleasure. So, two fingers to slick up his insides was the only prep that Finn gave him before he stuffed his cock inside, the blunt head catching on Jaime's rim before bottoming out in one thrust.

They both gasped, Finn bracing himself over Jaime, anchoring him down, and then he fucked him harder and deeper than ever before.

Jaime cried out his name, sobbing and hiccuping in pleasure at the sheer ecstasy of it, hands scrabbling for purchase as Finn punched his thick cock up into Jaime's belly relentlessly, driving him up onto his tip-toes every time.

It was never ending. Finn took Jaime higher and higher and higher with his praise and gentle commands, telling him that he was such a good boy, he was so good at this, he felt divine.

Finn told Jaime to take it as he heaved him back against his chest and held him tight around his belly and shoulders with firm, claw-tipped hands, pressing them together as Finn ground up into him while Jaime mewled. He knew he'd have new marks from this, cherished the proof of Finn's want written all over him, reminding him of the pleasure they took in each other.

Jaime's orgasm was a tidal wave—he saw it building long before it hit him full on, and yet he was still unprepared.

Voice cracking and pitching high, all Jaime could do was hold on, unable to support his own weight anymore as he took himself in hand and shouted Finn's name over and over while he came, cum spilling all over the counter, all over his own belly and hand.

Finn's arms banded even tighter. He grunted and thrust up into Jaime twice more before he came too, cock throbbing and jerking as he shoved himself deep inside and held tight, shouting his own climax.

Finn held Jaime up for a long while until their breathing slowed, nose buried in his hair as he softened inside of him.

Once Finn withdrew in a long, slow pull and Jaime wobbled back down off his tip-toes onto unsteady legs, Finn's cum slipping down the backs of his thighs, they stayed there, fingers tangled together as they exchanged wet, filthy kisses.

Long hours later, well after dark, they lay wrapped around each other before the fire and listened to the chilly spring rain patter on the roof.

Jaime peppered Finn with questions about all of the paranormal people in Silver Rapids, completely fascinated.

"I knew there was something up with that Jared guy at the bookstore!" Jaime exclaimed, twisting in Finn's arms. "He's definitely a paranormal, right?"

Finn chuckled. "Yes, he's a bear shifter. Polar bear, actually. Guy's a loner and doesn't really talk much to other people, but he's always been kind to me. He just doesn't take to strangers very well."

Jaime hummed. "And Andi? I want to meet her properly, now. No wonder her food is so delicious, it's literally magic."

Finn chuckled again and agreed, and wondered aloud if she'd be more inclined to share her culinary secrets with Jaime instead of him.

Silence stretched between them, comfortable and familiar. Finn lightly traced the tips of his claws up and down the soft underside of Jaime's arms in soothing strokes, just the way he liked, and Jaime knew that he wanted every night to feel like this, for the rest of his life.

Forever.

He turned his face toward Finn, pressing his cheek into the meat of his shoulder. "Finn?"

"Hmm?" Finn looked like he'd been dozing, but he cracked one eye open to look at Jaime.

"Why haven't you bitten me yet? I mean, why haven't we tried to, *you know*, while you're shifted?"

The sleepy daze fell away from his face, and Finn propped them both up a little straighter before answering, a smirk slashed across his face. "You've had my cock inside of you every which way, and you're calling sex *you know*? I've seen what you read baby, don't be shy."

Jaime glared, blush sitting high on his cheeks. "Fine. Why haven't you *fucked* me, knotted me, bitten me, and claimed me yet? I think I'm more than ready to take you," he sniffed, chin lifted.

Sweet delight shot through him as he saw the effect of his words on Finn, eyes going hazy for an entirely different reason, now. He shook his head as if to clear it, the move so lupine that Jaime snickered, but he saw Finn sober before he replied.

"First, you're going to need far more prep than you usually let me get to before I knot you. Second... I want to. And I know you want to, too. It's not doubt, I promise."

He paused, tucking a wayward lock of hair behind Jaime's ear. "When we take that step, I don't want it to be clouded by the fear and uncertainty we are in now. I want us both to be clear headed, in a home that we make ours. When we're both old and gray, I want to look back and remember all the love and happiness that we felt when I finally claim you, not those Salt Creek assholes."

Jaime smiled, leaning into his touch and opened his mouth to say that he agreed, but the shrill chime of the ringing phone cut him off.

So far, they had only communicated with Sheppard and Silas through text message on the secure line, and it was too late for this to be a casual check-in. Looking like his thoughts were similarly skewed, Finn reached over Jaime and snagged the phone off of the coffee table and answered, putting it on speaker.

"Sheppard, what's wrong? Has something happened?"

The line crackled and his voice was a bit tinny as Sheppard replied, "Is Jaime there with you?"

Looking even more alarmed, Finn tightened the arm still banded around his shoulders. "Yes."

Sheppard gave a relieved sigh, which sent Jaime's heart racing. Focusing on keeping his breathing steady, Jaime said, "I'm here, Sheppard. What's going on?"

"Bishop escaped. He was being transported to the courthouse for a pre-trial hearing this afternoon and the van crashed. He's in the wind."

Jaime couldn't feel his body. Finn shot up off of the couch and began pacing, hurling questions at Sheppard that Jaime didn't hear.

He could feel the walls closing in around him, the pull and bite of the bindings around his wrists and the gag making it hard to breathe. Sucking in great heaving breaths, he tried to move, to do something as he stared at the unmoving, dead eyes of Vera while she lay in a pool of her own blood. Hands scrambling, he tried to close the wound on her stomach, tried to put everything back inside where it should be, but he kept slipping and getting stuck in all of the blood covering him, gluing his hands and feet to the floor as he heard the approaching footsteps behind him, getting closer, closer, a dark shape looming in his periphery, before—

"Jaime, baby. Hey, shh. It's ok. Let's breathe together, yeah?"

The voice was different from Jackson Bishop's. A lower timber. He'd heard it before, had followed it out of the dark before.

It was safety.

Jaime swam back up to that voice, letting it guide him through the exercises from the pamphlet until he could open his eyes, until his breathing slowed enough to lift his head from where he'd curled tight into himself.

Finn was there. His Finn. Gentle and brave and so kind, the Finn who always stood shoulder to shoulder with him. The one who would always protect him when he needed it. He was there, and Jaime wasn't stuck in that house, in that closet, anymore. He'd gotten out, he'd survived, and now he was here with his Finn.

Wiping the tears from his eyes, Jaime took a long, wet breath. "I'm sorry."

Finn wrapped broad arms around him. "Oh, baby. Don't ever apologize for that. Not ever. That phone call hit us both sideways. I'm sorry for not stepping in to help sooner."

Jaime shook his head. "It was a shock to us both. If I don't get to apologize, neither do you."

Finn held him a while longer, and after gulping down some water, Jaime asked him to fill him in on what he'd missed.

Police weren't sure whether the wreck was an accident or intentional, but Bishop certainly had help. Most likely from the Salt Creek deputies that were in his escort, either through a coordinated effort or seizing a moment of opportunity.

Apparently, Sheppard said that DA Rivera had narrowed down both his identity leak and the main suspect in aiding Bishop's release to Detective Jones, which did actually shock Jaime a little. He was an ass, sure, but he had seemed invested in bringing justice to Vera.

More concerning, though, was his potential knowledge of Jaime and Finn's whereabouts. Detective Sutton was made aware that they were relocating to a secure safe house, and if Detective Jones somehow got ahold of their location and communicated it to Bishop or Jeffrey Dugan... Jaime shuddered.

Finn continued explaining that no one knew where Bishop was. Monroe PD's search area was too narrow, based on the potential movements and physical limitations of a human man, but the paranormals on the force were doing what they could with the help of other packs and shifters in the area to get a wider search party together.

It was difficult though, given that Bishop likely had help from Detective Jones and other Salt Creek deputies who weren't talking. Jeffrey Dugan's tail hadn't reported any suspicious activity, and though they suspected the two were connected, there was no proof that he'd helped with Bishop's escape, so they couldn't arrest him.

Dana, Detective Sutton, and DA Rivera all called one after the other through the secured line, updating him and asking if he was ok, if they were safe. Being blindsided by that first phone call had sucked, but Jaime did ok for the rest of the conversations. He kept his breathing steady, anyway.

Everyone seemed to agree that it was best for them to stay where they were for the moment. There was no proof that Detective Jones had compromised their location, and now that the trial was on hold, they had no reason to leave until Bishop was apprehended. The cabin was defensible, and was as good a place as any to hole up until Bishop was found. They all promised that they'd call to check in tomorrow.

Jaime felt strung out and thin, suddenly overly anxious about locked doors and open windows when he hadn't been before. Ready to go tuck into bed next to Finn, he started for the stairs when the phone rang again.

Finn answered, "Silas."

The relief and raw emotion in his voice brought tears to

Jaime's eyes, the ache in his chest from missing Sam sudden and overwhelming.

Finn darted his eyes up to Jaime, full of empathy and understanding. "He's here with me, yes, but just about to head up to bed. This is so fucked, Si."

They exchanged a few words, and it seemed that Silas didn't know anymore than anyone else, but then Finn's eyebrows shot up in surprise. "Something else you want to mention, brother?"

Jaime could only make out a few gruff mumbles in response. Finn again looked up at Jaime, this time in conspiring surprise. "Tell him that he's ok. Shaken by the news, but ok. Does he... I mean, does he want me to hand the phone over?"

Jaime narrowed his eyes in question. Finn's face fell a bit. "Well, ok. I'll say goodnight, then. Yeah, we'll talk tomorrow. Be safe." His face grew fond. "Yeah, you too, Si."

Hanging up, Finn heaved a great sigh and tossed the phone aside, bouncing on the couch cushions. With an unreadable look on his face, he said, "So, that was Silas. And Sam."

Jaime's brows shot up just like Finn's had. "Sam is with Silas? At your house? Why?"

Finn shook his head once in an unsure gesture. "I don't know. He wouldn't say anything, except that Sam needed to know you were safe."

Jaime's mouth tightened. "And he couldn't tell me that himself?"

Finn rubbed the back of his neck. "Ah, I'm not sure he thought you'd want to hear from him, after your... conversation, the other morning. Apparently, he just wanted you to know that he is thinking about you, and wants you to be safe."

Jaime rolled his eyes and started up the stairs, unable to stop his snide tone. "Helpful."

Finn didn't say anything more about it after that. He had to be tired and anxious too, and some part of Jaime knew his reaction wasn't entirely fair. Yes, Sam had ignored him for the better part of a year when he'd reached out, but he also knew that after what he'd said in Finn's bedroom, he'd probably need to be the one to re-open that line of communication.

Tomorrow. Maybe the next day. Not tonight, when all he wanted was to crash into bed and curl up in the safety and warmth of Finn's arms, too exhausted for anything else.

———

THE NEXT TWO days at the cabin were entirely different from the first two that they'd spent together.

Now, their tiny shelter really did feel like a safe house, and less like a sex den. The windows were too small, and yet too exposing, and the outhouse was too far for Jaime to comfortably go without Finn standing on the porch, keeping watch.

Finn was almost always in his partial shift now, always tense and alert, and he rarely left Jaime's side for longer than a few minutes at a time. Before, Jaime had passed the time that they weren't fucking each other like animals by reading, or doing one of the puzzles on the shelf. He'd even debated firing up his iPad, safely on airplane mode, and sketching a few things that had been on his mind.

Finn, mostly.

Finn had also read, going through thrillers nearly as quickly as Jaime read romances. And he'd take an hour or so here and there to run laps around the cabin in his wolf shift, burning energy and assessing their perimeter.

But not now. Now, he was glued to Jaime's side, their anxiety bouncing off of each other.

In theory, they didn't have anything to worry about. Bishop was still in the wind, but it had been two days with no sign of him, and with Detective Jones' continual denial that he had anything to do with Bishop, no one had any more concrete evidence that he knew where Finn and Jaime were.

Still, the not-knowing had changed the dynamic of their stay at the safe house.

On the evening of the fourth day there, Jaime was ready to pull his hair out from the anxiety and tension pouring from them both. Finn was staring at him nearly as much as he was staring out the windows, giving him those big, brown, puppy eyes like he expected Jaime to disappear into thin air.

Unable to stand it any longer, Jaime snapped, "I'm fine. Stop looking at me like I'm going to fall apart at any moment."

Finn looked down and shuffled his feet. "I'm sorry. I know I'm being a lot. I didn't realize how much I was counting on Bishop being locked up and unable to get to you again."

Guilt washed away Jaime's irritation. His shoulders dropped, and he padded over to Finn and reached for his hand. "No, don't apologize. I'm sorry. I'm not mad at you, I'm just anxious."

Jaime ran his fingers through his messy hair, lightly pulling. "I hate the waiting. I hate that we are both so tense, and I hate letting him control what I do, again. Over and over I've let this monster dictate where I go, and who I can and can't see, and how I feel. I hate that he's wormed his way into our lives, again. I'm just tired of it."

Finn didn't say anything—there really wasn't anything he could say. He pulled Jaime close, wrapping him up tightly.

After several long minutes of just holding each other, Jaime stood on his tip-toes to pull Finn's mouth down to his, the kiss moving from tender and sweet to filthy and hot, teeth clacking.

And then Finn was in his human form again, walking Jaime backwards until he dropped down onto the couch. Following him down, Finn's voice cracked on a plea. "Jaime, I need—"

Jaime knew what he needed. "I know. I know. Take it."

They came together quickly, frantically, all grasping hands and needy kisses and breathy gasps, thrusting hard over clothes pulled aside just enough. The hasty swipe of lube provided enough slick so that the stretch around Finn's girth simmered low at the base of Jaime's spine, making him cry out and see stars, his own cock throbbing in pleasure.

Finn was the only thing Jaime knew, after that. His weight on top of him, cradling him tight while he moved deeply inside, swallowing all of Jaime's gasps and whimpers, words full of hot praise and earnest love—Finn filled Jaime up, and there was no more room inside of him for anything else.

Finn exercised his need to protect, his fear of losing Jaime again in brutal, powerful thrusts, and Jaime took it all. He let the high tide of Finn completely overwhelm him, needing to feel covered, consumed, and held.

He whispered his own promises back to Finn—one for each time that he pounded deep into Jaime—that he would never leave, he was Finn's, and Finn was his.

Forever. Forever.

Jaime's words ripped Finn's orgasm from him, sobbing in pleasure and relief as he spilled deep inside, and fisted Jaime's cock until he came, too.

Finn was still trembling when the aftershocks finished, pressing kisses and high pitched whines into Jaime's neck, behind his ear, into his hair. So Jaime wrapped his arms around his love, and held him tight.

Still seated deep inside, neither willing to part just yet, Finn finally spoke. "We're together now. We're together, and I'll never let him rip you away from me again. I won't allow it. I won't."

Jaime placed soothing kisses along Finn's temple, sensing that the words were meant more for himself.

JAIME DRIFTED out of a fitful sleep the next morning when he felt Finn shift beside him. Pressing a lingering kiss to his temple, Finn whispered, "I'm going to go split more firewood, baby. I'll be back inside in a few minutes."

Jaime pressed his face back into the pillow, mumbling about eggs for breakfast.

Finn huffed out a laugh, and tromped down the stairs, shuffling around in the kitchen before he went outside.

Yes, he does always clomp around everywhere he goes.

Jaime smiled into the pillow and drifted off for a little while, allowing himself to wake up slowly. Finn came back inside only a few minutes later, though, shutting the door quietly behind him and softly treading up the stairs.

Smirking, voice still muffled by their bedding, Jaime said, "While I appreciate the effort to be quiet so that I can sleep in, I'm starving. What are you—"

He rolled over to look up at Finn, but it wasn't Finn looming over him.

"I should have fucking killed you a year ago."

CHAPTER 20

JAIME

"You really don't know how to pick your friends, kid. First that bitch, Vera, and now the Silver Rapids half-breed?"

Jaime had to be having a nightmare. That voice—Jackson Bishop's voice—yes, he was having a nightmare.

Bishop reached down and grabbed Jaime by the upper arm, claws digging in harshly as he yanked him from the bed. He looked Jaime up and down, clad only in his boxer briefs, nostrils flaring before his lip curled up in disgust.

"You'd be pretty if you weren't covered in that mutt's cum. Did you let him fuck you, or did he just take what he wanted?"

That shook Jaime out of his frozen stupor and he scrambled to get away, hitting and scratching and fighting Bishop's hold, all the while yelling and screaming for Finn.

Too late, he realized that Bishop was shifted, and of course he was, he was a fucking *wolf*, and Jaime's attempts to get away were swiftly rendered useless as Bishop wrapped a heavily muscled arm around Jaime's throat, ceasing his ability to scream, and pulled him downstairs.

Through the choking hold, scratching deep marks into Bishop's arms that began to heal and close right before his eyes, Jaime rasped out, "Finn is coming back soon—he'll kill you for this."

Bishop chuckled, and Jaime hated how the sound skittered up his spine. He threw Jaime onto the couch, and growled, "Don't fucking move."

Leaning back against the counter, Bishop smirked at Jaime's frantic attempt to cover himself with the blanket that was left sprawled there from the night before.

"He's not coming back inside anytime soon. It's just you and me, and we are going to have a conversation."

Jaime's breath started coming too fast. All he could picture was Finn, his beautiful, kind, and gentle Finn, sprawled out on the ground outside, torn open and ravaged the way Vera had been...

"Relax. He's not dead. Yet. Just tied up. Alpha Cain will decide what to do with him—he could be useful with the right motivation. You, though. You've been a fucking thorn in my side from the start."

Jaime couldn't get his voice to stop shaking. "How did you find me?"

"I didn't find *you*," Bishop spit. "You were a mistake the first time, too. One that I should have ended. I won't make the same mistake again. No, I'm not here for you. The Detective told me that reject alpha's Second would be here, but when I smelled you on him, so fresh, I knew you were inside. So I came to do what I should have done a year ago."

Jaime's mind was spinning, momentarily shocked out of his panicked worry for Finn. He couldn't process anything this monster was saying.

"But—the attack at my house. The Salt Creek wolves on the force leaked my identity to the press. Why would you—"

"Do you really think that we couldn't have killed you at any time in the last year if we had wanted to? Our contacts in Monroe PD knew who you were the whole time. They knew you never saw me, that all you have is a vague recollection of a phone call. We left you alive in hopes they'd blame the murder on you, and when that didn't happen, leaking your identity became a useful distraction while they organized my escape. You never mattered. You were always the sideshow. Vera was always the sideshow, too."

Jaime felt his world tilting upside down.

Finn. Where is Finn?

If Jaime could get out of here, if he could find him... Bishop chuckled again.

He had seen pictures of him of course, but up close he really was the monster of Jaime's nightmares. Not because of his dark eyes, or thinning blonde hair, or the elongated canines and claws, but because of the look in his eyes.

It was feral, barely contained rage. Hate. Contempt.

"You're not getting out of here alive, so stop looking like you're about to bolt. You can't outrun me, anyway." He gave Jaime another long, calculating look. "Your idiot brother hiring that security firm to protect you was the worst decision he could have made, but it turned out to be a lucky break for us. They didn't attack your house to kill you, kid. They were there for the reject and the mutt. Why do you think they waited until he showed up? Until they were separated? Attacking them at your house was the perfect cover—everyone would think that they were there for you."

Jaime shook his head. "But, *why?* They didn't get involved in all of this until they were hired to protect me. They haven't done anything— "

"They were the target from the very fucking beginning!" Bishop roared, an unhinged look in his eyes.

Had he always been like that, or had a year in prison messed with his head? Probably both.

"Second Dugan dispatched me to kill the reject alpha and his sorry excuse for a pack—the mutt outside, and the other one he lets boss him around. But his meddling wife stuck her nose where it didn't belong, and she found out about our plan. She threatened to go to the police if we didn't call it off. So, we pivoted. I was going to kill her, drive to the reject's house to kill him and the mutt who lived there too, and then plant everything on Sheppard. The DA is already suspicious that he's hiding shit from law enforcement through his business. They may have squabbled a bit about motive, but all of that evidence on him would have been too overwhelming. It would have been an easy sell."

He pushed off the counter, sauntering toward Jaime. "But then you showed up at her house that night, and it fucked everything up. We decided to hold off on the rest of the plan until things died down after her murder, but then the neighbors found that security camera footage and they arrested me. And I will not spend the rest of my life in prison because of one insignificant mistake. You'll not be the reason I rot in there. So, here we are."

Jaime felt like he was going to throw up. He couldn't put it all together right now, couldn't follow the thread of a thought through the clawing panic that Finn was just outside, hurt.

His voice was hoarse when he asked, "If you're just here to kill me, then why haven't you, yet? Why wait and draw this out, why tell me all of this?"

Bishop grinned, and it was the most horrible thing Jaime had ever seen. "I wanted you to know how insignificant you were before you died. That it had never been about you. You were just a means to an end, even now. And as for why I haven't killed you yet... I know your mutt mate will fight the bindings."

At Jaime's surprised look, he continued, "You both reek of the mating bond. I know he will get free eventually, and he will fight harder from sensing that you're still alive. Still afraid. It will give him a sense of hope, before I crush him."

The look Jaime was giving him must have been suitably horrified, because he gleefully went on. "I am going to kill you, but we need to break the mutt. He's the best collateral we have against the Silver Rapids alpha since he doesn't have a mate of his own, but his Second won't do what we want until we've fully destroyed his spirit."

He scraped his claws along the countertop. "So, we wait until he shows up, desperate to save you, and then I'll rip your guts out right in front of him. Just like I did to her."

Jaime's face hardened. Judging by the slightly put out look

on Bishop's face, it wasn't the reaction he was looking for. He wanted the fearful human he'd shoved in a closet last year. The helpless, confused man who sat trembling on the sofa while someone threatened to take away his life, threatened to break his mate's spirit. He'd clearly expected Jaime to cower, to beg in fear.

His mistake.

Jaime smiled, and it was almost the snarl that he'd seen on Finn's face that day in the truck, when they had found the Salt Creek wolves prowling around his house.

"I don't think you will."

Bishop raised an eyebrow, "You don't think I will?"

Jaime held up the phone he'd tucked into the folds of the blanket wrapped hastily around his waist after Bishop threw him on the couch. He'd hidden the three taps it took to call Silas as embarrassment, the poor human trembling to cover himself.

"Silas, how much of that did you hear?"

"*All of it.*" His voice was a deep, earth-shaking growl. Jaime had never heard anything like it before.

Bishop looked frazzled, caught off guard. Still, he chuckled. "You think I give a fuck if that cast-off heard what I said? A phone call isn't going to save you. He's four hours away in Silver Rapids, too far to help you now."

Jaime shifted back as Bishop moved toward him. "That may be true, but my mate isn't."

Finn burst through the door, splintering it to pieces as he took one giant leap, propelled by the corded muscle bunching in all four legs, claws and teeth slicing for Bishop. He barely had time to turn and shift before Finn was on him, jaws clamped tightly around Bishop's throat as he shook and ripped.

Jaime threw himself toward the staircase, scrambling up and out of the way of the two giant wolves as they tumbled and snarled, slamming into furniture and shaking the cabin with their heft.

But, to Jaime's overwhelming relief, it really wasn't much of a fight at all.

Maybe if Bishop hadn't been caught off guard, if he hadn't been distracted by Jaime's antics with the phone, it would have been more evenly matched. Or maybe Finn's training in the military gave him the upper hand. Or maybe Finn was just more motivated, with his mate's life at stake to fuel his rage and power.

Whatever the reason, it was quick.

No sooner had Jaime reached the loft and looked back down did he see Finn tear Bishop's throat to ribbons, his claws anchoring the other wolf down, pinning him.

He didn't stop there, though. Jaime could see the muscle and viscera around Bishop's throat trying to heal itself even as Finn continued to tear.

And now Jaime understood how Vera could have looked so destroyed after only a few seconds of being alone in the hallway. He knew now, the damage these wolves would be able to inflict on his fragile human body. How close to death he'd been, alone in this cabin with Bishop while he'd baited and distracted him, praying it would buy enough time for Finn to free himself from his bindings.

Jaime watched as Finn placed one giant paw on Bishop's head, claws digging in. He listened to the guttural sound of the trapped wolf as Finn dove in one final time, shredding his neck and yanking with his paw at the same time. He saw Bishop's head roll, separated from his body.

He watched as Finn panted and growled down at the dead wolf, waiting—making sure he was really dead.

On shaky legs that he couldn't feel, Jaime stood and slowly made his way downstairs. Stepping over the splintered coffee table, making sure not to cut his feet on the jagged pieces of wood, he moved to where Finn crouched, hovering over Bishop's body still in wolf form.

Standing where Finn would be able to see him, scent him, Jaime placed a hand on his flank.

Big, brown eyes, darker and wilder than he'd ever seen them, focused on him. Took him in. Jaime caught the moment that Finn was looking back at him again. Or, more of Finn, and less of the wolf inside.

Jaime cupped Finn's giant, gore-covered maw with both hands. "He's dead. Come on, let's clean you up."

He'd dropped the phone in his haste to get out of the way of the tumbling wolves, and didn't know where it was now. He should call Silas back, should call Sheppard and DA Rivera and Sam. He should tell them all that they were alright, that they were alive. But all of that could wait, because Finn, still a giant wolf, was giving him that vulnerable look.

As if, despite the ferociousness he had just demonstrated, one frightened glance from Jaime would gut him.

So Jaime led him over to the kitchen sink, wet down a towel with warm water and began cleaning the blood and viscera off of his face and neck. Lifting one giant paw at a time, he gently wiped down his claws and toe pads. Finn stood still the whole time, letting Jaime fuss.

Finally done, he left the soiled rag to soak and turned back to Finn. He was staring at him, eyes still warm and pleading. "I see you, Finn. And I am not afraid. Please, can I hold you?"

Finn's face melted. With a whine, a tremor passed through him and then thick, hairy arms were banding around him, Finn's lips and descended canines pressing into the skin of his neck, his hair, his collarbone. Jaime realized that he was trembling, too.

Between short kisses and demanding hands and too-tight hugs, soft, shaken, words passed back and forth between them. Apologies, and assurances that they were alright, and thank-you's spilled out in a rush, both talking over the other.

Jaime told Finn to stop apologizing.

Finn assured Jaime that he was ok, more than ok, he'd only been knocked out and tied up.

Jaime promised that Bishop hadn't hurt him either, hadn't touched him, that Finn arrived just in time and had saved him. Smacking kisses all over his face, wherever he could reach, Jaime continued to thank him for coming back, and told him that he was amazing.

That he loved him so much.

Finn pulled away, a grave look on his face. "I never wanted you to see me that way."

Jaime cupped his face, fierce pride swelling in his heart. "I am *glad* that I saw you that way. You are my mate, Finn. And I am yours. And if our roles were reversed, if you were the human and I was the wolf, I would have done the exact same thing. I would have torn him apart for threatening you. I will never accept an apology from you for that."

Finn blinked, and then yanked him back into his arms, channeling all of that ferocious will into a passionate kiss, demanding entrance with his tongue, consuming Jaime whole. Finn's kiss showered him with adoration and gratitude for being his mate. For seeing him, even his worst parts, and loving him. Not despite them, but because of them.

Jaime felt it all through that kiss, and fed his own pride and love into Finn through their connection. Eventually, they pulled apart long enough to realize the phone was ringing non-stop from somewhere under the destroyed coffee table.

"Shit. I called Silas when Bishop got here, he heard everything. He's probably panicking right now."

Jaime found the phone first, and picked up the call, putting it on speaker. "Silas. We're safe. We're fine, both of us. Finn got here in time."

He could hear white noise in the background, like Silas was in a vehicle. But the sob that came through the line wasn't Silas. "Jaime. Oh thank God, Jaime. We thought—all we heard was... Oh my God."

Sam. Sam was in the car, on the way to see him, and he was crying.

Silas spoke then, voice still a distorted rumble like it had been earlier. "Finny? Are you alright?"

Finn had one arm wrapped around Jaime, guiding him over the broken furniture to sit on the counter, away from the giant beheaded wolf across the room.

Yikes, they'd have to figure out how to deal with that.

"Si. I'm here, brother. I'm ok."

There was a long pause, but eventually Silas choked out, "Good."

Jaime stared at the mess before them, avoiding looking at the giant wolf's body as much as possible. He cleared his throat. "Um. So, not to put a damper on things, but there is a very large, very dead, decapitated wolf in the living room. Who is also a man. What are we going to do about that?"

He heard Sam's wet chuckle, and it warmed him.

Silas also cleared his throat, some of that grated rumble dissipating. "Sam recorded the entire conversation. Up until the phone cut out anyway, when we heard Jaime shout..." he took a deep breath. "We sent it to Sheppard. We're on our way; we have been since you first called. Sheppard is right behind us. We're letting him figure out how to handle Monroe PD. I suppose it's both better and significantly more complicated that he's dead in his wolf form. Anyone who isn't in the know will just think a very large animal attacked you, and you defended yourself. But if we decide to tell the DA the truth that Bishop is dead, things will get very weird."

Jaime heaved a sigh. "What about all that stuff about Jeffrey Dugan wanting the three of you dead? And his real motive for killing Vera? And why would he want to kill you, anyway?"

Finn looked up, shocked, and Jaime remembered that he hadn't heard the same things they all had. *I'll fill you in later*," he mouthed to him.

Bishop had called Silas a "reject alpha". Did this all have something to do with why he was kicked out of that pack as a child? Slowly, Silas answered. "I'm sure Sheppard is relaying the information we have about Jeffrey Dugan to DA Rivera as we speak, so that he's arrested and can't hurt anyone else."

Finn didn't let him dodge the question. "What does that mean, wanting to kill the three of us? Why target you? Us?"

There was a long pause, before Silas blew out a heavy sigh. "Alpha Cain is my Uncle. And he probably had his Second planning to kill me because none of his children inherited the alpha line. I did."

CHAPTER 21
FINN

Silas and Sam arrived at the safe house several hours later.

Jaime and Finn had washed and gotten dressed, but otherwise had left the cabin untouched. Their movements and routines as they switched places in the shower stall and dressed in the loft were familiar and hushed—there just wasn't much to say about the situation until they knew how Sheppard wanted to proceed. But being close to each other was a comfort.

Finn knew that Jaime was avoiding looking at Bishop's body, which was entirely fair. He didn't particularly want to look at it, either.

But Jaime did not look away from him, and in the end that's what mattered.

Jaime's adamance and pride that he would have defended Finn just the same had healed something in his soul. After being afraid for so long to finally bare everything —all of the violence and anger he was capable of, in all of his forms—only for Jaime to wash him, tend to him, and press sweet words of love and acceptance into his skin, was axis-shifting.

Finn had no idea how he'd gotten so lucky in having Jaime as his mate, but he would be thankful for him every day for the rest of his life, and he would never let himself doubt his devotion and love again.

They were in the process of loading up the truck when their brothers pulled up. Finn heard Jaime's breath catch at the sight of Sam, like he hadn't really believed he was coming until now.

Jaime stood there, fingers tangled in the hem of his shirt as he tracked Sam's movements. Sam halted, unreadable emotions playing across his face while he seemed to be debating with himself about what he should say, but then he threw himself forward, wrapping Jaime up in a tight embrace as they both began to cry.

Turning away to give them privacy, he saw Silas also rushing toward him, before he threw himself around Finn in a great bear hug.

Finn held him tight, patting him on the back. He wasn't sure what to make of Silas's confession over the phone, or why he would have kept that from him all these years. But it didn't matter.

He pulled back just enough to press his forehead into Silas's. "It doesn't change anything. You are my brother. My longest friend. I'll swing for the fences with you every day, *every day,* that's never going to change. I don't give a fuck that you're an alpha, or that your Uncle is a power-hungry murderer."

Honestly, he should have seen the alpha thing coming. He wasn't sure why he hadn't put it together before now—there were several times over the years that his instincts had known and responded to the alpha in Silas, even without Finn knowing.

He'd just always assumed that alpha's were... well, assholes. Controlling. He'd assumed that their need to order people around wouldn't let them function in a dynamic like the one the four of them had in the military, with Sheppard in command. And Silas had never balked at being given orders, nor had he ever chafed against Sheppard's direction at the security firm.

Silas just squeezed him harder, and tried to hide his tears.

And then Finn was crying, too.

It was at that moment that Sheppard pulled up. Stepping out of the truck, he took one look at the four of them, all teary-eyed and hugging each other, and said, "I'll be inside."

Silas released his grip on Finn, and stepped in to sweep Jaime up into his own bear hug. Finn thought that he might start crying all over again as he heard Silas rumble out how glad he was that Jaime was safe, how worried they'd been, how awful it had felt that they couldn't do anything, how happy he was that his brother found such a good man, such a good mate...

He was surprised out of his second round of tears, however, when Sam gave him an assessing look before throwing his arms around him too, squeezing hard. Finn just stood there, arms held out, as Sam embraced him around the middle. He was so short that his head barely came up to Finn's chest.

"Thank you for protecting my brother. I'm sorry for being an ass back at your house."

Finn's arms came around to pat him on the back, head tucked down. "You were protecting your brother from a stranger, I would have done the same."

Sam took a step back. He assessed Finn again with that intense gaze—weighing him. He nodded once, and Finn felt a wave of relief that he hadn't been found wanting.

Jaime sidled up next to them. He wrapped an arm around Finn's waist, giving him a gentle squeeze before he turned to Sam. "Can we talk?"

"You two can sit in the truck, Si and I will go in and catch up with Sheppard."

Finn pressed a kiss into Jaime's hair, and passed him the truck keys. He ushered Silas onto the porch, whose gaze was locked back on Sam.

As the boys stepped up into the truck, Finn turned to his dearest friend, lifting one brow. "So. You and Sam, huh?"

Silas tore his eyes away, and gave Finn a look. "I didn't pry into your business, you shouldn't pry into mine."

Finn guffawed. "You absolutely did pry into my business. You pried so far into my business, you started giving me dick anatomy lessons."

Silas groaned. "Please, Finny. I thought we'd agreed to never bring that up again."

He smiled at his brother. "Well? Are you two... getting to know each other?"

Silas refused to look at him. "There's a decapitated wolf in the house, and you're asking me about my love life?"

Finn nearly choked. "*Love* life? You've literally never called it that before. It's always been whoever you're currently fucking. Oh, Silas, have you thought this through? His brother is my mate. We will have to see him. Regularly. You can't just drop this guy forever when you get tired of him."

Silas did turn to him then, fire in his eyes. "Yes, I've fucking thought it through. No, I won't tell you any more than that. Back off."

Finn took a step back, hands held up. "Sorry. I didn't mean to... sorry."

Silas shook his head, clapping Finn on the back. "Me too. It's been a tough couple of days. I've been worried sick about you all. Let's just go inside, and figure out how we are going to deal with this mess, yeah?"

Finn nodded, and followed him into the cabin.

He couldn't shake the conversation, though. Silas had never balked at being teased about his occasional flings before. Something about this was different.

The sight of Sheppard heaving Bishop's decapitated head off the floor to inspect it brought him back to the situation at hand, however.

"Jesus, Finn." Silas whistled.

He wasn't proud of what he had done, but he wouldn't apologize for it either. "He had Jaime cornered. He was going to kill him. I did what I had to do."

"How did he get a jump on you?" Leave it to Sheppard to analyze every detail, and assess how to improve their training moving forward.

"I stepped out first thing this morning to use the outhouse and split some kindling. He got me when I was leaving the outhouse, hit me upside the head with something. When I woke up, I was gagged and bound. In the goddamn outhouse. I couldn't hear specific words, but I could hear his voice, and Jaime's, speaking to each other in the cabin. I could feel Jaime's fear."

He shivered, refusing to go back down that road right now. He'd have nightmares about this day for years, he knew.

"That sounds eerily similar to what he did to Jaime," Silas said, inspecting the places that Finn's claws had dug into Bishop's body to hold him down.

Finn had thought the same thing when he was frantically clawing and ripping at the ties around his arms, struggling to free himself. An all new sense of respect and pride came over him that Jaime had come so far after experiencing something so terrifying. "It didn't take me all that long to get out of the bindings once I woke up, but I'm not sure how long I was knocked out."

"The phone call was less than ten minutes," Silas answered roughly.

Ten minutes. It was such a narrow window of time, if he had woken up just a few minutes later... Another tremor passed through him.

Silas clapped him on the shoulder, sensing the direction of his thoughts. "You got there in time. Your mate is strong, and smart. Jaime walked Bishop into spilling all of his secrets like a fucking dog, and made him believe that he was in control the entire time. Don't dwell on what-if's, Finn. Not now that you're here, on the other side of it."

Finn nodded, grateful for the pep talk.

"Right," Sheppard said. "There's no sense in you two staying out here once we get this cleaned up, and it would be too difficult to come up with a convincing enough lie to explain to Gabriel why you're suddenly both back in Silver Rapids, walking around like Bishop isn't running around on the loose somewhere. I think we have to tell him."

Silas raised his eyebrows at Finn, mouthing, *"Gabriel?"*

Finn shrugged his shoulders—Damn Sheppard and his secretive ways. "Do you mean that we tell the DA that Bishop is dead, or that *The X-Files* is a documentary?" he asked.

Silas snorted.

Finn smiled—Jaime had made that joke a few nights ago, when he'd told him about all of the paranormal beings he knew of.

Sheppard looked at him flatly. "Both."

"Woah, boss. The DA? Really?"

Sheppard gave a single nod. "It will make our interactions with Monroe PD so much easier. There's already several shifters on the force, not including the Salt Creek wolves. I don't see a way around it."

They both nodded in agreement. Sheppard never did anything without thorough consideration, which meant that he'd been considering bringing the DA up to speed for a while. This was just the final straw.

Together, they heaved up Bishop's dead body and brought it outside, placing it between the cabin and the outhouse. Sheppard explained that he'd show the DA the phone call as proof of Jeffrey Dugan's involvement, and let him decide how to proceed with Bishop's case. He'd offer to show him the shifted body.

It went unspoken that they had the leverage in this situation, if he decided to turn on them. The DA couldn't really accuse Finn of murder, seeing as there was no human body. He didn't have much of a choice but to believe them.

They decided against cleaning up the cabin for now. As odd and unbelievable as the situation was, they didn't want to give the impression that they were covering anything up. Yes, Finn had killed Bishop, but it was in defense of his mate. The real problems would come from the Salt Creek pack if they decided to avenge Bishop, but Sheppard speculated that they would be too busy dealing with Jeffrey Dugan's arrest to worry too much about a low-ranking rogue.

Rounding the side of the cabin, they saw Sam and Jaime in another teary embrace, having emerged from the truck. They parted when the three wolves approached them, and when Jaime looked up at Finn he saw there was pain in his eyes, yes, but also a clarity and peace that hadn't been there before.

"We're getting ready to head back to Silver Rapids. Are you ready to go?" Finn asked gently.

Jaime nodded. "Let me use the bathroom first, then I'll be ready."

Sam said the same, giving Silas an unreadable look.

"SAM HAS A STALKER."

Finn whipped his head toward Jaime. They'd just pulled out onto the highway, having discussed Sheppard's plan to tell DA Rivera everything when they got back into town on the long, bumpy track from the cabin to the main road.

"A stalker? Since when?"

Jaime heaved a sigh. "Sam earns money online, somehow. He's never told me all the details. He said the stalker has popped up every now and then for years, but in the last year it got worse. They send threats that they know who Sam is in real life, know where he lives, that he has a younger brother."

Jaime paused, voice turning rough. "They've threatened to hurt Sam. To hurt me. He says it's why he pulled away. The stalker would send him pictures of his apartment, of us coming and going. He panicked, and thought the stalker would leave him alone if he just didn't leave the house very often. But he didn't want them to only see me, either."

Finn's heart ached. "So he pulled away from you."

Jaime nodded, eyes welling up again. Finn reached across the console, taking his hand. "I'm sorry, baby. Did he say why he didn't talk to you about this before now?"

Jaime huffed, and Finn could tell that question was still a sore spot between the two brothers. "He says he didn't want to burden me anymore than I already was. That I was already going through it with Bishop and Vera's murder, and he didn't want me to worry anymore. *He* thought he was a burden on *me*."

Jaime shook his head. He whispered, "I told him that's how I've felt for the last year. Like he didn't want anything to do with me, so he just threw money at me, instead."

Finn squeezed his hand again. "How do you feel?"

Jaime was quiet for a bit. "Better, I think. I understand more, now. Or, well, I have a better idea of what was happening. I don't understand why he didn't share that with me. I thought we were always a team. But... I'm better. I think we will be better, too, in the future. If we try."

Finn nodded. "Sometimes we do things out of love that don't make sense. But..."

Finn stopped, unsure if Jaime wanted his input.

Jaime looked over at him. "But?"

Slowly, he continued, "But, to me, it seems that he cares about you very much. It seems like the attempts to help you that felt overbearing and judgmental were just his need to do something, to make up for what he thought he wasn't able to do in other areas."

A small smile appeared on Jaime's face. "That's what he said."

"Do you believe him?"

Jaime glanced out the car window. "I don't think he's lying to me. I think he's telling the truth. But believing that is going to take a while yet, I think."

Therapy would help. Slowly mending what had broken between them would help. And Finn would help too, however and whenever he could.

He squeezed Jaime's hand again. "So, not to change the subject, but..." Jaime looked over at him, raising an eyebrow.

"I think there might be something going on between Silas and Sam."

Jaime's mouth dropped open. "Oh my *God,* really? Tell me everything."

And so the rest of their trip passed quickly, a lightness shared between them as they chatted about Sam and Silas, and how Sheppard had called the DA *Gabriel.* Jaime called his lawyer to let her know that he was headed back into town, and that the DA would have updates for her soon, and then Sheppard called to tell them to head straight to the security firm's office in Silver Rapids where DA Rivera had agreed to meet with them.

SITTING across from the DA in the security firm's large conference room with Jaime's hand in his, Finn was very thankful that he'd ended up going with the "rip the bandaid off" method of telling Jaime about wolf shifters, because Gabriel Rivera was not taking the "tell then show" method well.

He hadn't believed them at all, really, accusing Sheppard —who he called *Cam*—of fucking with him. Sheppard just sat there, raising one stoic eyebrow at the attorney before he stood, and began undressing.

Jaime groaned, putting his head in his hands. "Ugh, not you, too."

Sam looked from Sheppard to Jaime in alarm at that exclamation.

DA Rivera turned to the two brothers like they were the

only three sane people left in the world. "Jaime, what the hell is going on? Have they been feeding you this bullshit the entire time? Why didn't you tell me? I would have gotten you out, brought you somewhere safe. Jesus Christ Cam, why the fuck are you getting *naked*—"

His rant was cut off as Sheppard shifted, skipping right over the partial shift and going straight for the wolf.

Finn could tell that Jaime was surprised by the size of him, taking up nearly half of the conference room with his bulk, noticeably larger than Finn's wolf.

He smirked, and leaned into Jaime's ear. "My wolf is smaller than theirs, since I'm only half shifter. It makes me stealthier."

Jaime swallowed and nodded. "Uh-huh. Yes. I see that, now."

"Oh my God." DA Rivera looked like he was going to pass out.

Jaime stood, walking over to where he sat and put a supportive hand on his shoulder. "I know it's a lot to take in, but I promise, they're not scary. Well, they are if you're threatening to hurt someone they care about, but you aren't doing that, so we're all good. Right, Finn? All good?"

Before Finn could answer, Jaime's face lit up in the most adorable way, like he'd just had a great idea. "When they're happy, they purr!"

Silas choked. "Wait, what? Did you just say that Finn *purrs*?"

Sam was looking at Jaime like he had sprouted a second head.

Jaime gave Finn a sly smile. "Sometimes."

DA Rivera was still staring at Sheppard. "I'm sorry, have you all lost your goddamn minds? A man I've known for my entire life just turned into a giant *dog*. Will someone please explain this to me?"

"Good luck with that," Sam mumbled, shooting Finn a look.

"I did explain it to you already, Gabriel. You just chose not to believe me. Take a few minutes to digest, and then we can discuss arresting Jeffrey Dugan and what to do about Bishop's body." Sheppard had shifted back by now, and was putting his clothes back on.

"You're lucky they aren't telling you to completely ignore what you just saw *because it has nothing to do with you*," Sam groused, earning a look from Jaime.

DA Rivera ignored him though, eyes bugging out of his head as he watched Sheppard get dressed. "Bishop's *body*? Did you kill Jackson Bishop, Cam?"

Silas waved his hands around. "I'm sorry, can we please circle back to the purring? What the fuck is Jaime talking about, Finn?"

He blushed. "I don't purr. When I'm, um. *Content*. My chest makes a low rumbling noise."

Jaime snickered. "Content."

Silas raised an eyebrow, a smirk stretching across his face. "So, you purr."

"It's clearly a sex thing, and I don't want to hear about my brother's freaky wolfy fucking. Drop it," Sam sniped.

Jaime turned bright red in confirmation, and Silas gave Sam another one of those heated looks.

Ugh, it was going to start stinking in here if they didn't hurry this up.

DA Rivera had his face cupped in his hands, massaging his temples. "Will someone *please* tell me if Jackson Bishop is dead? And how he got that way? I've got searchers out looking for him, and there's a storm system coming in. If I can call them back, I need to know now."

The rest of their meeting went by slightly less chaotically, and DA Rivera mostly just listened to Sheppard's explanation of Bishop's attack, his death, and the phone call confession that implicated Jeffrey Dugan in Vera's murder.

Afterwards, he made his own phone calls to bring the searchers who were out looking for Bishop back in before the storm, and to have the team that was tailing Dugan bring him in for questioning. By the time they got him to the station, the arrest warrants would be ready to go.

Finn couldn't help but respect DA Rivera. He may be struggling with all of the wolfy business, but whatever history he had with Sheppard was apparently enough for him to take the man at his word about the phone call's merit. He told Sheppard to send it to him without even asking to listen, first. Which was good, because Finn wasn't in any kind of headspace to listen to that.

He wouldn't be for a while, probably.

Things were still tense between Sheppard and the DA, though, and oddly enough, it seemed like the glances that passed between them were more hurt-laden than anything else.

On their way out, DA Rivera told Jaime that no matter how they decided to handle Bishop's death, they clearly couldn't put him on trial for killing Vera anymore, but that he would more than likely have to testify at Jeffrey Dugan's trial when the time came.

Jaime nodded. Seeing as Bishop's trial had taken over six months to start from the time of his arrest, that was a future problem.

Right now, Finn desperately wanted to bring Jaime home. Whether that was back to his cabin, or to Finn's house, he didn't care. He just wanted a hot shower that they both fit into, and a bed, where he'd remind them both that they were alive—that they were together.

Then, maybe dinner at Andi's.

That would have to wait a little longer, however, because as they all walked out of the office together before going their separate ways, the group halted at who was standing before them.

Alpha Cain, head of the Salt Creek pack, stood in their parking lot, flanked by two partially shifted wolves on either side.

Finn had never met him before, but he'd seen pictures. He looked to be in his late fifties, maybe early sixties, with salt and pepper hair and light brown eyes, catching almost yellow in the afternoon light. He wasn't the largest man among the five of them that were facing off, but Finn could sense the overwhelming alpha presence, the command in his gaze.

He looked long and hard at Silas, before skipping over Jaime and Sam, sandwiched between them, to settle on Finn, and then Sheppard. His lip curled in contempt, before addressing DA Rivera. "So, they've told you. Good. That will make this conversation easier."

Finn thought it was a good thing that Sheppard had shown DA Rivera the full wolf shift after all, hoping it took away some of the shock of seeing the five partially shifted men before them now.

A low, rumbling growl, one Finn had never heard before, came from Silas. "What are you doing here, Cain?"

The four wolves flanking him snarled at the lack of respectful address, and Finn, Silas, and Sheppard all stepped forward at once, standing in front of the three humans with them.

They were outnumbered, but they had trained together, fought together as a pack before. If they were able to get the boys back inside, they might stand a chance of fending off the Salt Creek guards until Monroe PD could be called—

Alpha Cain held up a hand. "I'm not here for a confrontation, Nephew. Stand down."

Silas shook under the weight of the ignored command, but did not ease his protective stance in front of Sam. And this time, Sam wasn't trying to elbow his way around the larger man, seeming content to sidle closer to Jaime, angling his body protectively.

Silas asked him again, "What are you doing here?"

The alpha shook his head. "The mess that Jeffrey Dugan and Jackson Bishop caused was unfortunate. I came to say that they were not acting on my orders, and that I will not be protecting Jeffrey Dugan from being held accountable. Bishop's death was also unfortunate, but it's probably for the best that it was at your mutt's hands and not mine, for his insubordination."

Silas winced. "How do you know that he's dead?"

Alpha Cain gave him a look that said he wasn't fooled by the deflection. "I can smell his blood all over your Second."

Finn blinked at the address.

"Why should we believe that you had nothing to do with Vera's murder and the attack on Finn and Jaime?" DA Rivera looked a bit less frazzled now, having collected himself from the shock of their arrival.

Cain ignored the DA's question, but gave him an appraising look. "Prosecute Jeffrey Dugan and let that be the end of it, District Attorney Rivera. I would hate for the career that you've worked so hard for to be jeopardized over a few files you shouldn't be digging around in, anyway."

DA Rivera paled, and Sheppard's hackles rose, a low growl rumbling from him.

Cain turned his nasty smirk back on Silas. "And the same goes for you, Nephew. Let's set the past aside. I would hate for something bad to happen if you go poking your nose where it doesn't belong."

Sam did step forward, then. Not to bat Silas out of the way, but to stand in front of him. "Is that a threat?"

The alpha's gaze fell to Sam, like he'd just noticed him for the first time. His lips tipped up in a knowing smile that made Finn's skin crawl. "I would also hate for your growing pack to be held accountable for your meddling."

Silas's answering snarl was vicious and terrifying, and he wrapped an arm around Sam's shoulders, pulling him back into him. "Get out of here, and do not threaten me or mine again, Cain."

They stared at each other for another long minute, before the alpha cocked his head at his guard and they turned to leave, heading for two large SUVs with blacked out windows.

The group let out a collective sigh when they drove off, and as Finn turned toward Jaime, he caught DA Rivera's mumbled question to Sheppard.

"What have you all gotten yourselves into, Cam?"

PART FOUR
FULL

CHAPTER 22
JAIME

Jaime drove back home with the windows down, the evening air warm on his face. Spring was almost gone, now, fleeting as it was in Alaska, and the long days of summer were ahead of them.

He glanced out at the sea of blue and purple flanking the highway on his way around the lake, and thought of the lupine meadow he'd planted in his backyard last year.

A surge of emotion overcame him as he recalled how overjoyed he'd been to pull up to his house a few weeks ago with Finn, to find the first flowers just beginning to bloom. He'd waited all last summer to see it, only for them to go crispy and brown in the fall, no flowers in sight.

But not this year.

Jaime smiled. No longer did he yearn for what he couldn't have, because it was already his, waiting for him to return home.

He'd met Sam for dinner at Andi's, and she'd fed them

until they were bursting. She hadn't even let them order properly—she'd just sat them at their booth tucked into the back, and brought out plate after plate of incredible food.

Jaime had sweet-talked her into giving him the recipe for her Swedish meatballs, saying that he knew Finn wouldn't be able to recreate them as good as hers were, but they were just so delicious that he had to try.

She'd winked at him, like she knew he was buttering her up, but she'd obliged anyway.

Sam and Jaime had walked around Silver Rapids after that, popping into the same bookstore that he and Finn had gone into on their first outing together. Apparently, Sheppard and DA Rivera had called in some favors with the local media, because they hadn't mauled him since that first day at his house, and when he did catch someone staring for too long or taking pictures of him, Finn or Sam were usually there to glare until they went away.

But like Finn had said that very first day, something else would always come along to shift the spotlight, and Jaime was thankful that he was no longer at the center of that particular storm.

As for the Salt Creek pack, well, things were still tense, but no other threats had been made. They seemed content for now to leave Silas and his friends alone, including Jaime and Sam. Still, Finn whined at him to check in often whenever he went into town without a shifter with him, which really wasn't often.

But things were getting better between him and his brother, and tonight Jaime hadn't wanted a buffer between them. They weren't the same as before, but Jaime wasn't sure he would want to go back to that, if given the choice. He wanted to move forward—wanted to see what their friendship could grow into, if they tried to be more open with each other.

He knew Sam was still keeping things from him—he never wanted to talk about the stalker, and he always sidestepped any questions Jaime asked about Silas. But Jaime could tell that he was trying. Leaving his apartment to come to dinner and walk around town was a big step, and Jaime felt a pang of worry as he watched his confident and strong big brother glance over his shoulder every time he thought Jaime wasn't looking.

It unnerved him to see Sam that way, but Jaime knew all he could do was make sure Sam knew he could come to him, if he needed.

Jaime parked his car behind Finn's truck and walked through the front door, a warm golden light pouring out of the cabin windows in the blue dusk. Kicking off his shoes, he saw that Finn wasn't in his usual spot on the sofa, or in the kitchen.

It had taken a few weeks to settle into a routine together, but after their time at the cabin, neither Jaime or Finn wanted to live apart.

Sometimes Jaime would ride with Finn into Silver Rapids for the day, strolling around town and sitting in the local coffee shop while he drew on his tablet and built up his social media commission platform again. Other days he'd stay at home, enjoying the peaceful quiet of the lake as he cleaned out his art studio, readying it to use again.

He still met with his therapist once a week, and found it

easier to work on his exercises now that Bishop was dead and Jeffrey Dugan was in prison. But there were still nights when it felt difficult to breathe; when the walls were too close, and Jaime had to remind himself that he'd escaped.

Finn was always there, with his gentle words and deep voice guiding him back, guiding him home. And then his strong arms and soft lips would remind Jaime that he was loved, and protected, and wanted.

Jaime found Finn out back, sitting on a blanket in the lupine meadow and looking out at the full Flower Moon's reflection over the lake. His breath caught at the sight, and he hovered by the door to take in the beauty of the moment, listening to the soft hum of insects and the calling loons as the shore lapped gently against the rocky beach.

Quietly, he padded over and sat next to Finn, curling into his side. Peeking up through his lashes, Jaime saw such contentment on Finn's face that it took his breath away all over again. It was even more beautiful than the moon hanging low over the lupine all around them.

Their troubles hadn't gone away; Jaime was again on the hook to testify, now at Jeffrey Dugan's trial for Vera's murder, and the Salt Creek alpha's threat was hanging over them all. But none of that belonged in this moment.

"Hi," Jaime whispered into the peaceful night.

Looking down, a small smile appeared on Finn's lips. "Hi. How was dinner with Sam?"

Jaime gave him a coy smile in return. "Good. I brought you something."

Finn's eyes lit up. "Please tell me it's the recipe for the Swedish meatballs."

He grinned, and pulled the scrap of paper out of his jean pocket. "Dinner for tomorrow?"

Finn beamed, looking so happy, so light and open, that Jaime had to kiss him. It quickly turned hot, hands wandering as Jaime ran his tongue along Finn's canines and their legs tangled together when Finn rolled him onto his back.

But too soon, Finn grasped his shoulders and pulled them both apart so that he could sit back, hovering over where Jaime lay reclined on the blanket. He could see Finn's face in the glow through the windows and the light of the full moon reflecting off the lake, and noted the nervous downward cast of his eyes.

Placing his hand over Finn's and sitting back up next to him, he asked, "What's wrong?"

Finn shook his head. "Nothing's wrong. Absolutely nothing. I just, um. I was out here with the blanket and everything for a reason, waiting until you got home."

Jaime cocked his head in question, and Finn cleared his throat. "I wondered. Well, I thought that maybe, since we've been, um, working you up to it, I thought tonight we could—"

"Oh my God, are you finally going to knot me?" The thought made Jaime giddy, and yes, a little nervous, too.

Soon after they'd returned from the safe house, Jaime had received a package at his door in Finn's name. He hadn't thought anything of it until Finn snatched it out of his hands to unbox whatever was inside, blushing. And then nervously, with those warm eyes that should be illegal, he'd presented Jaime with his purchases.

Finn had bought him butt plugs.

Plugs, as in several of them. In varying sizes. He'd shuffled on his feet and rubbed the back of his neck as he explained that these would help to stretch Jaime gradually, so the knot wouldn't hurt or tear him.

Jaime, blushing furiously, was so touched and so horny that he'd shoved Finn backwards onto the sofa, snatched the lube they kept in a drawer downstairs for exactly this reason, and rode him, hard, until they were both shouting their climaxes.

They'd used the plugs nearly every night since—Finn was fastidious in making sure that Jaime was well prepared for the size and stretch of him. And they'd both fucking loved the sight and sensation of Jaime's hole stretching around them.

Surfacing from the fond memory, he watched as Finn clocked the shift in his scent, eyes darkening as arousal mixed with excitement pooled low in his belly. Still, he didn't move over Jaime like he expected, instead taking both of his hands in his.

"Yes. If you're ready, yes. But first..." He squeezed Jaime's hands, a tremor in his voice. "It was always you, for me. I've been yours from the moment we met. I love you. Will you, um, will you be my mate?"

In the purple and blue meadow of blooming lupine, with the full moon behind him, Jaime would remember this moment with Finn forever. His voice choked with tears and overwhelming love as he exclaimed, "Yes! Yes, Finn. You are mine, and I am yours. I love you, I love you, I love you. Please, make me your mate!"

Finn pulled Jaime forward, banding his arms around his middle as he yanked him up into his lap and pressed wet, sloppy kisses to his mouth, along his jaw, behind his ear, and down his neck.

He stopped there, lapping and grazing his teeth where Jaime's neck met his shoulder. Peering up, he growled, "Hold on."

Jaime squawked, scrambling for a grip on Finn's shoulders and wrapping his legs tightly around his waist as he stood, carrying him inside and up to their room. Jaime pouted, "Why did we have to come inside?"

Finn chuckled, tossing him down onto the soft bedding. "Because I don't want bugs in places they shouldn't be."

He'd clearly made an effort to prepare their bedroom for this before Jaime had arrived. The lights were off, but the space was lit in a warm glow from the gas fireplace, still necessary on chilly evenings, along with the soft fairy lights they'd strung up over their bed when Finn had moved in. They both loved the reminder of the good memories they shared together from the safe house.

Jaime giggled, and Finn continued, "Also... we might be, uh, stuck together for awhile, afterwards. I want us to be somewhere we can be comfortable."

Jaime's heart warmed. "So thoughtful, baby. Now, fuck me, please." He reached out with grabby hands and squirmed further into the soft pillows as Finn flashed him a wolfish grin and tugged off his shirt.

"With pleasure. But first..."

He dropped to his knees beside the bed, and yanked Jaime down by an ankle, hastily shucking his pants and underwear off while Jaime fought to get his shirt over his head. He hadn't quite managed it yet, arms still tangled up, when Finn swallowed his cock in one go.

"*Hah*—Finn!"

He must have found the lube because suddenly, two slick fingers were massaging over Jaime's rim, pushing in slowly as Finn suckled and lapped at his tip the way he knew drove Jaime wild.

Feet flexing over Finn's shoulders, Jaime fisted his hands in his soft hair and began arching up into the wet, sucking pulls before dropping down, hard, onto the now three fingers curling purposefully against his prostate, pleasure pulsing up his spine and down into his thighs with each motion, making his hole clench around Finn's fingers.

He hiccuped, "Finn... Finn. I'm n-not coming like this. I refuse—refuse. *Please* come fuck me with your—*mmmph!*"

Finn's lips pulled off Jaime's cock with a wet *pop* right as he stuffed the largest plug into his hole, holding it steady as Jaime huffed and shifted, adjusting to its girth, before he began gently fucking it in and out.

Finn's voice was all gravel through teeth. "I wish you could see your pretty pink hole, Jaime. See the way it sucks the biggest plug right back inside—so needy for a fat cock, hmm? But it's not enough, is it... you need more. You need *my* fat cock stuffing you full, yeah? *My* knot? Do you need your mate inside of you?"

Someday, Jaime would ask Finn where all of his filthy talk came from, but right now he just basked in it, head tipping back and arms spread above his head as soft *uh, uh, uh's* spilled from him while Finn opened him up. The stretch and pleasure-ache was so delicious as he lay loose and pliant under his ministrations.

"Answer me, baby." Finn smacked a cheek, exposed as he hefted a leg further up on his shoulder.

Jaime mewled. "Yeah, baby. Please, I need you to fuck me. I want your fat cock. Only yours. Only you. Knot me, Finn. Please!"

Finn slurped him down once again, Jaime's cock in his throat as he swallowed once, twice, three times... "Oh, God, Finn! *Nu-uh*, nooo—I don't—please, d-don't make me come too—too—too soon!"

He pulled off right at the last second, and Jaime sobbed from the sudden shove back from the edge while the plug was still pressed against his prostate, begging for more, less, anything...

Finn pulled the plug out, and while Jaime blinked up at the ceiling, stars dancing in his vision, he heard him hastily shuck his clothes off before climbing up and over Jaime, resting with just enough weight to press him down into the mattress, his heavy erection slotting along Jaime's in a way that was both familiar and new.

Finn, so tall and broad and hairy in this form, hovered over him, a smug look on his face as he rocked his overlarge cock against Jaime's.

He grasped for a trailing thread in his cotton-candy filled mind and followed it, snuffling as he pouted, "S'mean to do that."

Finn chuckled. "You're fucking adorable when I edge you. We should do it more often."

Jaime shook his head side to side. He did *not* think that would be very nice, but his head was too fuzzy to say so.

Finn leaned in, tongue and teeth and lips trailing up his neck before he tugged lightly on the shell of Jaime's ear. "Really, I don't think I'm going to last for more than a few seconds before I knot you, baby, and I need you close before we start."

He sounded nervous, and as Jaime finally focused on him, he saw those adoring eyes staring down at him. So he smiled, hands cupping Finn's face as he lifted up to kiss him. "I'm ready, Finn. I'm so ready. I love you. I want you. Make me your mate."

Something flashed in Finn's gaze, no longer soft, and Jaime had the sense that they were both there now, right at the front. Finn and his wolf were looking down at him, together—reverent, hungry, equally enamored and loving.

"How do you want me, Jaime?" His voice was all rumble.

Jaime had given that question quite a bit of consideration in all of his many fantasies about this night. He leaned up to give Finn one more lingering, wet kiss, full of teeth and heat, before he gently pushed him back.

Rolling until he was sitting up on his knees, his back to Finn, Jaime tucked a pillow under his hips for support before he folded forward. Arms stretched above his head, he grasped the pillows and tipped his ass up, arching his back.

Presenting.

The position received the reaction he was looking for. Finn snarled, and Jaime heard something deeper, something that made him shiver and then loosen everywhere, growl, "*Mate.*"

Clawed hands grasped Jaime's hips, tipping him up and arching his back even further as a constant, low litany of filthy praise left Finn's mouth. He shuddered when he felt Finn's hot, wet breaths on his loose rim before Finn lapped there—once, twice, followed by a scrape of teeth on the meat of Jaime's ass.

The shock of the cold lube swiped along his rim made him jolt, and Finn placed soothing, open mouthed kisses where he'd just nipped, shushing Jaime as he slicked himself up. "Shh, baby."

Jaime relaxed when he felt the mattress shift around him, Finn's knees bracketing him on either side as he leaned down and completely blanketed his large body over Jaime's. Finn reached up and tangled their fingers together, pressing his face into his hair. His heavy cock rested along Jaime's lower back, already leaking.

There was more of Finn in his voice as he spoke. "I love you. Tell me to stop if I hurt you."

Jaime tipped his face to the side and kissed him. "You won't. Please, I'm so ready."

But when Finn shifted, and the wide, blunt tip of his cock dragged down from the small of Jaime's back to snug up against his hole, leaving sticky wet trails of precum along his skin, he had a moment of doubt at just how much there was of Finn like this.

Jaime gasped when he pressed in, and tightened his grip on their linked fingers while Finn whispered that he was such a good boy, telling him to breathe through it, bear down, and Jaime couldn't think of anything at all except for Finn, and the pressure, right at the edge of burn before his rim gave way and the fat head caught and entered him.

The stretch had his eyes rolling back in pleasure. Jaime keened, trembling.

Finn ground out, "Fuck, look at you, baby. You're taking me so w-well—well." He was trembling above Jaime, too—restraint and overwhelm in his voice. Jaime released his hold on Finn's fingers and gripped his forearms braced on either side of him—needing an anchor as the pleasure consumed him.

He felt himself adjust to Finn's girth, felt the fat head sink a little further inside as Jaime's hole relaxed, sucking him in. "M'good... you can move, *please* move—*Ooh!*"

Finn rocked his hips into Jaime, cock thick and hard as he grunted and huffed into his hair, going deeper with every careful thrust inside. "Oh fuck, baby. You feel so good. You're so *tight*, so perfect. Mine, you're mine, Jaime. I'm in you, now."

Finn's hips fell out of rhythm, like he stopped himself from going further, and his voice broke on a plea. "Jaime, I can't—*hmmph*—hold back, anymore—"

He sounded wrecked, the low timber of his voice pitching high with every measured thrust in. Jaime heard the wolf, too, like he was also there to claim what was his. What was theirs.

Mate.

And Jaime was so ready to be claimed. "Give it to me. More—more. I want—*hiccup*—want you. Deeper."

Finn whined in gratitude, lifting up just enough to palm

the nape of Jaime's neck with one clawed hand, and his hip with the other.

"I love you," he growled.

And then Finn fucked into him hard, bottoming out.

Jaime howled, limbs scrambling for purchase as Finn began pumping into him in deep, brutal strokes. Jaime's cock, which had flagged during the initial press in, was a steel bar hanging between his legs, his balls tight as he shifted against the pillow from Finn's pounding. In this position, with his ass up and his back bowed beneath Finn's anchoring hold, Jaime felt his thrusts moving deeper inside of him than he ever thought possible.

It was euphoric.

Finn seemed to have completely lost himself in the pleasure, a jumble of praise and command tumbling out of his mouth between grunts and hitched breaths. "Take it—take it. That's right. Yes, my mate. My good boy. Right in your belly. You—you want my cock? My—cum? You want your mate to knot you? Breed you? Stuff you f-full—full?"

Finn was all around him, his entire world, everything he knew—over him and in him and holding him. His words washed over Jaime, and he could feel Finn so deep, he imagined that if he pressed on the soft pouch of his lower belly he would feel Finn moving there.

The thought had him mewling, wanting more, more, *more*. Finn shifted his hips just enough to hit Jaime's prostate, over and over and over, and he sobbed in pleasure, his orgasm floating just out of reach. Breaths hitching, he reached back to claw at Finn's hip, wanting him closer, deeper still.

"Finn—*nnngh*, please! Please! *Please!*"

Jaime didn't know what he was begging for, but Finn did. Finn always knew what he needed—and he always gave it to him.

The hand at Jaime's nape slid beneath him, wrapping across his chest and the opposite shoulder, angling Jaime's neck just so. Suddenly, Finn's teeth were there, hovering over that spot, teasing.

"Say—it. Say you're m-my mate. Say you want my claim —Jaime."

Finn's breath was hot against the sweaty, curling hairs at Jaime's nape. He felt the bond pulsing deep in his bones, a matching thrum to Finn's grinding cock against his prostate —something intrinsic within him calling out, needing to claim and be claimed.

Jaime was Finn's, and Finn was his.

His thrusts punched the words out of Jaime. "I want it. *Hiccup.* I'm yours—yours—yours. And you're mine, *hmmph*, mine. I want—it. *Please*, Finn. *Oh!*"

Jaime felt the swelling start, Finn's cock dragging even more on his withdrawals, catching on Jaime's rim deliciously as he stuffed him full again. His own erection was aching, the friction against the pillow just on the edge of not enough.

As the pressure from Finn's knot heightened even more, making Jaime wonder if they could do this—if it would fit— his teeth were in him, biting.

Claiming.

And then Finn's knot blew wide, Jaime's eyes rolling back when his rim swallowed and fluttered behind the bulge as the pleasure-pressure on his prostate throbbed up his spine.

Finn released the bite and sobbed, "Oh *fuck*, baby—baby, look at y-you. At us. You're so full—full of me. I'm going to b-breed you, now, *Jaime*!"

He leaned forward again, and gripped Jaime's hands in his, completely covering him. They came with a euphoric shout, one following just after the other. Jaime shot ropes of cum up the pillow beneath him as Finn anchored him down, making him take it, knot lodged deep as he rocked inside and pumped his cum into Jaime's belly with a muffled roar, face buried in Jaime's neck.

Jaime shook and twitched when his orgasm ripped his breath away, pathetic mewls and sobs the only sound coming from him as he squirmed beneath Finn, the movement pressing him further onto his knot.

It was all so much; the pleasure was overwhelming as Finn's thick cock kicked, spilling in him, his knot and teeth and claim all consuming.

Finn purred above him, his entire body a trembling mess while he continued to rock his hips in aborted motions, plugging Jaime up and filling him. He began lapping at the mating bite, shushing Jaime's wet, hitched breaths as the aftershocks moved through them both.

Time slipped from Jaime. Finn's chest rumbled while he hovered over him, still knotted deep inside. It could have been hours, or days, or maybe just a few minutes.

He was floating in that liminal space between consciousness and pleasure-induced black-out, stars dancing behind his eyes and only aware of Finn all around him, when he heard the soft words that would bind them together forever.

"I claim you, Jaime Lamont. In love, honor, and gratitude. You are mine, and I am yours."

Thick arms banded around his middle, keeping him close as they shifted to the side. Jaime whined at the stretch and pull on his rim, Finn's knot jostling as they adjusted before settling, spooned together.

He took Finn's hands again where they were wrapped around him, and with the weight of them on his heart, Jaime repeated the words that ached to be free.

"And I claim you, Finn Winters. In love, and honor, and gratitude. You are mine, and I am yours."

Whether it was a true physical connection, or some indefinable emotional bond, Jaime didn't know. But he felt those words wrap around his heart, felt them pull him further into Finn's embrace. And he swore that he could feel Finn's joy and wonder echoing his own, swelling along with the purr coming from deep in his chest.

Jaime knew that tug would always remain, a comforting presence connecting him to his love, his mate, forever.

Finn's knot finally softened, and cum spilled down Jaime's thighs, making them wet and sticky as he pulled out. He carried Jaime to their bathroom where they bathed together in the hot water, and as Finn fussed over the newly-healed mating marks that he'd left on Jaime's neck, as they exchanged hushed exclamations of awe and pleasure at the joining they'd just shared, as they pressed soft words of love into each other's skin—Jaime knew that this was always meant to be.

Whether they met a year ago, or five years from now, or in another lifetime altogether, they would always find their way home to each other.

EPILOGUE

JAIME

1 YEAR LATER

"Mr. Lamont, please state your name, and spell it for the record."

Fiddling with the tie that felt too tight around his throat, Jaime took a deep, steadying breath, and looked up. Not at DA Rivera, who had just called him to the witness stand to testify against Jeffrey Dugan, but at his mate, sitting in the front row.

Finn's eyes were already on him, full of warmth and pride that Jaime felt echoed deep in his chest.

Next to him sat Sam, whose gaze was the other side of Finn's coin. His pride was fierce, and the nod he gave was resolute in his trust that Jaime could do this.

And on the other side of Sam, was Silas. Silas, who had whooped and hollered, picking Jaime up and spinning him around before crushing them both in a bear hug the day after

326

he and Finn had claimed each other, exclaiming how happy he was that they were brothers now.

Finally, on the end sat Sheppard. Reserved as always, but his usually stoic features softened a touch as he smiled in support.

So much had happened since that day the media swarmed his house and Finn had thundered back into his life. They'd all been through a great deal together, and Jaime was thankful every day for them, for his family, and especially that they were all there to support him today.

Gaze skittering back to Finn, mooring him, he cleared his throat, and began.

———

JAIME'S HAND braced against the headboard, stopping his slide up every time Finn brutally fucked into him. "Yes, like that! Harder, please. Just like that—that, Finn. Fuck!"

Finn hiked Jaime's legs up higher on his shoulders, nearly bending him in half as he ground his hips down, whispering filth into his ear. "Is this what you need, baby? You n-need me all the way inside you, stuffing my cock deep in your—b-belly?"

Jaime mewled, unable to form words anymore. He could tell by the way his hole stretched around the base of Finn that his mate would come soon, and fuck, he was nearly there just from Finn pegging his prostate with his thick, blunt tip.

Jaime snaked his other hand between them, canting his hips up higher to give Finn the best angle, the angle that always had them both screaming each other's names, and took his cock in hand, pumping hard to bring himself over the edge.

"Come inside me, baby. I'm close. Fill me—fill me up. Up. Breed—breed me, *please*. Knot me and make your m-mate come."

That was something new they'd learned together after Finn had knotted him for the first time. No matter that he couldn't actually get Jaime pregnant, asking Finn to breed him was the equivalent of a vibrator on high direct to Finn's prostate, with how fast it made him blow his load deep in Jaime's ass.

And Jaime fucking loved it.

One day when Jaime was working on a watercolor commission for a local client from home, Finn had texted saying how bored he was, and how much he wished someone would call with an emergency request to get him out of all the paperwork piled up on his desk.

So, Jaime had slicked himself up, sat on the plug he hadn't used in ages because Finn knotted him so often, and snapped a selfie. He'd replied, telling Finn that he'd worked up quite the emergency situation at home and that he desperately needed Finn's help, before sending him the photo, captioned, *Breed me.*

Finn's truck had screeched into the driveway only a few minutes later, feet stomping up the stairs two at a time before he'd burst into their bedroom, bent Jaime over the dresser, and fucked him with a ferocity he hadn't seen before.

Later, as they'd laid tangled up in each other, panting heavily and Finn's knot pressed deep inside, he'd sheepishly explained that the thought of Jaime, alone, slick and ready to be bred while anyone could just happen by the house, had short-circuited his brain, sending him straight into wolfy *mine* territory.

Jaime had replied that he certainly wasn't complaining, and that they would absolutely be doing that again.

Jaime's hand was flying over his shaft now, while Finn snarled, "Your tight little hole is squeezing my cock back inside, baby. It's begging for my knot. Begging to be b-bred. Do you want your mate's cum? Do you want m-me to fuck into your belly and breed you? Do you want my load that badly, baby? Take my—cum!"

Finn gasped and buried himself deep, pressing his full body down and knot blowing wide as Jaime's hole swallowed around him. Jaime shouted his climax, tightening the fist around his cock as he shot all over his stomach and chest.

He wrapped shaky arms around Finn's shoulders, twitching through the electric pulses zinging through him while he basked in the pressure of Finn's knot pressed against his prostate, cum filling him up.

Dropping Jaime's legs off his shoulders, Finn rolled them until Jaime was mostly on top, legs and arms a jumble as they breathed through the come down, pleasure softly pulsing through him as he felt Finn's rumbling purr underneath. By the time his knot softened enough to pull out, and Jaime felt like he could form full sentences again, he was ready for a hot shower and Finn's Shepherd's pie.

Jaime told his mate so, who chuckled and shuffled them both into the bathroom, where Finn very attentively washed away the cum and lube dripping down his thighs.

And then sucked Jaime's cock down and swallowed around him until he was hard again and keening, pouting and begging until he splashed down Finn's throat, blearily watching him jerk himself off on his knees.

A LITTLE WHILE LATER, hair still damp and muscles pleasantly liquid and sore, Jaime sat in their dining nook and watched Finn pad around the kitchen, shirtless, slicing and sautéing and whatever else he was doing that was far less interesting than the bunch and stretch of his back muscles as he bent over.

Jaime really needed to buy him that damn apron.

"Thank you for being there, today. I know it had to be boring sitting through all of that, but it means a lot to me that you were there. And thank you for afterwards, upstairs. I needed that, too."

Finn turned toward him, a crease forming between his eyebrows. Jaime remembered the first time he saw that crease, and how much he'd wanted to smooth it away, so he stood up, padded over to his mate, and did just that.

Finn hooked an arm around his waist. "Of course, I was there. There was never any question about that."

Jaime smiled. "I know. But still, it's important to me that you know how much I appreciate it. How much I appreciate you. That there never was any question for you. I love you, and I am grateful for who you are."

It was Finn's turn to smile now, and he pressed a kiss to Jaime's temple before he turned back to their food. "I'm very proud of you. You did so well today. Whatever verdict the jury returns, you did Vera justice."

Jaime nodded. He had answered all of the questions that DA Rivera asked him without issue, feeling lighter after his story was finally out there. But then the defense attorney had peppered him with more difficult, pointed questions. She'd brought up things that Jaime hadn't thought were relevant, but that he'd been forced to testify about.

His job, his brother, his relationship with Finn, and thus the security firm. Feeling like he'd been put through the wringer, Jaime had finally stepped down after DA Rivera had helped him re-state some of the details he'd felt like the defense attorney had muddled.

Somehow, that took nearly all day, and Finn drove him home in a daze.

When they'd walked through the door, Finn kicking his shoes off next to Jaime's and offering to make them an early dinner before going to bed, a sudden swell of emotion had come over him. He was proud of himself for staying composed on the witness stand, yes, but for some reason, he hadn't been able to shake a horrible sense of *what-if*.

Jaime had seen a version of himself come home alone after testifying, without Finn. He'd seen himself warm up a frozen pot pie in the microwave, sit on the couch, and eat dinner, alone.

The emptiness he'd felt as he pictured it had Jaime pouncing on Finn, pulling him up the stairs and begging for his knot. Finn, as always, had sensed what he needed, and gave it to him.

Brutally, over and over.

Jaime needed Finn to know that he saw that, saw his unwavering support, and would always be grateful for it.

As Finn slid their Shepherd's pie into the oven to bake, Jaime thought about what Finn might be needing, and asked something that he'd been wondering about for a long time.

"Have you ever thought about getting another dog?"

Finn turned wide eyes toward him and leaned back against the counter. He opened his mouth to answer, but then stopped, taking a moment to consider. "I didn't want to at first, after Luna died. I couldn't handle the thought of giving my heart away again."

He smiled softly at Jaime, and continued, "But now, with you. Yes, I have thought about it. A lot, actually. I was debating over whether to ask if you'd like to get a puppy together. Or maybe find a shelter to adopt from."

Jaime cocked his head. "Why were you debating asking me that? Of course, I would love to get a dog with you, Finn. We'd be fucking fantastic dog dads. I'll get us all matching sweaters. The Christmas cards will be adorable."

Finn chuckled, eyes bright. "Well, the thing is... there's something else that I've also been wanting to ask you, and I was debating on which to do first. There might be travel involved in the second request, and I'd hate to leave our new puppy at home without us so soon."

Jaime was lost. "Do you want to go on a vacation? I agree, I think we should do that before we get a puppy—Finn, what is so funny?"

That mirthful look still on his face and eyes glowing, Finn plucked something out of one of the kitchen drawers that Jaime never had any reason to look inside anymore, and sidled up to him, crowding Jaime back against the counter. Reflexively, he grasped Finn's forearms and began running his fingers through the soft hair there.

Finn's voice was teasing, a knowing smile slashed across his face. "So, you agree? We should do the other thing, first? Get that out of the way before we dive headfirst into puppy parenthood?"

Angling his head up, Jaime narrowed his eyes in suspicion at the amused grin on Finn's face. "What am I missing?"

Finn's laughter settled into a warm, joyful smile, and he held out his open palm before Jaime, presenting him with a brushed gold wedding band.

"Will you marry me, Jaime?"

Jaime blinked. Blinked again. "Oh."

Finn smirked. "Oh?"

Jaime batted at Finn's chest. "Yes, *oh*. And, not fair! You're not supposed to tease me after proposing, you're supposed to confess your undying love for me, and tell me how much you can't live without me, and how good I am at sucking your dick, and—"

Finn cocked an eyebrow at him. "I think I said all of that and quite a bit more an hour ago upstairs, when you were clawing my back up and screaming my name while I was balls deep inside of you. But if you'd like, I'm happy to repeat myself."

Jaime swatted at his chest again, blushing at the memory. "Alright. I suppose we have done and said all of that today, already. And, yes. I will marry you. Honestly, I thought mating was it for wolf shifters, I didn't know you all had ceremonies like humans do—"

Finn shut him up with a kiss, deep and intense.

Pulling away, he pressed his forehead to Jaime's and slid the ring onto his finger. "I love you, so very much. You are mine, and I am yours. We're forever, baby. But I'd also really fucking love to call you my husband, loudly, so that guy we always see at the grocery store stops checking you out."

Jaime threw his head back and cackled. Wiping at his eyes, he answered, "Babe, that guy is checking *you* out, not me. You just only notice him when he's looking at me, and trying to figure out how I bagged these swoon-worthy broad shoulders of yours." He ran his hands appreciatively along them to emphasize his point, beaming at the glint of the golden band on his left hand.

Finn cataloged that, briefly. "Huh."

Jaime gripped Finn by the shoulders. "I love you, too. And yes, it would bring me so much joy to call you my husband. Yes, I will marry you, and we can go on an amazing honeymoon, and then we can get a puppy, and then we can grow old and gray together. I want all of it, with you."

Finn gave him that midnight sun smile. "All of it, with you."

ACKNOWLEDGMENTS

I started writing *Under the Lupine Moon* alone, with my fluffy dog on my lap, hoping that someday at least one other person would fall in love with Finn and Jaime's story as much as I have. As I write this thank you, I still have my fluffy dog on my lap, but I am overwhelmingly grateful for how many people have joined me on this journey.

To my best friend Kelsey, I haven't let you read this yet, but it's been so fun to build our passion projects together and learn new things alongside you. Thank you for always being a good sounding board. To my other best friend Lindsay, who also hasn't read this yet, thank you for cheering me on as I go. I'm always rooting for you, too! To my family, who, you guessed it, hasn't read this, thank you for always believing in my creative dreams.

To my beta-reader, last-minute proofreader, wisdom-giver, video-camera-hugger, and new friend, Thea Verdone, thank you for all of your time and support (she *has* read this). You swooped in and saved the day just when it was needed most, and I'll always be grateful for your kindness!

To my new author friends, it's been such a joy finding community with you all. Thank you for all of the hype that you've given my debut!

And to Bookstagram and the bookish community, your love and interest in *Under the Lupine Moon* has been more than I could have ever hoped for. Thank you so much for every single way that you have supported this book. I can't wait to share more of the Silver Rapids wolves with you.

Alright, let's get sappy. [Trigger warning] for medical diagnosis. My heart knew that I needed this book before my head did. At the beginning of April (2024), I experienced some incredibly scary physical and mental health problems, and was admitted to the hospital where they diagnosed me with multiple sclerosis. The diagnosis and treatment of my symptoms put me out of commission for over a week, and I wondered what my future would look like with this life-long disease. Thankfully, I am feeling much better now, and treatment for MS nowadays is such that I have high hopes for an active and healthy lifestyle for many years. But, through it all, this book has kept me present and focused, and has given me so much joy to hold on to during a very difficult season in my life.

So, I hope this book can be a warm hug for anyone out there who is also going through something hard. And remember, there is always an *after* the *after*. Keep looking at the moon.

ABOUT THE AUTHOR

A. Knightley lives in the wilds of the Midwest with her dog. She loves to write paranormal romance stories with heaping doses of spice and happily ever afters. *Under the Lupine Moon* is A. Knightley's debut novel, and she can't wait to share what's happening next in Silver Rapids. To stay up to date with what she's working on next, you can connect on Instagram @author.aknightley.

WHAT'S NEXT?

Do you want to find out what all of those heated looks between Silas and Sam are really about, and what the Silver Rapids wolves are up to next? Find out in Book 2 of the series, coming in early 2025! Follow A. Knightley on Instagram (@author.aknightley) for updates and announcements.

ALSO BY A. KNIGHTLEY

THE SILVER RAPIDS SERIES

Under the Lupine Moon, Book 1

By the Blood Moon, Bonus Story

* 9 7 9 8 9 9 0 6 5 4 1 1 2 *